Assault
in
Asheville

AN AMANDA RITTENHOUSE MYSTERY

Other Books by Kate Merrill

Romance
Northern Lights (as Christie Cole)
Flames of Summer

Diana Rittenhouse Mystery Series
A Lethal Listing
Blood Brothers
Crimes of Commission
Dooley Is Dead
Buyer Beware

Amanda Rittenhouse Mystery Series
Murder at Metrolina
Homicide in Hatteras
Murder at Midterm
Assault in Asheville

Miss Addie's Gift: Portrait of an American Folk Artist

About the Author

Kate, a longtime art gallery owner and passionate writer, lives with her wife on a lake in North Carolina. When she is not writing or creating driftwood sculpture, she enjoys swimming, boating, playing with her cats, and allowing her strong-headed Golden Retriever to take her for a walk.

Assault
in
Asheville

AN AMANDA RITTENHOUSE MYSTERY

Kate Merrill

BELLA
BOOKS
2020

Bella Books, Inc.
P.O. Box 10543
Tallahassee, FL 32302

First Bella Books Edition 2020

Editor: Alissa McGowan
Cover Designer: Judith Fellows

ISBN: 978-1-64247-128-1

Acknowledgments

Special thanks to Linda, Jessica, and the staff at Bella Books, to Alissa McGowan for her invaluable editing help, and to the North Carolina mountains, a uniquely haunting setting.

Dedication

To Dianne & John
Nita & Sandra
Alice & Ranice
and my other wonderful mountain friends.

PROLOGUE

Chicago, 1969

Nick Rossi backed away from the pot of boiling pasta water, leaned against the doorjamb, and mopped the sweat off his face with a paper towel. Joey worked the grill, Rose stirred the sauce, and through the small window in the swinging door, Nick saw the dinner crowd streaming into his papa's restaurant.

Summer in the city was not the best time to slave in a hot kitchen, but it paid Nick's tuition to the American Academy of Art, an undertaking his father thought was *verimento stupido*—a complete waste of time. Today, Saturday, Nick's special new friend from painting class was demonstrating against the Vietnam War in Lincoln Park. Nick longed to be with him, drinking beer and cursing President Nixon. Instead, he frowned as Joey propped the back door open, allowing the smells of grilling sausage, peppers, and onion to spill into the alleyway, while not a breath of fresh air came into the kitchen.

Out in the dining room, Papa, in a crisp white shirt, bow tie, and black trousers, greeted the customers with an obsequious smile. Nick was angry with Papa for groveling to the likes of

Capo Alfonso and his soldiers, who were gathering in their favorite booth in the corner near the bar. Papa had risked his life fighting his former countrymen and fascism. He had been overseas when Nick was born, and Mama had died in childbirth, so now father and son resided in a low rent tenement serving spaghetti to the local lowlife.

As Nick fumed and dreamed of a better life, a black limousine pulled into the alley and four men climbed out. His heart jumped into his throat as he recognized Pietro Roman, better known as Milwaukee Pete, boss of The Chicago Outfit and bitter rival of Capo Alfonso.

"No, you cannot come in here!" Joey backed away from the grill and waved his spatula at Mr. Roman. Rose ran into the bathroom and locked the door.

But Roman and his men rampaged through the kitchen, automatic weapons attached to the sleeves of their dark suits like lethal hands.

While Nick attempted to block the door to the dining room, he absurdly noted that Roman was movie-star handsome in his expensive suit, with raven black hair and a swarthy complexion. His heavy cologne made Nick nauseous with fear.

"Step aside, Nicky." Roman winked, shoving him away as the four charged into the restaurant.

Frozen by shock, Nick cowered behind the swinging door as people screamed. Gunfire shattered the night and scattered the patrons. Some fled into the street, while others dove under the tables. But Roman's men had only one target—Capo Alfonso's booth near the bar.

Every muscle in Nick's young body turned to jelly as he sagged and covered his ears. In slow motion, Alfonso's head exploded. Riddled by bullets, his soldiers danced like spastic marionettes before sliding to the floor.

Nick should have covered his eyes, because when it was all over and the intruders retreated back through the kitchen, into the alley, and the limo left the scene, five were dead. The carnage left the black and white linoleum tiles red with gore, and the fifth man, an innocent bystander, lay on his back. His arms were outstretched like Christ on the cross. His surprised eyes stared up at the tin ceiling as a bright crimson rose bloomed on his crisp white dress shirt.

Nick Rossi's father was dead, and life would never be the same.

CHAPTER ONE

Fifty years later...

Amanda Rittenhouse backed away from the pot of boiling pasta water, leaned against the doorjamb and mopped the sweat off her face with a paper towel. Her lover, Sara Orlando, who usually did the cooking, was seated on the couch in their living room, whispering words of comfort and encouragement to their friend Maya. Beyond the tall French doors that opened to the deck, Lake Norman lay in steel gray silence beneath a frozen January sky. The frigid day perfectly matched the cold atmosphere inside. All was not well between herself and Sara, and for the life of her, Amanda could not understand exactly why.

Winter in North Carolina was not a great time to travel to Washington, DC, but Sara was going in two days—without Amanda. Maya's lover Sharon, whom everyone called Shar, was their newly-elected US Congresswoman. She was the youngest woman ever chosen for the House of Representatives and was already residing in the Capitol. In spite of a government shutdown, she was vigorously protesting President McDonald, advancing her progressive agenda, making all kinds of mischief and a name for herself. Shar longed for Maya to be with her, drinking margaritas and cursing the Republicans, but Maya, Assistant District Attorney for the City of Charlotte, was not at all sure she was ready to join her—at least not in any permanent way.

Be careful what you wish for. They had all worked hard campaigning for their friend, had been shocked and elated when she won, but love was complicated. Now, when push came to shove, it seemed Shar's victory might tear the couple apart. It also seemed that Amanda and Sara might become collateral damage.

When she carried the chilled wine into the living room, she saw their heads together; Sara's long, silken black hair mingling with Maya's close-cropped Afro—Sara's porcelain cheek almost touching Maya's dark one.

"I don't know what to do!" Maya moaned.

"It'll be all right. Once you're face-to-face, you'll work it out," said Sara-the-shrink as her fingers brushed the back of Maya's hand.

Amanda's temper flared. Sure, Sara was a psychiatrist, while Amanda was just a starving artist, but how come Sara always got to be Comforter-in-Chief? Hell, Sara should be in the kitchen making the spaghetti sauce. True, Sara had known Maya and Shar forever, while Amanda had only been with Sara for five years.

Still Sara needed to get her priorities straight. This was not the weekend for her to leave. It was Amanda's special weekend.

She set the wineglasses down hard on the cocktail table, interrupting the therapy session, and poured without ceremony, splashing a drop of blood red Chianti on the glass.

"What?" Sara blinked in surprise and moved away from Maya.

"What time do you leave Friday morning?"

"First thing. We talked about this, babe."

Usually Amanda loved it, but at the moment, she did not want Sara to *babe* her. "Well, Moby Dyke's running on empty.

You'll have to pay to fill her up." Her old, white, whale-like van was a gas guzzler. Sara had commandeered it to help Maya haul Shar's stuff to Washington. "Can I use your Miata while you're gone?"

"Why not? I'd keep the convertible top up, though," Sara answered uneasily.

"I'll pay for all the gas, Mandy," Maya said. "I really appreciate you letting us use your car."

"No problem," she grumbled ungraciously.

"And I am so sorry we'll miss the unveiling of your sculpture," Maya continued. "I know how hard you worked on that piece, and it's absolutely awesome. I just wish the opening was next weekend instead."

"So do I." Sara gazed up at her with those amazing green eyes. "I would not have missed your opening for the world, you know that. But Shar is desperate. She's down to her last pair of undies."

So why is that our problem? Amanda wanted to scream. Why did Sara have to go? Why couldn't Maya make the trip alone? Yes, none of them were rich enough to buy whole new wardrobes, and it would take several sets of strong arms to shift the dresser Shar had begged them to bring. But still…

"I'll make it up to you," Sara said seductively. "And as soon as I get back, we'll visit your sculpture in its new home. I'll take you to dinner and out on the town, I promise."

Amanda wanted to be reasonable. She wasn't jealous. And yet the whole idea of them leaving her alone to face the biggest art event of her young life—all those strangers—made her sick to her stomach.

"I think I've burned the garlic bread," she mumbled, and then stomped back into the kitchen.

CHAPTER TWO

Into the night...

Maya hadn't left until midnight, so Amanda was sleep-deprived. Consequently, the day of work had left her weary to the bone, yet each aching muscle was a badge of accomplishment. Her sore wrists and bruised hands marked the completion of a labor of love, because today she had mounted *Icarus*, her twelve-foot welded steel sculpture, into its marble base. Its soaring aluminum wings were polished, and a billowing silver drop cloth had been lowered from the bank ceiling on a long wire cord, clothing the artwork in secrecy until its unveiling tomorrow night.

Prepping for the big opening had actually been a blessing. The frenetic commute from Davidson into the city, the comradery and support from both the executives who had purchased her piece and the laborers who had helped install it, had taken her mind off the tensions at home. The day had allowed her to recalibrate her thinking, to regain her perspective and to count herself lucky.

To begin with, she'd never expected to sell *Icarus* to the same folks at Wells Fargo who had bought her first major commission four years ago. They had paid a price well beyond her wildest dreams. The monumental sculpture had required a year of intensive work. At the same time, she and her friends had been striving to elect Shar. The idea of electing a liberal lesbian in deep red North Carolina had seemed like a pipe dream. Indeed the effort had initiated an assassination attempt and a murder and had almost cost Amanda her life. So the fact that Shar had won was an unexpected gift and certainly not the cause of her current worries. Amanda was thrilled by the midterm results and the unprecedented number of diverse women elected to Congress. However, she sometimes wondered if either Sara or Maya, both ambitious women, wished they had run instead. With Shar embarking on her glamorous new career, did they feel jealousy or discontent?

Driving home as the sun set off her left shoulder, Amanda thought about how different she was from Sara. It had always been a huge part of the attraction. While Sara was professionally driven to help the addicts, parolees, and homeless she counseled for the City of Charlotte, Amanda was laid-back. If she didn't feel like picking up a welding torch on any given day, she'd avoid her studio and kick back with a good book.

Sara's Puerto Rican heritage gave her luminous porcelain skin, raven black hair and boundless energy. She was a small, buxom bundle of intense emotion. Amanda's Nordic roots gave her pale blond hair, worn short as duck down, a tall, lanky build and skin prone to freckles. As for energy? Much of the time she was just plain lazy.

Sara was experienced, with many lovers in her past. Amanda, not so much—only one other, in fact. But so far these differences had served them well. Better than well. They were spectacular together. Sara was the love of her life.

Feeling much better, Amanda arrived at their condominium complex, pressed the remote, and the door to their two-car garage lifted. First she noticed she had plenty of room to drive

Sara's Miata inside, because her van was missing. Next, craning her neck around, she saw Moby Dyke backed up to their front door and packed to the gills. Funny. She'd thought the plan was for the girls to load up tomorrow morning, then leave for DC directly from Maya's house. They must have changed their minds, decided to get a jump on things.

Likely they'd been working hard, just as she had, and surely Maya intended to spend the night. Bummer. She'd been looking forward to some quality time alone with Sara, a chance to rekindle the spark that had been missing these past few weeks. She wanted to tell Sara how amazing it felt to see her sculpture lifted and suspended in a glory of completion. Even though Sara would miss her opening reception, sharing the elation of today was maybe even more important. She had envisioned them cuddling together with wine and leftover spaghetti, then early to bed for a night of lovemaking.

Sex had never been a problem.

But now, as she trudged up the few steps to their door, weariness invaded each bone in her body, and she adjusted her expectations. Now they would share the food, the drink and the evening with Maya. Not what she had hoped for.

Inserting the key and twisting the lock, Amanda entered quietly to a dark foyer. Instead of the noise and laughter she'd expected, the silence was profound except for soft music, the seductive voice of Norah Jones, coming from the living room.

Had they already collapsed and fallen asleep? Not wanting to disturb, she tiptoed toward the music. The room was dark, but ambient light from the deck leaked through the fog at the French doors. The space was empty. She figured Sara was in the master, Maya in the guest bedroom. Feeling deserted and peevish, Amanda stared into the gloom and caught a shadow of movement from the corner of her eye. Then a dark shape lifted above the back of the couch—Sara's head.

Her eyelids were heavy above startled green eyes as she shifted upwards to a sitting position. Amanda rushed around to give her a kiss, but then she saw the second head—Maya's—nestled in Sara's lap like a little black pussy.

Neither woman was asleep.

Quite the contrary.

Amanda could not breathe. Her chest constricted in what felt like cardiac arrest. She could not hear their words of desperate protest as she turned and somehow fled out the door and back into the night.

CHAPTER THREE

Too close to the sun...

Friday night was unseasonably warm as their car moved south on Interstate 77 toward Charlotte. Her mom, Diana, was elegant in an autumn rust pantsuit, cream blouse, and a silk scarf patterned with the colors of fallen leaves. Her stepdad, Trout, who was driving Mom's old Crown Victoria, looked decidedly less comfortable in tan slacks, brown corduroy sportcoat, and a hated tie.

Amanda fidgeted in the backseat, wondering how she'd made it to her parents' home the night before, blinded by tears and grinding the gears in Sara's stupid little sports car. Luckily they'd both been asleep when she arrived, so she hadn't had to explain her hysteria. Luckier still, they'd bought her excuse this morning—that Sara had left early for DC, so she'd figured she might as well come up to the lake cottage and ride to the opening with them.

Mom had purchased Amanda's dress for the occasion—a low-cut, buttery silk sheath with vivid blue piping, flared sleeves and skirt—colors Mom swore brought out her hair and eyes. Her high-heeled sandals had lace wrapped around her toes and thin straps strangling her ankles. They were supposed to be the hot new thing, but they made Amanda feel like she was walking on tiptoe and did nothing for her destroyed self-image, especially if they caused her to trip during the presentation.

"Relax, honey." Mom reached over the seat and patted her knee. "You look beautiful. Your speech will go fine, and it'll all be over soon."

Her reassurances did not help. The party could not be over soon enough.

As her stepfather parked outside the new Ballantine Wells Fargo branch office, she wondered how she'd get through a speech, when her tongue couldn't get through the next sentence.

She hated being the center of attention, was scared of meeting strangers, suffered from stage fright, and was sick with depression. She had not spoken to Sara since the betrayal, but she'd accidently heard one voice mail before turning off her cell phone.

Please call me, Mandy! It wasn't what you think. I swear!

Like hell it wasn't!

"Look, Ginny, Trev and Lissa are here!" Trout pointed to the little family exiting a Subaru. Clearly the sight of them made him feel less a stranger.

It didn't help her, though. Much as she loved her stepsister, who had proven to be a soulmate, adored the husband and her niece, tonight she wished they would all just go away.

On the other hand, if she could just hang with family rather than make idle chitchat with the society crowd, she might survive. She was grateful when Trout, always the southern gentleman, helped her from the car, and with Mom on his other arm, walked her toward the bank. Tonight she needed all the balance she could get.

As they moved up the freshly poured concrete sidewalk, expertly bordered by pansies, snowdrops, and phlox—blooms to take the landscaping well into a North Carolina winter—she couldn't help being impressed by the modern architecture of the building that would be the permanent home for her sculpture. She was less happy with the full parking lot. The organizers had instructed her to arrive at eight, one hour later than the other guests and just in time for the unveiling, so she could make a grand entrance.

"Are you ready, honey?" Mom asked as they paused at the electronic entry doors.

"Ready as I'll ever be." She took a deep breath and they stepped inside.

The large lobby was completely transformed for the event. Instead of the bright lights she'd used to supervise the installation, the space was now dramatically illuminated by a ring of tall, electric tiki lamps, which encircled the covered sculpture. Banquet tables bordering a makeshift dance floor were covered with silver cloths and laden with a feast of hors d'oeuvres, while waiters in tuxedos circulated with trays of drinks. A string quartet played upbeat classical music and well-dressed patrons milled around, laughing and toasting one another.

God help me! Sara, how could you do this?

"Oh, here's the guest of honor!" Suddenly she felt a man's hand on her arm. Spinning around, she recognized Peter Smith, the acquisitions scout who had purchased her work. The tall elderly man with a unique moustache beamed as she haltingly introduced her parents.

"I hope you all enjoy the party," he said. "And I know you're mighty proud of your talented daughter."

As Mom and Trout mumbled in the affirmative, a second tiny hand tugged at Amanda's skirt.

"*I'm* proud of Aunt Mandy!" Lissa piped up, her red curls bouncing. "But why aren't there any other kids here?"

Everyone laughed as Ginny and her handsome husband, Trev, joined the group.

"Don't worry, Lissa," Trev said. "We won't stay long, just until you see Aunt Mandy's big bird."

In spite of herself, she was touched that they'd taken the time to come. She knew Friday night was the busiest time at Buffalo Guys, the nightclub owned by Trev and Ginny, so they must have hired extra help in order to get away. And with an infant son at home, the gesture was even more impressive.

"I have a little bird!" Lissa held up a champagne glass filled with bright pink liquid and yes, a plastic cockatiel perched on her straw.

"Are you drinking a cocktail, young lady?" Diana frowned.

"You bet she is, Grandma." Ginny winked. "A cranberry juice cocktail!"

At that point, Peter Smith bowed and took his leave, holding up a hand of fingers. "Five minutes till curtain. Get ready, Amanda. I'll be calling you up to the podium."

Before she had time to faint, Ginny drew her aside.

"Mandy, have you called Sara?" she whispered urgently.

Amanda miserably shook her head.

"Well, you need to call her. I don't know what the hell happened, but she's called me three times."

Trev interrupted just in time and pulled Ginny away. "Sorry, Mandy, but we'll have to leave right after the unveiling. Our little red-headed monkey here hasn't eaten yet. We figure a quick trip to McDonald's is in order."

"No problem," Amanda mumbled.

"Just call Sara!" Ginny hissed as Trev dragged her off into the crowd.

All too soon, the tiki lamps blinked and the quartet did its rendition of a drumroll. Peter Smith called out her name over a microphone and Trout escorted her to a spotlight near the base of the sculpture.

She clung to his arm. "Stay with me, Trout!" she pleaded.

"I'll be right here, Manda Bear," he promised.

The audience got quiet as a mechanical winch in the ceiling began cranking the cord and lifting the silver tarp off *Icarus*. Suddenly, the tarp flew completely away, a trumpet sounded, and a collective gasp went up as the sculpture was fully revealed in a theatrical flood of colored lights.

When Amanda turned to look, she was stunned by *Icarus's* beauty—silver wings reaching upward, he seemed to spin skyward with grace and majesty. In that amazing moment, she had absolutely no recollection of giving birth to such a thing as her eyes flooded with tears.

Perhaps by loving Sara, I flew too close to the sun. Like Icarus, my waxen wings have melted and I will plunge to my death.

"Good job, girl!" Trout shouted in her ear.

Only then did she realize everyone was clapping.

Someone yelled, "Speech, speech, let's hear from the artist!"

Her fingers trembled on the mic. "Thank you, everyone," she choked. "All I can say is, hope you enjoy it."

It was enough.

CHAPTER FOUR

Trouble…

As the house lights came up, she was only vaguely aware of the crush of humanity congratulating her, shaking her hand. Dazed, she watched the beautiful people milling around the room, many smiling and nodding in her direction. Then suddenly she recognized a face she'd never in a million years expect to see at an art event.

Detective Rick Molerno from the Charlotte Homicide Division approached with a woman on his arm. He had spotted her and was heading in their direction like a determined funnel cloud, with the sexy woman in tow. He had not changed since she'd first encountered him while exhibiting at Metrolina— same short black hair, same square jaw with afternoon shadow, same rumpled suit.

Just seeing him brought back bad memories.

Bracing herself for his comments, she was shaken when his date initiated the contact. Even at emotional zero, Amanda noticed that the woman with a black buzz cut was hot. Maybe ten years older than Amanda, she was almost the same height. The woman was slim, energetic and tan. Her strapless violet gown showed plenty of cleavage, and her smoky gray-green eyes seemed to undress Amanda in a way blatantly unseemly for Rick's date.

"Ms. Rittenhouse, I really love your work. *Icarus* is magnificent. It's an honor to meet you."

Her voice was as deep and smoky as her eyes. Amanda couldn't decide if her over-the-top praise was sincere or snide. "Th-thank you," she stuttered.

Rick wore his usual sardonic smirk, hands in pockets as he rocked back and forth in scuffed shoes. "Amanda, meet Gina Molerno," he said. "Gina is an artist, too—paints crazy big abstracts. She's the one who dragged me out tonight."

"Pleased to meet you." Amanda shook the woman's hand, then turned back to Rick. "I didn't know you were married, Detective Molerno."

The man coughed out a laugh that turned a few heads. "Hell no, Gina's not my *wife*. She's my *sister*."

Oh, Amanda thought as Gina held on to her fingers a beat too long. As those gray-green eyes continued to stare, she sensed trouble.

At the same time, Rick looked back and forth between them, seemingly amused. "So, Amanda, where's your pal Sara Orlando this fine evening?"

Gina's ears pricked. "Who is Sara?"

He offered a wolfish grin. "Believe it or not, I arrested Ms. Orlando about four years ago—the charge was murder."

"The murder charge was insane!" Amanda longed to disappear. The terrifying incident had occurred when she and Sara had first met and were exhibiting together.

"As it turned out, your girlfriend was completely innocent. But it was exciting for a few weeks, wasn't it?" The detective smirked.

"Why don't you get lost and buy yourself a drink, Ricky?" Gina gave her brother a little shove toward the bar. "I'm sure they have hard liquor as well as this watered-down champagne. I'd like to chat with this woman on my own."

The surly detective left immediately, claiming he had no interest in "art talk." They watched him slouch off in search of scotch and soda.

"My big brother means well," Gina said. "This isn't his scene."

"Not mine, either." Amanda desperately wanted to shelter in her parents' home, kick off her stupid high heels, and brood about Sara.

"Really? Don't you enjoy basking in all this glory?"

She shot the woman a dark look, still not sure whether Gina was offering approval or making fun. "You paint abstracts? Where do you show your work?" she asked tiredly, not really caring about the answer.

"Hey, tonight's not about me, Mandy. It's about you."

She'd never given Gina permission to use her nickname. The woman was unmistakably flirting. She looked for her parents, hoping to escape, but they were still out on the dance floor. Clearly they would not be leaving anytime soon.

"Listen, Mandy," Gina continued. "I actually have an ulterior motive. There's a woman here I'd really like you to meet." She latched onto Amanda's hand.

Having no choice, she allowed Gina to lead her across the room. Along the way, she noticed the party had turned from stuffy to raucous. A gang of young bank execs were playing an improvised game of beer pong, tossing small mint balls into plastic champagne glasses.

"She's right over there…" Gina pointed to a tall, willowy woman in her late forties. She had flowing blond hair, wore a gown similar to Amanda's, and was lost in earnest conversation with Peter Smith, who was keeping a wary eye on the antics of the Wells Fargo boys. "Amanda Rittenhouse, meet Lila Franken. Lila's a sculptor, too."

As Gina introduced them, Amanda pulled out of her funk and was awestruck. "Oh my God! It's such a pleasure to meet you, Ms. Franken. I've studied your work and read your textbook…" She waved toward *Icarus*. "Can't you see your influence? You're the closest I've ever had to a mentor, but I never expected to meet you in person!" She realized she was gushing, but every word she'd uttered was God's own truth. She had admired Lila Franken's metal sculpture forever. "What in the world are you doing down here? I thought you worked out of New York."

"I was in New York for many years, but circumstances beyond my control brought me to North Carolina…" Lila paused for a meaningful look at Gina. "I now have a studio outside my home on Lake Norman—just like you, I understand."

"Mine's not really a studio—more like a garage—and it's only temporary," Amanda confessed. "It belongs to my stepfather, and actually I'm looking for a bigger space…" She clamped her jaw shut. She'd been running off at the mouth, an unfortunate byproduct of coming face-to-face with one's idol—a sculpture superstar. Embarrassed, she was grateful when Peter Smith came to her rescue.

"Lila is the new director of the Mooresville Art Guild," he said. "Were you aware of that, Amanda? It's close to where you live."

"I-I wasn't aware," she stammered. Why was she behaving like a clueless groupie? Part had to do with the rumors she'd heard about her idol being a lesbian—making the hero-worship even more delicious. But when she looked from Lila to Gina, she thought, no way. Everything about Gina, from her in-your-face flirting to her funky sense of style was more like Ginny— while Lila had the grace and sophistication of Amanda's mom. They just didn't belong together.

Lila saw her staring and smiled. "So you are looking for new studio space, Ms. Rittenhouse? Maybe I can offer a few suggestions…"

CHAPTER FIVE

A proposal...

Peter guided them to a private office and opened the door. "You ladies can enjoy some peace in here, so help yourselves." With that, he left, presumably to check on the champagne pong guys.

"Okay, let's talk." Lila led the way. With Amanda in the middle and Gina bringing up the rear, she couldn't escape. They all took seats around a brand new desk still smelling of its packing crate.

"It was my idea, actually," Gina began. "I heard about this space opening up only yesterday. It would be perfect for you, Mandy. Perfect for Lila, too. To be honest, I asked her first, but I can't get her to leave Mooresville."

Amanda was still dazed to be in Lila's company. Being offered a workspace her idol had rejected was beyond belief. "Where is it?"

The two women glanced at one another.

Gina said, "That's the thing, it's in the mountains—Asheville. You'd have to relocate, but I think it would be a good career move for you."

"I agree." Lila nodded. "It's in an amazing area called the River Arts District. Basically, this is a neighborhood of twenty-some old industrial warehouses and factories that have been repurposed over the years as working artist studios and retail space. Almost two hundred artists exhibit there in all kinds of mediums, and it's a destination for collectors from all over the world."

Gina paused to wink at Lila. "It's a happening place, Mandy. The rent is affordable, sales are great, and the town of Asheville is artsy-fartsy awesome—cultural diversity, progressive people, and a number-one destination for lesbians."

Heat crawled up Amanda's face. Did she have a big purple "L" tattooed on her forehead? And why the hard-sell from these women?

Gina noticed her discomfort. "Relax, Mandy. I only knew you were gay because my brother told me. When Rick was working the Metrolina murder he got to know Sara Orlando pretty well. Having a sister like me, who is way out of the closet, he was able to put it together."

The explanation only served to make her more self-conscious. She fidgeted in her chair and tugged at her dress to better cover her knees. Hearing Sara's name spoken was agony. "I can't leave town right now," she muttered.

Gina groaned and rolled her eyes. "Told you so, Lila. She's as bad as you are. I bet this is about Sara. Seems like whenever the opportunity of a lifetime knocks, you partnered-up lesbians can't answer the door. Am I right, Mandy? Is this about Sara?"

Amanda rose to leave, but Lila put a gentle hand on her shoulder.

"Please don't go, Ms. Rittenhouse. Gina always shoves her nose in where it doesn't belong, and in my opinion, it's unforgivable." She frowned at Gina. "But she is right about me. I gave up New York to be with my partner in North Carolina, and she's the reason I'm not jumping at this opportunity in Asheville. All this was my fault, because the moment I saw *Icarus* unveiled I asked Gina to approach you about the space. So please forgive us both."

Lila's kind words calmed her, and she was shamefully flattered by the praise. So she sat very still, twisted her hands in her lap, and listened to the string quartet. The group had switched from classical to soft, danceable popular music, and the party was winding down.

"Nothing to forgive," she said at last. "I really appreciate you telling me about this, but I just can't relocate right now."

Lila nodded in understanding, but Gina made one last pitch. "Look, Mandy, I'm driving up to Asheville tomorrow to stay with some friends for the weekend, and I have a proposal. Why don't you tag along and at least take a look at the River Arts District?"

"Leave her alone." Lila gave Gina's hand a little smack. "*No* means *no*. Don't you get that?"

While the two squabbled, a loud argument was escalating right outside their door. It involved Gina's brother and a handsome newcomer whose voice she recognized immediately. Sara's twin brother, Marc.

She gasped. "Will you excuse me, please?" Without waiting for a response, Amanda rushed toward the noise, leaving the women gaping after her, their mouths hanging open in surprise.

CHAPTER SIX

The sixty-four thousand dollar question…

The two men were shoving one another. Amanda knew there was no love lost between Marc Orlando and Rick Molerno. During the Metrolina murder investigation, the detective had first accused Marc, then Sara, of the homicide. The animosity began there.

She pushed between them. "Stop it, Marc! What the hell do you think you're doing?" She delivered a sharp little punch to his arm, and he spun around in surprise.

Seeing Sara's twin always jolted her, but tonight it was a punch to her gut. They were so much alike. Although Marc was taller and more muscular than his sister, he had her silken black hair, square jaw and intense eyes. At the moment those eyes were wide with amusement.

"That's no way to treat a patron of the arts, Mandy. I made a special effort to be here tonight." He grinned with perfect white teeth. "Rick and I were just playing around. Weren't we, Molerno?"

The detective laughed. "We had a minor disagreement about your sculpture. Marc says it's a bird. I say it's a sailboat. So which is it?"

Completely confused, she looked from one to the other. Since when had these guys become such great pals? "It's a doomed young man with delusions of grandeur." She frowned.

"So we were both wrong." Marc shook Rick's hand, then noticed her confusion. "Weird, isn't it? Believe it or not, Rick and I reconnected at one of his sister's painting classes. I see you've met Gina, so you know she's an artist. The style I've been fooling around with is similar to her work, so I figured she could teach me a thing or two."

"You take art classes from Gina?" She knew Marc enjoyed painting as a hobby. One of his big splashy abstracts hung directly over the bed where she and Sara made love. The thought made her sad all over again.

Rick picked up the conversation. "So one day I visited the classroom to check up on my little sister and found this shady character working at an easel. We decided to let bygones be bygones, had a couple of beers, and the rest is history."

She tossed up her hands and gaped at them.

"So now that Amanda has intervened to keep the peace, I'll leave you two to chat." With that Rick went in search of a waiter serving drinks.

"It's a small world after all," Marc sang under his breath. "But seriously, Mandy, I was planning to come to your unveiling all along. Sorry I'm a little late. I got held up at work."

"No problem."

Marc was gorgeous in a gray suit, deep navy dress shirt and colorful silk tie. Many women in the room were watching him, and no doubt he'd choose one to take home tonight. One-night stands were his specialty.

"Besides, Sara would kill me if I didn't put in an appearance," he teased. "Where is my sister, anyway?"

"You don't know?"

Marc spread his hands and lifted his eyebrows. "Isn't she with you?"

That was the sixty-four thousand dollar question. "I'd guess Sara is in Washington, DC, about now."

Now it was Marc's turn to gape. He blinked a couple of times, then took her to a quiet corner. "Are you okay, Mandy?" He tentatively touched her sleeve. "You guys didn't have a fight, did you?"

"Of course not," she lied and tried to compose herself. "Sara's helping Maya move Shar's stuff to her new apartment."

"Well, that's cool." Marc had worked hard on Shar's campaign, so he was as anxious as the rest of them to see Shar well established in Washington. At the same time, he had a short attention span and was soon eyeing an attractive blond woman who had been flirting hard from the sidelines of the dance floor. "Give me a call when Sara contacts you, okay? I want an update about Shar kicking Republican ass."

Marc kissed her cheek, then made a beeline for the blonde. The party was breaking up. Soon Mom and Trout would take her home, and in the meantime, Gina and Lila had left the office and were moving toward the exit door.

Impulsively, she headed them off and grabbed Gina's arm. "Wait! I've changed my mind. If the offer's still good, Gina, I'd like to go to Asheville with you tomorrow."

CHAPTER SEVEN

Stranger danger…

Amanda's impromptu trip to Asheville raised two eyebrows—her mother's. Mom hovered while she hurriedly packed some casual clothes and her all-purpose black party dress in a tag-along and rolled it to the back porch to wait for Gina.

"What's going on with you, Mandy? You never said one word about going to the mountains. Good thing you left some of your clothes here with us."

She sighed and stared at her mother, who still looked slightly hungover from their late night at the unveiling. "It was a last minute decision. I've never seen the Appalachians, so when Gina offered, I figured why not?"

She couldn't admit she was exploring new studio space, which implied she was moving away, because then her mother would panic and try to change her mind. She and Mom had only recently reunited, after many years of estrangement, which had been entirely Amanda's fault. They had come to know and love one another all over again. Mom had even rented her and Sara the condo for way below market value. Mom had lived in the condo before she met Trout, the new love of her life. So Amanda did not want to leave her now, no matter how tempting the Asheville space might be.

She certainly couldn't tell Mom how she'd caught Sara with Maya, for Diana would be truly devastated.

"But who is Gina?" Mom persisted. "You don't even know this woman."

"True, but her brother is a cop, so I don't think I have anything to fear." She laughed uneasily, because while she knew Gina posed no criminal stranger danger, she was not entirely sure Gina had a platonic friendship in mind, and she didn't want to be fighting off unwelcome advances all weekend.

Mom shook her head and cinched her bathrobe tighter against the cold breeze blowing across the porch. "Well, all the pretty autumn leaves are down now, but the hills should be beautiful all the same. You will be home for your stepfather's birthday, won't you?"

"Of course. Trout's birthday is Thursday, and I'll be back Monday evening at the latest."

Her mother seemed unconvinced, but when old Ursie padded out to join them, yawned and tucked her long, grizzled Doberman nose into Diana's hand, her mother exhaled in resignation. "Well, that's okay then, because Ginny's roasting a big turkey and everyone will be here. I sure hope Sara can join us."

Amanda tried to keep the exasperation out of her voice. "I'm not sure about that."

"Well, why don't you ask her? I don't know what's wrong with the two of you, but Sara's been calling me all morning wanting to speak with you. Can't you find a few minutes to call her back?"

Mom was pissed. Sometimes Amanda thought she liked Sara better than she liked her. Ever since she'd come out as a lesbian and introduced Sara as her partner, Mom had been a fan. If they ever broke up, Diana would hate it.

Amanda was mightily relieved when a metallic green pickup truck came roaring down the gravel road, kicking up a cloud of dust. It had to be Gina, since Trout's cottage was the only destination at the end of the path.

Sure enough, Gina hopped down from the driver's seat, lifted a brisk salute to the bill of a pink ball cap concealing her gelled punk cut, and grinned at them. Today she wore skin-tight jeans with holes at the knees, high-heeled black boots, and a vintage leather bomber jacket splattered with droplets of colorful oil paint.

"Hi, guys," she called. "Let's get a move on, Mandy!"

After the briefest of introductions, Gina opened the truck bed and tossed Amanda's luggage in along with racks of paintings stacked for delivery.

"What's all this?" Amanda wondered.

"It's my new Nissan Frontier. Isn't it cool?"

"No, I mean, is this your art?"

"Yeah, I'm taking a load to Asheville. You asked last night where I show my work, so now you'll see one of my venues in person."

Seconds later they were on the road. When they reached River Highway and Amanda suggested they turn west for a scenic shortcut to Route 40, Gina ignored her, made a right, and headed toward Mooresville.

"I need a Starbucks fix," she explained as she sped a good fifteen miles an hour above the speed limit.

Amanda fastened her seatbelt and prayed the Iredell County sheriff was not on patrol. Clearly Gina was a take-charge kinda gal. It seemed the last thing she needed was a jolt of caffeine, but Amanda held her tongue as they skidded into the restaurant's parking lot.

"I'm having a double cappuccino. What can I bring you, Mandy?"

"I'm good. I'll just wait in the truck."

She watched Gina bustle through the crowd of early Saturday coffee drinkers. In the unforgiving light of morning, she looked older than she had at last night's party. Fine age lines webbed the corners of her eyes and mouth, and she moved with the exaggerated energy of someone determined to ignore the little aches and pains creeping up on her. Amanda now guessed her age at mid- to late-forties, about fifteen years her senior. She was able to assume all this because Gina Molerno reminded Amanda of her ex-partner, Rachel, and the similarities plucked a bittersweet chord on her heartstrings.

God, the last thing she needed in her life was another Rachel, who, incidentally, had also been a painter. They had lived together for a decade in Sarasota, Florida, until their hurtful breakup had sent Amanda running to North Carolina. Been there, done that. And yet Gina was not at all like Rachel. Where Rachel had been serious, refined, and polite to a fault— Gina was brash, flamboyant, and unafraid to speak her mind. So other than age and profession, the only thing they had in common was that both were magnetically attractive.

"Ready to rock 'n' roll?" Suddenly Gina was at the door, handing her a steaming coffee as she climbed into the driver's seat. "Hold that while I buckle up, will you?" Her fingers deliberately touched Amanda's in the passing of the cup.

As they drove north on Interstate 77, connecting with Route 40 near Statesville and then turning west toward the mountains, Amanda did not attempt to help with navigation since Gina obviously knew the way. In fact, Amanda did not converse much at all. She was too busy remembering the last time she'd been at that intersection with Maya, Shar, and Sara. Instead of turning west that summer, they'd gone east to North Carolina's Outer Banks and the eventful vacation where she'd fallen deeply in love.

She'd been aware of Gina watching her as the miles unraveled and a haunting blend of violin and Native American flute music came from the CD player—a disc Gina enthusiastically described as "authentic mountain music." But apparently she was not paying strict enough attention, because Gina abruptly ejected the CD and turned to face her.

"Enough already," she said. "Now, Mandy, tell me all about your love life."

CHAPTER EIGHT

Gina's story…

Amanda scooted as far away from Gina as she could get in the claustrophobic cab. The question about her private life was offensive from the lips of a near-stranger, not to mention the last thing she wanted to talk about.

"Oh, c'mon, Mandy. You know my brother told me all about you and Sara, but I didn't see her with you at the party last night."

Amanda gazed at the forest whizzing past her window at breakneck speed. The trees were barren and stick-like, a dizzying tangle of gray braced for winter. In the distance, the foothills slept in the morning haze.

Instead of answering, she said, "Did your brother the detective fix your speeding tickets, too? We're out of his jurisdiction now, Gina, so you better slow down."

Her companion barked out a smoky laugh and eased up on the accelerator. "Sorry. You're not the first person to complain about my driving. I always go too fast and I'm way too pushy. I apologize. You don't have to tell me about Sara if you don't want to."

"There's nothing to tell. Sara's out of town." She gave the easy explanation of Sara's visit to DC—to help Shar get settled.

Gina then raved about the awesome new congresswoman, whom she had of course supported, and seemed somewhat starstruck by their friendship with Shar. Yet Amanda remained uneasy, because Mom had forced her to turn on her cell phone so they could keep in touch, and she knew Sara would keep calling. She had set her phone to vibrate, not wanting to have a private conversation in front of Gina. But the phone lay in her pants pocket, against her thigh, like a snake threatening to strike at any minute.

"Do you and Sara live together?" Gina could not leave it alone.

"Yes," Amanda mumbled unhappily, and in a desperate bid to change the subject, asked, "Are *you* with anyone, Gina?"

The question proved to be a perfect deflection, but a sore subject, because it opened up Gina's emotional floodgates and initiated a long, bitter rant about a woman named Red. The two had a long and stormy off-again-on-again history. Over the past two decades, Gina and Red had shared apartments, even bought a house together, but at the moment their love affair was over—Gina's choice.

"You say Red is a homicide detective, and she's your brother's partner?" Amanda was fascinated.

"That's the big problem, isn't it?" Gina moaned and gripped the steering wheel. "Rick introduced us years ago. The two of them are really close, you know? Cops share this weird bond. They have each other's backs and depend on one another in life and death situations."

She continued to explain the conflict, which sounded almost incestuous. When Gina and Red first became lovers, Rick, who had just gotten divorced from his wife, highly disapproved of the relationship. He claimed not to mind that the two most important women in his life were gay, yet he displayed a response much like jealousy.

"Sometimes I wondered if Red was more passionate about me or my brother. Too much intensity all the time, and Rick was always around—in our home, our lives, with me stuck in the middle."

As Gina talked, her eyes blurred with tears and she recklessly sped up to eighty miles per hour. "I asked Red a million times to get off the streets, where she faced danger every day. She could have gotten a desk job anytime, but hunting criminals gave her this insane rush. But then she got shot!"

"Please pull over Gina and let me drive for a while," Amanda begged. As interesting as all this was, she did not want to end up as roadkill.

"So when she got hurt and almost died, I waited until she was out of the hospital and then begged her one last time to get off the streets. But she said no."

Amanda touched Gina's arm. "Pull over right now."

Amazingly, Gina suddenly slowed up. Fortunately a weigh station appeared on the horizon, so she drove off the highway and stopped. As the woman got her sobbing under control, she handed Amanda the keys, stepped out of the truck, and they switched places.

After a quick scan of the dashboard and operating systems, Amanda nodded. *I can do this.* Automatic shift—piece of cake. After all, Gina's Nissan was much like Moby Dyke. Soon they were back on the road, cruising at a sedate sixty-five miles per hour.

Eventually Gina was able to speak again. "So I left Red for good. It's over."

"I'm sorry." Amanda recalled how, when she had been shot—twice—Sara had stuck with her and visited the hospital every day. It seemed odd that Gina would abandon her lover under such circumstances, and she wondered how final their current separation would prove to be. Considering her past history with Red, Gina's story might well have another chapter yet to be written with her police lady.

Would she and Sara get another chapter, too?

Just then kick-ass mountains suddenly jutted their breast-like peaks high in the near-distant sky, and the snake in her pocket bit her thigh. When her cell phone vibrated, she knew at her core it was Sara. She also knew she had to answer sometime if she wanted to retain what was left of her sanity. Gina was lost in her own thoughts, gazing out at the landscape, and did not notice her distress. Deciding to let Sara's call go to voice mail, Amanda cast about for a way to communicate in private.

"Hey, Gina, I really need to pee. Is there a rest stop nearby?"

As she snapped out of her reverie, Gina's amazing gray-green eyes, ravaged red from tears, soon came alive with sassy humor. "You and me both, sister. That double cappuccino is busting my bladder, but we're in luck. There's a truck stop dead ahead."

CHAPTER NINE

Love's...

Love's Truck Stop. The name was topic-appropriate to their first hour of road trip conversation, and she was thrilled when Gina rushed from the truck the minute they parked. Gina's urgent call of nature gave Amanda the perfect opportunity to check her voice mail without an audience.

She unfastened her seatbelt, opened the door, and lowered her sneakers to the pavement. Noise assaulted her ears from the roaring highway, idling diesel trucks and chattering travelers. Seeking a quiet spot and a breath of carbon monoxide-free air, she made her way through a maze of monster tires and gas pumps, and finally located a well-worn bench behind the huge convenience store. The bench sat in a tattered grass plot outside the rear entrance to public showers and the restaurant kitchen. Here the noise was somewhat muted and the air smelled of cooking grease rather than exhaust fumes.

Taking a seat, she rolled her neck and saw a red valentine heart soaring atop one of those tall pods designed to attract traffic from miles away. The Love's logo floated in front of a mountain range that resembled a naked blue woman lying on her back, and as Amanda checked her voice mail and confirmed her caller had indeed been Sara, her heart began to palpitate and her mouth went dry. Perhaps it was fatigue from the night before, or emotional overload, but as she beheld the surreal scene before her, she felt disoriented and adrift. Where was she and what the hell was she doing?

She inhaled, held her breath and listened to Sara's familiar voice in the alien place. Was it her imagination, or did she hear tears as her lover begged her to call back? She touched the screen and shakily returned the call. After enduring an unusually long interlude of silence while her call networked through the southeastern United States and sailed up to Washington, Sara picked up on the first ring.

"Oh, thank God you called, Mandy. I am so, so sorry!"

The tearful apology failed to convince her, nor was she moved by the shaky edge in Sara's voice.

Sara pushed on. "I'm a stupid fool, but I promise, what you saw meant nothing! If you give me a chance, maybe I can explain. I know how bad it looked, but we never went all the way. I was trying to comfort her, and yes, it got out of hand. Maya and I both understood immediately that it was a terrible mistake. We've never been anything more than good friends. Surely you know that? Will you ever forgive me?"

Certainly Amanda had always known how close Sara and Maya were, and admittedly, a time or two in her life, she herself had allowed physical attraction to mistakenly intrude in a friendship, but forgive Sara? Just like that?

"I don't know," she answered honestly.

"Mandy, I'm so ashamed, and I can only imagine how hurt you feel. How can I make it up to you?"

Amanda squeezed her eyes shut tight and tried to process.

As she looked around the parking lot, her gaze fell on a driver asleep in his rig, his head thrown back on the rest, mouth hanging open in a snore.

"I have to think about this," she choked out.

"Please, Mandy, I…"

But before Sara could finish the sentence, a new truck drove up and crawled close past the bench, belching and hooting like a locomotive.

"What the hell was that?" Sara cried. "Where are you, anyway?"

She recalled seeing a sign right before she pulled in. "Pisgah Forest, I think?"

"You're in the *mountains*?"

"Looks that way." She glanced at the heart sign. "We're at a place called Love's Truck Stop, would you believe?" she answered bitterly.

For a long moment, silence echoed from Washington, DC.

"Dare I ask, why are you at a truck stop in the Blue Ridge Mountains?"

Fair question. "I don't exactly know. Some people I met at the unveiling thought I'd enjoy seeing Asheville, especially the River Arts District."

"Absolutely! It's a great town and a world-class center of the arts, but who are you traveling with?"

"The woman I'm with is a friend of your brother, Marc. He introduced us last night."

"A friend of Marc's? What's her name?"

Amanda stalled. "He takes a painting class from her, I believe."

"C'mon, Mandy, who is she?"

"Her name is Gina." She heard wheels grinding all the way from DC as Sara processed the information.

"Gina Molerno *the lesbian*? Good God! Everyone knows that whenever that woman is fighting with her girlfriend, she's on the make for anyone with an X chromosome. Has she moved on you yet?"

Amanda bristled. Where did Sara get off being jealous right now? Plus, she did not appreciate being described as any old X chromosome. "You know Gina, do you?"

"No, I've never met the woman, but Marc's told me everything I need to know."

"Gina is actually quite attractive. I think I'm going to enjoy our time together."

"Give me a break," Sara said angrily.

Five minutes into the conversation, and already they were fighting. The snoring trucker woke up and started his engine, drowning out any hope for further discussion.

"I can't hear you!" Sara complained.

"Yeah, we can't talk right now," Amanda growled. "Maybe I'll call when I've settled in…"

But the connection was already broken, by accident or design, she was not sure. Either way, she knew Sara would wait a few minutes and then call back, but Amanda wasn't up for it. Besides, Gina would return any minute, and she didn't want her to overhear an argument. So she shut her phone down completely, took one last look at the absurd floating heart, and felt bluer than the naked mountain lady sleeping on her back.

CHAPTER TEN

Gaining altitude…

As Amanda ducked into Love's to use the restroom, she passed Gina coming out.

"Hey, Mandy, hold my coffee while I show you the present I bought you." Gina handed her a cup of supercharged Java Amore while she picked through a bag of purchases and held up a T-shirt. "Check it out! You can't visit Asheville without a nod to all the aging hippies living there."

The psychedelic orange and chartreuse tie-dyed shirt depicted a classic black peace symbol incorporating the Love's logo, with the words "Make Love, Not War."

"Wow, thanks! But you shouldn't have…"

Gina tucked the shirt back in her bag and repossessed her coffee. She held up the two-fingered peace salute. "Go in peace, girlfriend." And then she headed for the truck.

The store smelled like leather, popcorn, and hotdogs. It offered souvenirs ranging from gospel CDs to biker chains and sold lots of NoDoz. After a quick trip to the bathroom, Amanda purchased two chili dogs and two caffeine-free colas. She was starving and she figured Gina could use some food in her belly to soak up all the liquid stimulation she was drinking.

Soon Gina was driving toward a town called Black Mountain as they companionably chewed on hotdogs. By unspoken agreement, they'd stopped discussing romantic disappointments, and Amanda gradually felt less bruised by the phone call with Sara as the scenery seduced her.

"Those mountain ranges are called the Seven Sisters." Gina gestured at the horizon. "The sisters step up in height, one after another, to their father, Graybeard Mountain."

"So, what's the folk story behind them?" She hoped that Gina would spin some yarns about the North Carolina mountains.

But Gina shrugged. "Beats me. I never pay much attention to that woo-woo stuff."

Disappointed, Amanda fell silent and designed her own fable as she gazed at the misty haunting peaks drifting toward infinity. Naturally the legend should include unrequited love, doomed Indian maidens and heroes—better yet, heroines.

"Where are we staying in Asheville?" she asked.

"Now *that* is an interesting story. We're staying at the home of an elderly professor of mine, Carl Fischer, which he shares with a man named Ron Dunifon. Ron's about my age, at least twenty years younger than Carl."

From the twinkle in Gina's eye, Amanda knew something juicy was up. "Are these guys gay?"

Gina giggled. "Well, that's the mystery, isn't it? Carl taught in the art department at Appalachian State in Boone, and that's when I met him, back in the mid-nineties."

"So Mr. Fischer teaches painting?"

"No, he taught ceramics—he's a potter, retired now. But I took a few of his classes, and somehow we became friends. When I graduated with my BFA and returned to Charlotte, Carl kept in touch and encouraged me to keep painting. He's been a mentor, a father figure all these years."

As Gina spoke, Amanda realized how little she knew about this woman. Did she and her brother even have living parents? "So what about Ron?"

"Well, I share display space with him in downtown Asheville at a place that used to be an old Woolworth's building. Now Ron is definitely gay. I met him at the Pride parade up here two years ago. Professionally he's a practical nurse, but he aspires to be an artist. He's not a good painter yet—too tight and realistic for my taste—but he tries real hard. In fact, he's doing me a huge favor by subleasing a few walls to me. Otherwise I couldn't show here because they require their artists to live locally."

Gina went on to explain that the Woolworth Walk, like many antique malls, was manned by a rotating staff of exhibitors who watched one another's booths and rang up sales for each other—so the artists could have other day jobs. The River Arts District, by contrast, required the artists to work daily and attend to their own sales. In short, the River Arts lessees were onsite owners and operators of their individual businesses.

"So if I chose to lease space in the place you brought me to see, I would definitely have to move here," Amanda concluded.

"Right."

"But in the Woolworth's building I could show my sculpture from long distance?"

"Only if you could find a local like Ron. And the building is full up, with a waiting list."

Amanda reminded herself it didn't matter anyway, because she was only looking, with no intention of leaving her family— or Sara, if they could somehow mend their relationship. "How did Carl and Ron get together?"

"Honestly, I'm not sure, but I bet we figure it out this weekend." Gina winked. "And as for Carl being gay, who the hell knows? I've seen him with women, but I used to hear rumors that he swung both ways."

"You think he's bi?"

"Could be, but for Ron's sake, I wish he were gay, because I think Ron's in love with him. Observe them together, will you? I'd like to know what you think, Mandy."

As they neared the city of Asheville they drove steeply uphill, gaining altitude. Slower trucks moved to the right, as did travelers who wanted to savor the amazing view. Amanda's ears popped.

"This is exciting," she confessed as they drove into town toward Biltmore Village and Gina described the grandeurs of George Vanderbilt's 178,000-square-foot chateau down the road. The nineteenth-century millionaire was a railroad magnate who had left his mark on the city. "Is this the town center?"

"Nope, we'll keep moving into old Asheville and I'll give you a quick tour." They passed a huge medical complex spanning both sides of the avenue. "That's where Ron works part-time—Mission Hospital. He actually became a nurse when his partner died of AIDS many years ago."

"That's so sad," Amanda mumbled as they continued past a nightclub called The Orange Peel and entered what was obviously the happening downtown district. The place took her by surprise. Instead of trendy and modern like Sarasota, this town dated from the late eighteen hundreds. Two- and three-storied wood and brick storefronts were now occupied by boutique art galleries, ethnic and new age restaurants, and an old movie theater. Folks of all ages crowded the streets, enjoying the festive atmosphere. A large group waved signs to protest the current government shutdown, now in its third week.

The bustling shopping district snaked uphill for several blocks, with active streets, park areas, and enchanting alleyways. The imposing backdrop of eternal mountains lent a mystical atmosphere.

"You're right, Gina, I feel like I've stepped back into the sixties." She saw millennials, couples straight and gay, country and city types, and older pairs holding hands as they peeked into used book stores or browsed through vintage vinyl record albums. "What fun! These people look like they might actually buy art."

"Absolutely. In my space, I've sold to visitors from all over the world. You will be tempted to live here, Mandy. I promise."

CHAPTER ELEVEN

Meeting strangers…

They continued north through town on Merrimon Avenue. "This road leads to the village of Weaverville," Gina explained. "Carl's house is near Beaver Lake on the outskirts of Asheville. I've never been there before, but I understand it's impressive. He's quite rich, you know."

Amanda did not know, but she was curious. "So where'd he get his money?"

"It's a mystery. He's made a good income from the sale of his pottery because everyone wants to collect his work. But still, I've never heard of a wealthy potter—or professor, for that matter. Who knows, maybe Carl won the lottery?" Gina laughed and slowed with the rush hour traffic.

"Are Carl and Ron native North Carolinians?"

"Ron is Asheville born and bred. The way he tells it, his family were right-wing rednecks. He grew up piss-poor and got tossed out on his ass when his conservative, Bible-beating parents discovered he was gay. So I guess he literally pulled himself up by his bootstraps, worked his way through college with some help from his partner, then got his nursing degree on his own. Thing is, when you meet him, you'll never guess he came from trailer trash."

"What about Carl?'

"His official bio says he's originally from the Midwest. He got his BFA and MFA degrees from Indiana University and taught there for many years before he quit to become a professional potter in Brown County, Indiana. Then somehow he fell in love with the Appalachians and made his way to Boone, where I met him at the university. When Carl retired and moved to Asheville he became a mover and a shaker in the River Arts Community."

"You seem to know a lot about them."

"Ron, yeah, he's an open book. Carl, not so much. He never talks about the past and tends to live in the present."

Amanda was suddenly eager to meet these men. Ron sounded brave and sympathetic, like someone she could relate to, while Carl, unlike other elderly people she'd met who often dwelled on their lost youths, was apparently engaged in the here and now.

At the same time, she was nervous about meeting strangers. "Are you sure they won't mind putting me up for a couple of nights?"

"They'll love it, my dear." Gina chuckled. "These guys are social butterflies and they adore company—especially a fresh face with new gossip. Believe it or not, while Asheville may seem wildly cosmopolitan, much of that is due to the constantly shifting tourists. The smaller population of permanent residents—especially the arts crowd—has its little inner circles and cliques, like an ingrown toenail."

Maybe she would not be tempted to live here, after all. Amanda watched the eclectic homes crawling by beyond the truck's windshield. She and Rachel had lived center stage in a similar arts district in Sarasota, where everyone knew everyone else's business. At times the drama was claustrophobic—a lifestyle she was not anxious to repeat.

She had noticed that within the Asheville city limits, the residences had varied from older stately brick Victorians, to original Craftsman-style structures behind tangled gardens, to simple ranches and even some abandoned farmhouses. But here in the suburbs, the lot sizes were larger, with expensive new construction carved into the surrounding hills. Soon Gina made a left onto a hidden gravel lane that stood alone between the developments.

"This is it, 101 Merrimon Avenue," Gina said. "I almost missed it. Leave it to Carl to hide in plain sight."

Amanda knew exactly what she meant. The secretive entrance to Carl Fischer's home was sandwiched between two affluent developments so that most travelers would fly by without noticing. As they drove through a heavily forested area, up and down the rolling terrain, she saw no sign of neighbors. When they finally entered a clearing at the top of a hill and approached a large, contemporary structure that blended with the rocks, the trees, and the sky, it felt like they were in the wilderness.

"Wow, I figured Carl liked his privacy, but this is ridiculous," Gina said.

"The house is really beautiful, though. I've never seen architecture quite like it."

"Yes, it's Carl's own design. When he taught pottery he emphasized that form should follow function and believed pots should be as natural and earthy as the clay they are made from. Seems like he feels the same way about his house."

Gina was right. The organic flow of natural materials and stone walls, shingles that merged in color and texture with the rough rock ledge behind the house, and the many glass windows reflecting the outdoors made the house seem almost transparent, like it had grown from the land rather than been placed upon it. A crushed stone driveway wound around the structure, and an old barn, obviously renovated, stood behind the parking area in back.

The drama was heightened by an orange and blue sunset mirrored in the plate glass. "It's ethereal—otherworldly," Amanda commented as they retrieved their luggage and moved along a flagstone path flanked with native wildflowers gone to seed. They stepped up onto a porch canopied by laurel and rhododendrons. The cold air was scented with pine.

"Ready?" Gina pressed a bell beside the forest green door.

"Ready as I'll ever be." She held her breath as classic Westminster chimes echoed from deep inside the house.

Suddenly the door opened.

A thin, extremely tall man with bony wrists stared at them in the dim light from wall sconces. He had the trace of an afternoon shadow on his pale, skull-like face and reminded her of Lurch from *The Addams Family*. The dark embers of his eyes below thinning black hair were none too friendly when he scowled and said, "Who the hell are you?"

CHAPTER TWELVE

Ron and Carl...

Gina gave the man a playful shove. "Cut it out, Ron!"

He stumbled backward, laughing as he pulled Gina into his long arms. "You guys are late. We expected you an hour ago. Steaks are marinated, the salad is tossed, and I'm dying for a drink." He winked at Amanda. "Gina said she was bringing a friend, but you are so *young*. Cradle robbing, are we, Gina?"

Once she recovered from fright, Amanda hoped she was not blushing. She held out her hand. "Pleased to meet you, Mr. Dunifon, and I'm not all that young."

"It's a matter of perspective. When you are pushing fifty like Gina and me, you kids in your twenties look like babies. And another thing, call me Ron or I'll really feel ancient. Same with Carl. If you dare call him Professor Fischer he'll toss you out of the house."

She didn't bother to point out that she was actually a mature thirty.

Ron gave her hand a firm shake, then they moved down the hall and paused at the base of a steel spiral staircase, where the light was much brighter. While Gina formally introduced them, she noted that Ron was not as scary as he'd first seemed. Yes he was tall, slim, and pale, with thinning dark hair and smoldering eyes—but he was also quite friendly and excessively civilized. From his pressed denim work shirt to knife-creased tan slacks and Gucci loafers, Ron was urbane and beautifully mannered, with only a soft trace of southern accent. Like Gina had said, it was hard to believe he'd come from such a rough background.

He pointed at the staircase. "You ladies will be sleeping upstairs. I assume you want the room with the queen-sized bed?" He gave Gina a sly grin.

"Yes!" Gina answered immediately.

"No!" Amanda gasped. "What are the options? We're not a couple, you know."

"What a pity." He spread his hands. "I'm afraid the other bedroom has only bunk beds."

"I'll take it!" she exclaimed.

Ron offered to carry their bags up, but they both said no. Seconds later, they walked down a rustic hallway to their separate rooms, with Gina acting devastated by the fact that they weren't rooming together. She opened the door to the queen bed suite, which overlooked the mountains. "See what you're missing, Mandy?"

The view was truly spectacular, but Amanda said, "I'll survive," and continued to the end of the hall, where the bunk bed room faced the side of a cliff. But the space was large and fun, decorated with colorful bedspreads and sports posters that would appeal to teenage boys. For the first time, she wondered if Carl Fischer had grandchildren.

She especially appreciated the room's private bath, where she took care of business, washed her face, and brushed her teeth. Gina had promised that the dress code in the Fischer household was casual, so she decided the wrinkled slacks and striped cotton blouse she was wearing would suffice. Adding a pullover sweater to ward off the chill, she stepped into the hall and met a transformed Gina. The woman had traded the torn jeans, black boots, pink ball cap and paint-splattered bomber jacket for a sleek cranberry suede pantsuit, ivory silk blouse, handmade jewelry and artsy sandals.

She felt at a distinct disadvantage. "Not fair. Why did you change?"

"You look great. Don't worry about it."

Feeling like the fool who arrives at a Halloween party in a clown suit only to find everyone else in street clothes, Amanda slunk down the stairs behind her turncoat friend as her dread of meeting Professor Fischer escalated. They followed the music, a CD playing classical guitar, into a great room featuring a high-timbered ceiling, comfy leather furniture, rich Oriental rugs, and a huge stone fireplace with logs burning on the open hearth.

Ron stood near the fireplace fussing with a cart of hors d'oeuvres. He glanced at Amanda, then wolf whistled at Gina. "The bar is open, girls. What can I fix you to drink?"

As Gina placed an order for a whiskey sour, Amanda cast about looking for Carl Fischer. Soon she spotted a bushy white head slowly rising from the depths of a wingback chair. Although his back was toward her, she could see the man was having trouble standing. But when he finally made it with the help of a gnarled cane and turned to face her, she gasped in surprise.

Because Carl Fischer was a ghost. He was the spitting image of her long-dead Grandpa Whitaker—or at least, he was the essence of how she remembered that kindly old gentleman. He had the same rugged build stooped by age, same handsome face lined with time's wisdom, and same sparkling blue eyes lit by intelligence.

Noting her surprise, their eyes locked and Carl's brows shot up. "What's wrong, young lady?"

"Oh…" she stuttered. "It's just that you remind me of someone."

His laugh was the same booming bass from her childhood. "I get that a lot," he said. "Your grandpa, right?"

"Right," she confessed, suddenly at ease. Only his voice was different—slower delivery, words more enunciated than the lickety-split dialect of her New England grandfather. Also, she need not have worried about her attire because Carl wore baggy corduroys, an oversize wool sweater, and bedroom slippers that looked like the ancient hound lying near his chair had been chewing on them. She crossed the room and eagerly held out her hand. "I'm Amanda Rittenhouse, sir. Pleased to meet you."

After the expected admonishment that she must call him *Carl*, he took her hand in both of his and she recognized the rough, dry texture of a potter's skin. The bloodhound lifted his droopy eyes.

"This is Barney," Carl said. "Give him one of these and he's your friend for life."

She obediently handed the dog a bone-shaped biscuit and was rewarded with a double thump of his tail.

"Barney's old like me. His eyesight is shot, and he's not up to running anymore, but his nose is still first class."

She patted the bloodhound's silky brown head, then moved aside so Gina could give Carl a big hug. They embraced for several seconds before he held Gina at arm's length for a full appraisal.

"You look marvelous, my dear. I've missed your outrageous company." Then added, as an aside not intended for public consumption, but Amanda heard anyway, "I'm so sorry you broke up with Red. Are you okay?"

"Red who?" Gina shrugged. "Where's my drink, Ron?"

After that, everyone was animated to action. Carl splashed more scotch into his glass and then shuffled toward a large set of French doors at the end of a wide hallway that opened off the great room. Since Ron had a pitcher of whiskey sours already made up, Amanda asked for one of those, and then the women followed Ron as he rolled the hors d'oeuvres cart after Carl, with old Barney bringing up the rear.

"Carl always wants his cocktails on the outdoor patio so he can enjoy the sunset," Ron explained, then noticed their apprehension. "Yes, it's a little chilly, but the firepit is roaring. You'll be fine."

Along the way, she glanced to her left through an open door to the master suite. The room included a king bed facing a window wall framing twilight and early stars, ceiling-high shelving for a pottery display, and sadly, a wheelchair and side table crowded with bottles of prescription meds. Before she could speculate as to the nature of Carl's illness, they passed through the glass doors to magic.

Beyond the leaping flames from the pit and a knee-high wooden railing ringing the deck, across an open field at the edge of a small lake, the mountain range lay in dark undulating silhouette under a riotous orange, pink, violet, and blue sunset. The dying sun stretched out blinding golden arms as it sank behind the big old barn across the driveway. And as they dropped into lounge chairs, the night wove a fabric of delicious food, fine conversation, and way too much to drink.

CHAPTER THIRTEEN

Succubus…

By midnight Amanda was tipsy. She clung to the winding steel railing and pulled herself up the staircase to their bedrooms. Had she been sober, she never would have agreed to join Gina in her room for coffee.

"All the comforts of home," Gina said as she shoved a disposable two-cup pillow of coffee into the little machine and started it brewing. "Ron thinks of everything."

"Yes, he does." She had a coffee machine in her room, too. And Ron's perfectly grilled steaks, salad, homemade apple pie, and expertly turned-out hospitality made her feel like she was vacationing in a five-star resort hotel. She flopped down on the bed to keep her head from spinning.

"But I'm really worried about Carl," Gina said. "He's aged so much since I saw him two years ago, and he seems so frail."

"Well, he told us he has rheumatoid arthritis that affects all his joints but especially his feet and hands." He had also explained that while he intended to keep making pottery, he would move his equipment from the River Arts District to the barn behind the house, where Ron currently lived and painted. Carl had said his work was no longer of the quality he felt comfortable selling.

"It's sad, Mandy. Carl was so vital before." Gina poured their coffee and pulled a chair up near the bed.

Amanda sat upright so she could drink hers. Then she wondered what would become of Ron when Carl moved his stuff to the barn. Would he be invited to stay, or would he have to go? She took a gulp, hoping the caffeine would clear the fog from her brain.

Just before sunset, she'd studied the enormous bank barn behind the house. "That barn seems big enough for several artists," she said to Gina. "From what I've gathered, Ron takes good care of Carl. He shops, cooks, cleans, and even does nursing duty when the need arises. Do you think Carl will ask him to leave?"

"Why would he?" Gina frowned. "But what about the other thing, Mandy? Do you think they have a relationship? Are they lovers?"

Clearly Gina was deeply disturbed by the situation. In the dim glow of the bedside lamp she looked exhausted, her face appearing older than her forty-some years. Gina was also disturbingly sexy. She had shed her suede jacket and kicked off her artsy sandals. As she lifted her bare feet to the bed and relaxed back in the chair, Amanda noticed the soft mounds of her breasts under the silk blouse and the tiny pulse at the base of her throat. She considered her answer.

"Well, I don't think they are lovers, Gina. By the way Ron looks at Carl it's obvious he cares deeply for him, but I don't think his affection is reciprocated. Carl seems to regard him as a father would a son, or a teacher would a student. You said Carl's been with women, and I think he's straight."

Gina sighed and shook her head. "I hate it that Carl's gotten old, and in the end I'm afraid Ron will get hurt." She abruptly stood up to brew more coffee and close the drapes, and then she moved toward the bathroom. "Do you want some Tylenol?" she called over her shoulder.

"No, thanks. I'm good." While Gina was gone, Amanda took the opportunity to turn on her cell phone and listen to her voice mail. As she'd expected, Sara had left five messages since their upsetting conversation at Love's Truck Stop. She began by again apologizing for her irresponsible conduct with Maya, and then she apologized for her jealous outburst about Gina. The calls that followed were anxious and worried. She desperately feared Amanda was avoiding her—which was precisely the truth. Should Amanda respond? But it was already twelve thirty. By any decent standard it was too late to call.

"Fretting about Sara, are we?" Gina suddenly appeared in a gauzy yellow bathrobe.

The woman had washed her face. Without makeup she seemed younger, focused, sober and dangerous. Clearly she was naked under that robe, so Amanda quickly moved off the bed and into the chair when Gina handed her more coffee.

Gina flopped onto the bed where Amanda had been and delivered one of her smoky laughs. "Get over it, Mandy. I won't touch you unless you want me to. I see you are looking at my tattoo."

Oh God, she was! The four-leaf clover on Gina's left shoulder blade was clearly visible where the robe hung low and Amanda was staring. She redirected her gaze and slipped the phone into her pants pocket.

"No, I was just trying to remember our schedule for tomorrow."

"Sure you were." Gina's look was sultry and skeptical.

Seated on the edge of the bed, her shapely legs crossed at the knee, she began jiggling her foot in Amanda's direction. She was exactly like the succubus, a folklore creature that had always captured Amanda's imagination. This demon in female form was a supernatural entity that appeared in dreams and took the form of a woman in order to seduce her victim, ready or not.

Amanda was definitely not ready, although a subtle tightening south of her belly said she could have been, had circumstances been different.

"No, seriously, what's the plan for tomorrow?"

Gina finished her coffee and successfully slam-dunked the cup into the wastebasket. "Okay, first it's breakfast with the boys, then you come with Ron and me while I deliver my work to the Woolworth's building. Tomorrow night we play dress-up and the guys take us to the farewell party for Carl in the River Arts District, where you can check out that space for lease. Got it?" She placed her hand on Amanda's knee.

The contact sent an unwelcome charge up her leg. "Got it. Sounds like a busy day."

"So you need a good night's sleep, Mandy." Gina pointedly turned down the covers and patted a pillow. "Hop in and we'll both get some shut-eye."

She jumped up from the chair so fast she almost toppled the little coffee machine. "No thanks, Gina. I'm going to my room to make a phone call."

Before the woman could object, she was sprinting toward the bunk beds. Gina's laughter followed her all the way down the hall.

CHAPTER FOURTEEN

Portrait…

Everyone was in a good mood at breakfast. Gina and Ron were eager to visit their gallery, Carl was rested and much more vigorous after a good night's sleep, and Amanda was relieved because she'd finally had a loving conversation with Sara. Wisely, she'd waited until morning to call, and they had both seemed equally determined to patch up their differences.

Sara had again apologized, not only for her own behavior, but also for Maya, who had also offered to get on the phone and beg for forgiveness. Maya had even confessed the incident to Shar, who wanted desperately to get their friendships back on track. After all, the four had always been close, and had shared many wonderful adventures. And after five passionate years together, it hurt Amanda to her core to even contemplate losing Sara. But now it seemed everything might be all right.

"You're looking chipper this morning," Gina quipped over eggs, waffles, and bacon. "I suppose you and Sara had great phone sex?"

Amanda kicked her under the table, Ron choked on his juice, and Carl changed the subject to his philosophy of pot making. The gist was that mankind began making clay vessels to haul water and store food, but over the years the craft had been elevated to fine arts status by snooty critics and greedy artists who charged and expected big bucks for their work.

"Of course, I'm also guilty of accepting too much money for my stuff," he ruefully admitted. "But I have never deluded myself into believing my pots were anything more than utilitarian."

Carl pooh-poohed Gina's protestations that his ceramics were way more—beautiful, almost mystical in their grace and completely worthy of the critics' hyperbole. Amanda liked his down-to-earth disdain of the often pretentious art world. It was a discussion that could have lasted all day, but instead was terminated after second cups of coffee.

Yet as the three of them prepared to leave, Carl was determined to put an exclamation point on his thesis. "Wait, look at this!" He picked up a small object and tossed it across the room to Amanda. Fortunately, she caught it. "That grotesque little thing is a face jug made by Davis Pottery in Edgemont, South Carolina. It was created in the mid-eighteen hundreds by a slave, and today it's worth fifty thousand dollars, give or take…" He paused for effect.

Amanda gaped at the tiny crooked jug with sad eyes, a wide nose, oversized ears, and prominent teeth in its grinning mouth. The modeled visage was both exceedingly ugly and emotionally compelling. "God, I could have dropped it!"

Carl shrugged. "Don't worry, that thing won't break easily. Some poor slave made that jug and sneaked it into the kiln amongst the legitimate dinnerware his master was firing, and it's survived this long. It is authentic American folk art, but like so many other pure ideas, it's been bastardized. Today potters manufacture them by the hundreds and sell them to a public that can't get enough. Disgusting!" he finished with a snort.

"Thanks for the lecture, Professor, but we're outta here," Ron said. "Since you require us back here by happy hour, we need to get our work done."

They left in a hurry. Ron led the procession in his white Ford Fusion, while Gina and Amanda followed in the Nissan Frontier. Once they were clear of the property, Gina rolled her eyes and said, "Hate to say it, but Red collects those new face jugs. Carl would make fun of her if he knew. Owns a cabinet full of them. Go figure."

"I can't believe that little jug is so valuable. I hope Carl has it insured."

"I'm sure he does," Gina said. "Between his home and his art collection, his estate is worth several million, but he's never cared much for material things."

Amanda, who had been broke all her life, decided it was easy to be dismissive of material possessions when one was rich. Then suddenly she remembered how her room with bunk beds seemed to be designed for children. "Does Carl have a family?"

"Carl has no one. He was an only child. His parents are dead, and he claims he doesn't even have a cousin once-removed on his family tree. He's never been married and says he doesn't care to be."

"Would Carl ever leave his fortune to Ron?"

Gina grunted. "Who knows? I'd say Ron deserves it, and without Carl's support he'd definitely be hard up for money. In addition to everything else he's done for Carl, Ron has supplied him with a substitute family. His twin nephews visit often and Carl adores them, but that doesn't mean he'd remember any of them in his will."

They fell silent as they drove into town and turned onto Hayward Street. Somehow Ron had snagged two parking spaces directly in front of Woolworth's, which he straddled until they could pull in behind him. He propped the building's doors while Gina opened the truck's bed and began unloading her paintings. Forming a chain, they passed the large abstracts hand to hand until everything was stacked inside.

This was Amanda's first opportunity to see the work. Like Sara's brother had explained the night of the unveiling, Gina's style was similar to Marc's fledgling attempts—bold, undulating colors in motion, a combination of flat, opaque shapes that either lay on the surface of the canvas or receded back through transparent glazes of wash.

"I like them!" she exclaimed. "Good job, Gina. I prefer the organic shapes to the straight-edged abstracts."

"Did you say *orgasmic* shapes?" Gina teased.

"Oh, give it a rest." Amanda turned her back and started hauling the art to the empty white booth where Ron was waiting. When Gina left to move their vehicles, Amanda asked, "Is Gina always such a flirt? It's like she's on the make twenty-four-seven."

He laughed. "Yeah, she comes on strong, but just ignore her. Her heart belongs to Red, believe me."

Once Gina's paintings were safely stashed in her space, Ron nervously invited Amanda to visit his adjacent booth. "Remember, I just started painting two years ago, so please don't judge me too harshly."

While Ron paced, she opened her mind and slowly inspected the several dozen landscapes hung on the pegboard. They were mostly traditional mountain scenes, meticulously rendered in tight, painstaking detail. There were also a few studies of the barn at sunset, rivers and creeks—all painted in the same careful style. It struck her that while the art was competent and would appeal to the general public that reliably appreciated realism, it seemed Ron was holding back. Like the man himself, the art was too neat, timid, and reserved. It captured nothing of the emotion she sensed just beneath his outward calm.

As she searched for an encouraging response, she noticed a piece placed on the floor facing the wall. Impulsively, she picked it up and was shocked by what she saw. The portrait of Carl Fischer had been accomplished with the slicing strokes of a palette knife. Raw primary colors made up the sharp plains of his brow, cheekbones, and chin. Carl's blue eyes burned with intensity. The study was both angry and loving, born of the artist's conflicted emotions for a man he had captured perfectly.

"Oh my God, Ron!" She held it up. "This study of Carl is exquisite. How did you do this? It's completely different from all your other work."

But Ron was paralyzed, unable to speak as his deep brown eyes widened in something like fear. Finally the trance broke. He crossed the space with two long strides and snatched the painting from her hands. "You weren't supposed to see that," he shouted as he put it down again, facing the wall.

"But why not? It's really good, Ron."

"It's private. Don't you get that?"

She was stunned by his fury, but before she could form an apology, a stranger entered the booth. The handsome young man in his early twenties had short blond hair bleached almost white by the sun. Of medium build, he was buff and muscular, with amused dark eyes behind trendy black-rimmed glasses. The faded jeans, rumpled Metallica T-shirt, and tan skin made him look like he'd just stepped off a surfboard.

He stuck out his hand to Ron. "Dude, I'm glad you finally showed. I've been hanging all day so I could buy one of your paintings."

As Ron shook the man's hand, his anger evaporated, transformed to self-consciousness and attraction. It was obvious that the young man was seducing him on several levels.

"You want to buy one of *my* paintings?" Ron stammered as his pale face blushed red.

"Yeah, man, I do." The surfer went to the wall and retrieved the painting of Carl Fischer. "This one. It's awesome."

CHAPTER FIFTEEN

Surfer dude…

"That painting is not for sale," Ron insisted as he pried the piece from the man's hands.

Amanda backed out of the booth. She could not believe this was happening.

"C'mon, Mr. Dunifon," the kid said. "You know you'll sell it. Everything is negotiable."

As soon as she was certain the situation was under control, that the men would not start a fistfight over the portrait, she fled to Gina's space and found her friend sorting pegboard hooks. "Gina, you won't believe what's happening over in Ron's space!"

But Gina held up her hand. "I don't care. Don't bother me. I need to hang my paintings and I want no distractions."

"Okay, do you want some help?"

"No, I prefer to work alone."

She was determined not to take offense at Gina's attitude. After all, she herself suffered from the diva complex—that proprietary relationship of an artist to her space. She also preferred working solo, so she got it.

"Sorry, Mandy. Why don't you check out the rest of Woolworth Walk while I work, and then we'll hook up for lunch at the soda fountain."

"Sounds like a plan." With that, she struck out on her own, as she'd been itching to do since they'd arrived—this was her kind of place. The main floor and basement of the old five and dime had been fitted with a maze of display cubicles—160 artists in all—showing everything from jewelry, crafts, and paintings to bins of prints and posters. It reminded her of the times she'd shown at Metrolina in Charlotte and at the outdoor festivals in Florida. She talked to exhibitors and discovered that Ron Dunifon was well-liked by the group. She also found out that the young surfer dude was named Larry Goldberg. He'd been in and out of the building for several days looking for Ron and had even asked for Ron's address—which none of the artists were willing to supply.

"Larry's not local," one woman told her. "Far as I can tell, he's a drifter." She also said she'd be surprised if Larry could afford to buy one of Ron's paintings, since he seemed to have no money. "You just know he's hungry. He hangs around the soda fountain watching us eat, but all he's bought so far is a bag of chips."

Suddenly Amanda was hungry, too. She texted Gina, who wasn't ready to take a break, then hopped up onto one of the red leather pod seats at the counter and marveled at the fully-restored glass, mirrors, and stainless steel fixtures. She felt like she'd time-traveled to the 1950s. While many of the menu items were new age chic—organic coffee and Chai latte—she ordered a classic chocolate soda, club sandwich, and potato salad. She felt not the least bit guilty about her choices until Larry Goldberg slid onto a stool beside her.

"You're Mandy, right?" He then introduced himself and stared until she offered him half her sandwich.

"Are you sure?" Without waiting for an answer, he spread out a napkin, took the half, plus her pickle, and greedily ate.

Now what? She noticed he had no painting, so she figured his negotiations with Ron had been unsuccessful.

He caught her drift and said through a mouthful of food, "Mr. Dunifon said he'd sell me any of his other paintings, just not the one of Professor Fischer." He paused to swallow. "I couldn't afford it anyway, but I will have money tomorrow."

Was he planning to rob a bank? "So where are you from, Larry?" she asked.

He shrugged and wiped his fingers on a new napkin. "Hey, do you think Mr. Dunifon is gay?"

"Why do you ask?" she coldly replied.

He grinned, exposing perfect white teeth. "No reason. It's just that I think he likes me."

This kid was only a few years younger than she, but he was acting like a baby. "Why do you think he likes you?"

The look he leveled at her was neither childish nor naïve. If anything, it was creepy and slightly lascivious. "C'mon, Mandy, we can sense these things, right? I know he's interested because he offered me a job, just like that!" He snapped his fingers. "I'll be bar-tending at Professor Fischer's big farewell party tonight, so I guess I'll see you there."

With that, he hopped off the stool, dug two quarters from his jeans, left the tip, and then he was gone.

CHAPTER SIXTEEN

Trouble in paradise…

She told Gina about the surfer dude while they were dressing for the party. "I don't get it. Ron behaved like a smitten teenager around that kid, and I can't believe he hired him to bartend at Carl's party."

"Oh, Ron's only human. Who wouldn't be flattered by the attention of some young hot thing?" Gina's eyes roved deliberately up and down Amanda's all-purpose black dress. "Besides, I suspect Ron was planning to serve the drinks himself. This Larry person will free him up to enjoy the party."

"Maybe so, but what about that amazing portrait of Carl? Have you ever known Ron to paint something like that?"

Gina frowned as she slithered into an electric blue gown. The matching jacket was patterned with tiny silver sequins. "No, never. Ron doesn't like human subjects, and that loose style you described is completely out of character. What I don't understand is, if he doesn't want anyone to see or buy that painting, why did he take it to his booth?"

She had no answer. Perhaps it was a Freudian thing, like Ron secretly wanted someone to comment or ask about the nature of his relationship with Carl—whatever that was. The more she thought about the portrait, the more conflicted the image seemed—the colors and execution were both passionate and angry. Was it a reflection of Ron's feelings for Carl? What did she know? That sort of analysis was Sara's thing, and God she missed Sara.

"All ready?" Gina ran fingers through her short, gelled hair, creating little peaks that absurdly reminded Amanda of the Statue of Liberty.

Compared to Amanda, who felt downright dowdy in her old dress and Goodwill trench coat, which she would carry over her arm and wear only if she was freezing, Gina was a fashion statement—bizarre, but appealing.

"Sure, I'm ready."

They were behind schedule. The work at the Woolworth Walk had taken longer than expected, but Ron insisted that was okay because Carl, the guest of honor, should arrive fashionably late. But as they wound down the stairs, instead of the mellow music that usually issued from the great room, they heard the men's voices raised in a heated argument.

"Uh-oh, trouble in paradise," Gina whispered as she gave Amanda an apprehensive glance. "I wonder what's wrong?"

It took only seconds to discover that the disagreement involved the little face jug. Carl wore a smug smile as he held the object in the palm of his big hand. He also wore a black tuxedo, bow tie, and crazy red suspenders.

"Why shouldn't I take it?" Carl demanded. "This little guy is my good luck charm. Besides, everyone will be interested in its history."

"Especially that obnoxious Millie Buncombe." Ron spat out the name. "She's been trying to get her hands on your face jug for years."

"She's been trying to get her hands on *me*, Ron. There's a difference."

Although Carl was in high spirits, Ron was clearly agitated. The dignified effect of his custom-tailored dark suit, designer shirt, and silk tie was spoiled by his flushed complexion and snarling lips.

"Leave it at home, Carl. It's too valuable to show in public."

Completely ignoring him, Carl pocketed the face jug and winked as the women entered the room. "Don't mind Ron, he's just nervous. The way he's carrying on, you'd think *he* was the one at center stage. Not that I'm looking forward to being pawed over, with everyone shedding crocodile tears at my exit from the art world, but I can endure it for one night."

She didn't know what to make of them squabbling like the Odd Couple and hoped they'd calm down because they all had to drive to the party together. She checked her watch. "Shouldn't we get going?"

Right on cue, Ron held his arm out for Carl, like an escort prepared to depart with his date. "Let's go, old man," he said affectionately.

But Carl held back and gazed uneasily at the floor. Finally, he cleared his throat. "Well, there's been a change of plans. You three go ahead without me. I'll be along directly."

Ron did a double-take. "What the hell? You don't drive, Carl. How will you get there?"

"Gladys is coming for me," he said, barely above a whisper.

"What?" Ron roared. "When did this happen?"

Still unable to meet Ron's eyes, Carl mumbled, "Last minute. Would have mentioned it sooner, but she only called a short while ago. It means a lot to Gladys, so let's not make a scene."

Obviously a scene was about to be made. While Amanda and Gina glanced uneasily at one another, Ron ticked like a time bomb. His face got even redder as he clenched and unclenched his fists.

"Don't be like this," Carl pleaded. Just as the tension was edging toward an explosion, the doorbell rang. "That will be Gladys now," Carl announced with relief and moved toward the sound.

When Ron tried to block his way, Gina sprang forward like an electric blue panther and grabbed Ron's arm. "Behave yourself!" she growled.

Amanda stood mute and dumbfounded, wondering what would happen next. She did not have to wait long, because while

Carl was shuffling toward the front door, Ron did an abrupt about-face. With Gina still clinging to his left arm, he snatched Amanda with his right hand and dragged them both toward the French doors in the rear. Nudging the old bloodhound into the kitchen, he locked the doors behind them as he shooed the two women outside.

"My car's out back," he said.

"Shouldn't we stay to meet Gladys?" Amanda timidly asked.

"Yeah, Ron, you were really rude. Who the hell is Gladys?" Gina demanded.

"Gladys Uplander is Carl's girlfriend," Ron snapped. "They've been dating for almost a year."

CHAPTER SEVENTEEN

Dangerous game...

The drive to the River Arts District was unnaturally silent. While Ron labored to get his anger and disappointment under control, neither Gina nor she dared broach the subject of Gladys Uplander. Along the way, Amanda again enjoyed the diversity and charm of the architecture and watched the sun gliding down the sky toward the distant mountains. Minus all the drama, Asheville was a fascinating place, so she was determined to have fun this evening,

"We are now entering the District," Gina narrated. "Check it out, Mandy. Isn't it cool that all these old warehouses have been repurposed for studios?"

They had come through town on Haywood Road and now Ron was zigzagging through the River Arts District—Roberts Street, Depot Street, Lyman Street—past buildings called The Wedge, Odyssey, Pink Dog, Hatchery, Grain Silo, and many others. They crossed a railroad track and he explained that the French Broad River was dead ahead, flowing toward Tennessee and bordering the District to the west. By the time they could see Cotton Mill Studios, their destination, Amanda was in sensory overload, but Ron was calmer.

"It's too much to take in all at once," she said. "And where are all the people?"

"Most of the studios close at five. Carl's place is open because of his party," Ron explained.

As they approached the two-story redbrick mill, one of the parking lots was indeed filled with cars, and as Ron picked a space, she watched an older model Mercedes sedan park in a handicapped spot near the front door. Carl stepped from the passenger seat, then came around to open the driver's door. Gladys was tall, her long silver hair braided and wrapped atop her head. The couple moved arm-in-arm up a short flight of concrete stairs, and even at a distance, Gladys projected an aura of elegance. When Ron hesitated to step from their car, Amanda sensed he wanted the pair to be well inside before they made an entrance.

By the time Amanda's trio walked into a spacious white studio space so crowded she could barely see the displays of Carl's pottery lining the walls, Carl and Gladys were already across the room, surrounded by vocal well-wishers. When Amanda rose on tiptoe to locate the guest of honor, she realized that Carl had removed the little face jug from his pocket and placed it prominently on a pedestal. Apparently he was giving a mini lecture to those nearby.

Ron, who was much taller than Amanda, had not missed that bit of theater. "I wish he hadn't done that. Now look, that horrible Millie Buncombe is making her move."

By then Gina's curiosity was piqued. She took Amanda's arm and guided them through the crowd for a closer look at the women in Carl's life. Leaving Ron behind, they broke into the inner circle, where a flamboyant groupie—obviously Millie Buncombe—had picked up the jug and was lovingly fondling it.

"Oh Carl, it is even more beautiful than I imagined…and so historically significant. I say again, this little guy belongs in my folk art museum."

The imposing woman in her late sixties was at least six feet tall with a graying blond ponytail falling halfway down her back. She was eccentrically dressed in a burlap dress that could have been assembled from a collection of grain sacks sewn together. Her distinctive outer coat of many colors resembled a patchwork quilt. From the surrounding chatter, Amanda gathered Ms. Buncombe was the founder/director of something called The North Carolina Artifacts Museum.

"But, Millie," Carl objected, "the face jug is from South Carolina. It wouldn't fit in with your exhibits of Native American art." When he tried to pry the piece from her hands, she wouldn't let go.

Next Millie appealed to Gladys. "Help me here, will you? Maybe you can convince Carl to bequeath the jug to my museum in his will?"

But Gladys Uplander fled to the sidelines and refused to get involved.

Eventually Carl repossessed the jug and put it back on the pedestal. "First, Millie, I'm not ready to make a will yet, and second, I plan to leave the face jug to Brother Wolf. Let them auction it off to the highest bidder. That way it can do some real good."

"What is Brother Wolf?" Amanda whispered.

"It's an animal shelter here in Asheville. Lots of artists support it," Gina answered.

Amanda thought the donation was a great idea, but Millie did not. When she spun around in disgust, her huge coat nearly swept a large cobalt vase off a nearby table.

Luckily a handy waiter prevented the fall, then demanded that Ms. Buncombe give him her coat.

"Listen up, folks! I'll take everyone's outerwear, if you don't mind. We've set up a coat rack at the end of the landing, and you can pick them up when you leave."

"Are you giving us claim tickets?" Millie demanded as she reluctantly gave up her patchwork quilt.

"No, ma'am, but I reckon you won't have any trouble recognizing this garment."

Gladys stepped forward and graciously gave up her stole, then Amanda eagerly relinquished her ratty Goodwill trench coat. As the rest of the guests followed suit, she and Gina introduced themselves to Gladys. The woman must have heard all about them on the ride over.

"Yes, Carl told me how much he's enjoyed having you as guests. It's a nice change of pace for him, welcoming young women into his bachelor's pad."

Stepping in with a mischievous grin, Carl wrapped his arm around Gladys. "I also enjoy having a more mature woman around my house and look forward to much more of her company in the future."

When Carl kissed Gladys's cheek, Amanda sensed the two were more than just casually dating, possibly heading for marriage. Her heart broke for Ron.

Within minutes the pair was whisked away by adoring fans.

"What do you think?" Gina asked the moment they left.

"Well, I think it's serious."

"Me too. What can we do about it?"

"For heaven's sake, Gina, it's none of our business. I think we should forget about it and start drinking."

When she looked toward the makeshift bar at the end of the room, she saw Ron's stricken face above the crowd. He had witnessed the loving exchange between Carl and Gladys. Larry Goldberg stood directly in front of him, all decked out in a rented tux. When Carl and Gladys turned and headed for the bar, Ron waited until he was sure Carl was watching, and then he pulled Larry back against him in what could only be described as an intimate hug.

They were playing a very dangerous game, and Amanda wanted no part of it.

CHAPTER EIGHTEEN

Standing room only…

Amanda was attending the party for one reason only—to consider the space as a potential showcase for her work—so she extracted Gina from the soap opera and requested a grand tour. The walls were lined with Carl's pottery, and as they roamed the perimeter, she realized his work was much as he had described. Everything had a utilitarian function—vases, bowls, cups, and plates. He favored earth tone glazes. His high-fire stoneware was decorated with the russet, green, and blue tones achieved by adding cobalt, iron, and copper oxides. Yet these pieces far exceeded pure utility. Carl's style was delicate and graceful, and the pots were not cheap.

She longed to buy a certain teapot to commemorate her visit, but changed her mind when she saw the price tag.

"His work is amazing, is it not?" The voice at her elbow belonged to a movie-star handsome man in a dark Armani suit. His raven black hair and swarthy complexion made him seem Middle Eastern or Southern European, and although he was likely in his mid-fifties, he was vigorous and fit. "Do you know the artist?" he asked. "I would like to buy or commission a complete set of dinnerware."

No accent. The stranger was American, and he intended to spend big bucks tonight.

"Yes, we are friends of Carl's, but we don't represent him." Gina quickly grasped the situation. "You wait right here with Amanda while I find someone to help you."

"Please tell Professor Fischer that Al Cabella wishes to make a purchase." When Gina left, he turned his hundred-kilowatt smile on Amanda. "This is my first time in Asheville. What about you?"

"My first visit, too. It's an interesting town."

"Indeed it is." He moved in closer. "I should think it would be especially exciting staying at the Fischer home."

She backed up a pace. How did this man know where she was staying?

He chuckled. "No, I do not have a crystal ball, Amanda. I met Ron Dunifon earlier. He told me."

She accepted the explanation, yet something was off about Al Cabella. He was too smooth, almost predatory—or else she was naturally antagonized by a man whose suit cost more than her entire wardrobe.

He began to pace. "I wonder what is taking so long? I really want to meet the professor."

"I'm sure he'll be here soon." But Carl was nowhere in sight. "Or I'm certain Mr. Dunifon could write up the sale…"

"No!" Cabella roared. "I do not deal with employees, only the artist."

His aura of entitlement rubbed her the wrong way. Ron was no employee, and this was Carl's big night. He was expected to schmooze with everyone, not just this bozo. At the same time, she didn't want her host to lose a big sale.

"If you'll excuse me, Mr. Cabella, I will go find Professor Fischer."

Pushing her way through the crowd, she desperately searched for Carl. In her rush, she clumsily bumped into a guest balancing pink champagne, causing the poor guy to spill it all over his crisp white dress shirt.

"God, I am so sorry!" She snatched a wad of paper napkins from a nearby table and started daubing at the stain, but he roughly caught her hand.

"Leave it. I'm fine!"

Her victim, a handsome African American man, was big, buff, and bald—like a football player who had wandered off the field. He seemed less angry than frantic as his narrowed black eyes darted in the direction from which she had just come.

"That man you were just with—where did he go?"

Glancing over her shoulder, she saw with dismay that the customer was gone. Now she was double screwed. She'd lost the sale and spilled on a guest. But when she tried to apologize, he held up one enormous hand.

"No problem, it's not your fault. I wasn't paying attention."

When he smiled, his face lit up, his eyes relaxed, and for the first time she understood that perhaps she had not been responsible for the collision. In retrospect, it seemed this man had been rushing toward Mr. Cabella. But what was the connection? This guy in his too short, off-the rack trousers and scuffed loafers was in a different league than Cabella—more like a bodyguard than an art lover.

"Have you seen Professor Fischer?" he asked.

"Not recently, sorry."

With that, the man ran his big hand over his shiny ebony head, nodded, and wandered off toward the back of the room.

Somewhat at a loss, she was thrilled when Surfer Dude approached and offered her a drink.

"Can you make me a rum and tonic?"

"No problem, Mandy." He made a silly bow, then hurried away to do her bidding.

When he finally returned, she noticed the crowd had thinned considerably. "Where is everyone, Larry?"

"That's what took me so long. It seems Professor Fischer has this thing about watching the sunset from outside, so everyone's gone up to the roof. I had to move all the bar stuff up there."

"The roof?"

"Yeah, it's rad. They're even dancing up there."

Not knowing her way around, she took a big gulp of her drink and followed Larry. They took a half flight of stairs to a mezzanine with the coat rack and restrooms at one end, then shoved through a narrow door at the other end, which led up to the roof.

The cold evening air instantly raised goosebumps on her bare arms. The crude, cramped space consisted of a tarred floor, a hulking heating unit clanking away, and a flimsy wooden railing around the perimeter. She hated heights, so she clung to the inner wall and decided that if she rented this place, the roof might be okay for a summer lunch, but it was ill-suited for a fancy party with standing room only.

Most of the folks she'd seen downstairs had come up to indulge Carl's sunset fetish, and sure enough, the sky was ablaze with dramatic color. Many were gathered near the western railing where Carl held court. Someone had tuned a boom box to big band dance music and even more bizarre, a female artist Amanda had met at Woolworth's that afternoon was doing performance art with a framed square of mirror glass. She was capturing the sunset rays on her mirror, then redirecting the colors to dance on a brick chimney—to psychedelic effect.

All at once Gina was at her side, balancing a fruity alcoholic beverage. "Crazy scene."

"No kidding," Amanda agreed. "But I'm afraid we've lost Carl a sale."

"Maybe not. That Cabella jerk is up here somewhere. Last I saw he was heading in Carl's direction."

Gina's Statue of Liberty peaks were backlit by a rosy glow, and the mountains looked like roiling dark waves—like on the Hudson River, perhaps? While she made this absurd connection of Gina as Lady Liberty welcoming the world's huddled masses, the moment was shattered by a piercing scream.

She and Gina recoiled in terror as Gladys Uplander's screaming continued and others joined in. Gina dropped her glass when a human stampede rushed toward the source, while Amanda hugged the wall.

Ron stumbled in their direction. His eyes were wide with panic and his fingers trembled as he dialed 911 on his cell phone.

"What the hell happened?" Gina shouted above the din.

"It's Carl," Ron sobbed. "He fell off the roof!"

CHAPTER NINETEEN

Emergency response…

She was speechless as the chaos around her intensified. When Ron finished his call, assured that help was on its way, Gina pulled him into her arms and held him.

Eventually Amanda found her voice. "How did he fall?"

Ron was too paralyzed to respond, but a passerby brought them up to speed. "I don't know. It looked like Professor Fischer just stumbled, and that useless fence shattered with his weight."

Next Al Cabella stalked up. "I never got a chance to talk to him. Looks like I will not be buying that dinnerware, after all."

With that, the man left the roof, leaving her with the distinct impression he cared more about his acquisition than Carl's horrible accident. In the meantime, she calculated the drop from the roof to the parking lot below and feared a fall would surely be fatal. She blinked back tears as people peered over the edge.

Larry shouted, "I can't see him down there. It's too dark."

The young performance artist joined the lookie-loos and angled her mirror over the rail, twisting it up and down for a better look at the concrete. The two women who had been flanking Carl—Gladys and Millie—approached Gina and Amanda.

"It was insane," Gladys choked. "I turned away for one minute, heard Carl shuffle behind me and then he was gone."

"This is terrible, so terrible!" Millie's long gray ponytail swayed as she shook her head and obsessively twisted her hands together. "Why doesn't the ambulance come? They're taking forever!" With that, she strode toward the stairs and started down, only to be shouldered aside by the muscular man Amanda had spilled champagne on earlier.

"Hey, you guys!" the girl with the mirror called from the edge. "We need more than an ambulance. Someone call the fire department. Ask for a hook n' ladder, or one of those cherry pickers."

The tide of humanity, including Ron, flowed toward the girl to see what was what. Gina went too, leaving the acrophobic Amanda and a grieving Gladys behind. Impulsively, she took the older woman's hand

"I'm so sorry, Gladys."

"I can't believe it," she whimpered again and again. "It wasn't like Carl had too much to drink. He'd been nursing the same scotch all evening."

On the other hand, Amanda knew arthritis made Carl unsteady, and he'd left his fancy gnarled cane back at the house.

Suddenly the crowd gasped. People took out their cell phones. They used their flashlights or took pictures, lighting up the night like electronic fireflies.

Gina's eyes were wide as pie plates when she rejoined them. "It's a miracle!" she cried. "Carl never hit the ground. He's hung up on a ventilator valve, dangling from the wall."

"How can that be?" Gladys was in shock. "Carl is hanging on the wall? Is he moving or speaking?"

"I couldn't tell," Gina said. "Last I saw, that big black guy was dragging a mattress from the back of an old van. I guess he's planning to place it under Carl in case he falls."

Amanda heard sirens speeding ever closer, then felt Ron at her arm. Sharing a common thought, figuring they could help more on the ground than from this bird's nest, all four clattered down the stairs. They reached the mezzanine, then the gallery floor, but when they tried to go out to the street there was a chain of uniformed police officers blocking the door.

"Sorry, folks, everyone must wait inside," the officer in charge said. "The emergency vehicles are arriving and you'll only be in the way."

"But I'm the victim's partner," Ron argued. "We live together. You have to let me pass."

"But I am Carl's fiancée," Gladys interrupted. "Please, I need to be with him."

The officer was stumped. As he looked from Ron to Gladys, trying to determine which one was the significant other, he finally gave up and let them both out.

Amanda saw a glare of pure hatred pass between them as they rounded the corner of the building.

"*Fiancée?*" Gina mused. "For real?"

But Amanda was more interested in the emergency response. Two patrol cars were haphazardly parked out front and as she watched, a fire truck careened around the nearest corner, closely followed by an ambulance. At the same time, a black limousine, with Al Cabella in the passenger seat, glided away from the curb. He'd managed to slip out before the cops arrived.

"Jesus Christ, what a mess!" Gina sank onto a folding chair as the full horror of the situation hit home. "I really love that old man." She dropped her face into her hands.

Although Amanda barely knew him, Carl seemed like a kind and decent person. Certainly he did not deserve such a tragic ending to his big night of celebration. As she contemplated the unfairness of it all, she noticed that Surfer Dude had his nose pressed against the only tiny window in the rear. Apparently he had a good view of the rescue effort.

"Jeez, it looks like they're gonna save him," the makeshift bartender groaned.

"The kid sounds disappointed," Gina observed.

"Well, some people love a car wreck. They want to see blood and gore," she said with disgust.

"Hey, they're lifting one of those hydraulic baskets with a fireman in it!" Larry Goldberg held his captive audience spellbound. "Now he's reaching out for Professor Fischer…" The kid paused for effect as everyone held their breath. "Okay, they're bringing him down. Yeah, now they're putting him on a stretcher."

"Is Carl alive?" Millie Buncombe shouted.

"How should I know, lady?" Larry continued to hog the window. "But he's in the ambulance now, and some lady hopped in with him."

Gina snorted. "It seems like Gladys won the spousal privilege."

Precisely on cue, Ron Dunifon appeared in the doorway. He pushed through the police line and approached them. "Carl is unconscious. He's pretty banged up, but the paramedics say he's going to make it."

"Oh, that's wonderful, Ron!"

When Amanda touched him, he broke into tears. At the same time, he began to laugh hysterically. The combination gave him the hiccups.

"What's so funny?" she demanded.

When he finally got the fit under control, Ron said, "Those Goddamned red suspenders. I begged Carl not to wear them tonight, but what do you know? Those stupid suspenders saved his life."

CHAPTER TWENTY

The stable door…

Once the EMS team and fire engine left, the shell-shocked guests milled about consuming too much alcohol and polishing off the food. They hassled the cops, demanding to know when they'd be permitted to leave the premises, but the authorities were questioning everyone about Carl's accident and making a list of anyone who had been in close proximity when he fell. From what Amanda overheard, no one had a clear idea of what had actually happened.

"Carl is going to be all right. That's all that really matters." Ron sighed. Since hearing the good news he'd relaxed considerably, but he was still fretting about not being present at the hospital. "I should be at his side, not Gladys. She claimed they were engaged, but that's a crock of shit."

Amanda and Gina exchanged a look. Was it possible that Carl had actually asked Gladys to marry him and conveniently forgotten to tell Ron?

Amanda was more concerned with the logistics of getting home soon, but they were dependent on Ron for a ride. She was certain he'd want to stop by the hospital first, and although she was worried about Carl, she really wanted to lock herself in the bunk bed room for some quiet phone time with Sara. They had made a date to call one another at ten o'clock come hell or high water, and it was already eight.

Just then Ron's phone rang. He snatched it from his pocket and answered immediately. From the sour look on his face and his monosyllabic responses, the conversation was not cordial. He signed off and rammed the phone back in his pocket.

"Bitch!" he snarled. "That was Gladys. She's all bent out of shape because she had to leave her Mercedes here, and now she doesn't know how she'll get home from the hospital."

Amanda suspected Gladys was not an Uber customer. "Can't she call a taxi?"

Ron snorted derisively. "No, because she intends to take Carl home with her when they release him."

"They're releasing Carl?" Gina said. "So that's a good thing."

"Yes, but he should be coming home with *me*!" Ron roared. He fixed on Gina. "Look, I need you to do me a big favor. Gladys has an ignition key hidden under her fender and she told me where to find it. I'll drive my car to the hospital while you and Mandy follow in Gladys's Mercedes. Once I have Carl safely in my car, we'll take him home and leave the Mercedes for Gladys."

Gina threw up her hands in exasperation. "That's crazy. What makes you think Gladys will go along with that plan?"

"Or what makes you think the cops will let us go anytime soon?" But as Amanda nervously checked her watch, she noticed that people were actually leaving the building. "Oh, I guess the police ran out of questions," she amended.

Ron gleefully clapped his hands. "Okay, let's get this show on the road. I'll pay Larry and tell him how to close up, then I'll pick up Carl's stuff and we're off."

After Ron strode away to accomplish his missions, Gina groaned, "What a night. I can't wait to shuck these clothes and kick off my heels."

All Amanda wanted was some pillow talk with Sara.

As they moved toward the mezzanine to retrieve their coats, however, Ron's shrill scream stopped them in their tracks. Those around him also began shouting—so much so that two of the uniforms rushed toward the commotion, while the other two again blocked the door.

Out of nowhere, the football guy with the champagne stain materialized at their side. "Now what?" he growled. He frowned at Amanda, then stomped toward the noise.

"It's gone!" Ron shouted. "Someone stole the damned face jug!"

Millie Buncombe babbled incoherently, while the clueless cops struggled to understand why everyone was freaking out about some silly little jug. When the crowd made it clear how valuable the artifact was—with wild estimates ranging from worthless to hundreds of thousands of dollars—the cops got very serious.

"Oh man, now we have to search everyone," the officer in charge complained. He instructed his team to go through purses, backpacks, pockets, and coats before folks could exit.

"Isn't that like barring the stable door after the horse already escaped?" Gina asked.

"Sure, lots of people have already left." Including Al Cabella, Amanda noted. "But let's grab our coats and get in line, otherwise we'll never get home."

The cops gave Ron a pass. They figured that if he had stolen the jug, he'd already had ample time to hide it outside the building, so they did not search him at all. Ron gave Gina instructions about retrieving the Mercedes key, then took off for the hospital to deal with Gladys.

Gina quickly got her cape and Amanda got her Goodwill trench coat, putting them close to the front of the line behind Millie Buncombe and several others. The officer in change, Sergeant Rollins, was surprisingly overweight, with a gray comb-over and an astonishing twirled moustache. His men did the searching. It wasn't airport security, but it was quite thorough, and no one got past Sergeant Rollins's belly until the men gave their thumbs-up.

The football guy stood to one side, arms crossed, watching with an amused smile. Millie was not amused. When one of the officers took her quilted coat of many colors and gave her a pat-down, she batted his hands away and got as red-faced as the portly sergeant.

Amanda would have laughed out loud at the fuss had she not been so annoyed. Once Millie was allowed to leave, the room calmed down. As Amanda waited her turn, she thought about Sara and tried to picture what she was doing at that moment in Washington, DC—so far away.

"We're next," Gina whispered as she handed the cops her cape. "I can't wait to get the hell outta here."

Her sentiments exactly. It was already nine o'clock. They let Gina go, and Amanda handed them her trench coat. "Hey, I'll meet you at the Mercedes," she called to her friend's retreating back.

One man gave her the pat-down, while another searched her bag. The last officer in line went through her coat pockets. She was sniffing the cold fresh air of freedom when Sergeant Rollins roughly grabbed her by both arms.

"What's wrong?" she gasped. His hot breath smelled like tuna canapes. While the sergeant tightened his grip, cop number two went through her wallet.

"Miss Amanda Rittenhouse?" he asked. She nodded miserably as cop number three held up the small object he'd found in her coat pocket—Carl's face jug!

"I believe this is what we've been looking for," the sergeant said. "You need to come down to the station."

CHAPTER TWENTY-ONE

On her own...

The room got quiet and everyone stared. "No, it's a mistake. I didn't take it!" Amanda exclaimed.

"Then how did it get in your pocket?" the sergeant snidely asked as he and the cop with her purse led her out the door. "Excitement's over, folks," he called to the crowd. "Go on home."

Cell phones came out, blinding her with myriad flashing accusations. The cops had slipped the face jug into an evidence bag and returned her trench coat. They unhanded her momentarily so she could get her arms through the coat sleeves before the cold night air engulfed her.

"But I didn't steal it!" she whimpered as they pushed her toward a white patrol unit with "POLICE" written large on its sides. As she frantically scanned the parking lot for a glimpse of Gina, it seemed everyone from the party was hanging around to watch her walk of shame.

"Mandy, what's happening?" Suddenly Gina came up from behind, eyes stretched wide in confusion. She trotted alongside Amanda's captors as they fast-walked her to the car.

"They found the face jug in my pocket. They think I stole it!" Under different circumstances she would have been mortally embarrassed. As it was, she was scared shitless as they opened the rear door, pressed the top of her head, and guided her inside.

"You cops are crazy!" Gina shouted. "Mandy would never steal that stupid jug. She's totally innocent."

"Back off and let us do our job, ma'am." The sergeant elbowed Gina aside before leveraging his bulk into the passenger seat.

"Where are you taking her?" Gina pounded on his window. The police officers were not inclined to answer.

"Follow us, Gina!" she pleaded through the window glass. At the same time, the door locking mechanism clicked into place and she was truly a prisoner.

"But I have to go to the hospital," Gina protested. "Ron is waiting."

"Seriously?" Amanda hollered. If the woman didn't help her now, she would never forgive her. But then the unit's siren burped out a single sharp warning. The crowd parted and their car started moving, leaving Gina gaping indecisively in their wake.

She trembled as they drove down unfamiliar streets. The car's interior stank of industrial aerosol and fear. *Dear God in heaven, this isn't happening.*

From the scratchy chatter on the radio up front, she gathered these cops were from Adams District, West Asheville. They were debating where to take her.

"Haywood or Court Plaza?" the driver asked.

"Aw, just take her to Haywood till we figure out what's happening," the sergeant said.

She assumed Haywood was their home base, and minutes later they stopped outside a building called Police Research Center, with Fire Station 6 off to the right. She saw the same fire truck that had just rescued Carl pulling into the garage, where a group of firefighters were waiting in the brightly lit space to high-five their returning heroes.

Her knees shook as they helped her from the car and marched her past a flagpole, then down a short walkway through the station house door. Looking over her shoulder, she saw no sign of Gina in Gladys's Mercedes. Either she was still trying to break into the car, or she'd headed for the hospital.

Amanda was on her own.

Without ceremony, the two officers rushed her through a small lobby into a private office with a plain table, four minimal chairs, and a bubbling water cooler. Sergeant Rollins switched on a harsh overhead light.

"Make yourself at home, ma'am," he said, not unkindly. "I'll be back in a few minutes."

"Wait, don't I get a phone call?" The other cop still had her purse, with her phone.

When the heavy man laughed, his belly jiggled inside his black uniform shirt. "Sure you do, lady." He took her bag from his sidekick and dropped it on the table. "Knock yourself out. Call whoever you want." With that they left, locking the door behind them.

She sank onto a chair and clamped her jaw shut to keep her teeth from chattering. Strange streets, strange city, and she herself was a stranger. These people knew nothing about her. She had no character witnesses to speak on her behalf. She had known Ron, Carl, and even Gina less than three days. They might be inclined to give her the benefit of the doubt, but they had all been present when Carl announced that his jug was worth fifty thousand dollars. For all they knew she was a habitual kleptomaniac, and the artifact was indisputably found in her pocket.

The thermostat on the wall claimed the room was heated to seventy-three degrees, yet she was freezing. The big wall clock said ten o'clock, time to call Sara. She cinched the belt of her coat tighter and took a shaky breath. Common sense told her she should call a lawyer, or at least her mom. Yet she knew no lawyers in this horrible town, and calling her family, all too far away to help, would only upset them. So she took out her phone and followed her heart.

CHAPTER TWENTY-TWO

Cops n' robbers…

The conversation with Sara was fraught with emotion. While she haltingly explained her bizarre predicament, Sara made little sounds of comfort and distress. At times Amanda couldn't distinguish the sniffing back of tears from the snorts of fury.

"It's not fair. Why do these things always happen to you?"

"They happen to *both* of us, Sara." During the five years they'd known each other, Sara had been detained as a murder suspect, Amanda had been shot—twice—and they'd both been kidnapped by a crazed killer during a beach vacation. "But I've never been arrested for theft, and I swear I was minding my own business."

"It's not fair," Sara repeated. "I'm coming home to be with you, babe."

"Don't bother. Maya would be *so* disappointed." She realized too late just how snarky she had sounded.

But Sara ignored the barb. "Well, just hang in there, Mandy. I predict this whole misunderstanding will be cleared up tonight. They will release you and you'll be back in Mooresville tomorrow."

"Don't hold your breath." She knew Sara's prediction was wishful thinking, and by the lack of conviction in her voice, Sara knew it, too. "I'm afraid Trout will have to celebrate his birthday without me."

"Don't say that, Mandy. I'm sure Trout, your mom, Ginny—the whole crew—will be blowing out birthday candles with you on Thursday."

"You know what, Sara? Trout really wanted you to be there, too."

Sara was silent a moment, then said, "Someone's with you at the jail, right? The lovely Gina, no doubt."

"At the moment, I'm on my own," Amanda answered coldly.

"Well shit, that's ridiculous. Where's Carl? Where's Ron? Don't you have *any* support?"

Amanda realized she'd been so self-absorbed, she'd neglected to tell Sara about Carl's fall, but she decided not to pile on. "I'll be okay," she said. Although judging from the angry voices coming from the hall outside, she wasn't so sure.

"I can't stand it!" Sara exclaimed. "I'm coming home, Mandy, so let's make plans…"

"Wait, Sara, I honestly can't talk right now." The argument raging right outside the door escalated, and then Gina burst in with an angry Sergeant Rollins right behind her. "I'll call you back later, I promise…"

"Please, Mandy—"

"Sorry, gotta go."

She hung up just as Gina jabbed her middle finger in the sergeant's face and hollered,

"I arrived fifteen minutes ago, but this ape wouldn't let me see you!"

Amanda was shaken, needy, and upset about hanging up on Sara. She longed to beam herself across the miles to the safety of her lover's arms. "What is it, Gina?"

"For starters, why not say, 'So glad you came to my rescue. Thank you, Gina.'"

The woman's sarcasm did not sit well. She watched as Gina vamped her way across the room, scorched by the sergeant's watchful eyes. She propped one electric blue hip on the table, seductively crossing her legs.

"You don't have to say one word to these goons," Gina advised. "And I assume you didn't use your one phone call to contact a lawyer?"

Rollins guffawed. "You've been watching too many cops n' robbers movies, Ms. Molerno. Your friend isn't under arrest—yet."

"Did you read her the Miranda Rights?" Gina persisted.

"Nope, and we didn't cuff her, torture her, or deprive her of bathroom breaks." The officer was mellowing to the game as he stared at Gina's legs.

"My brother is a detective in Charlotte," Gina huffed. "So just because we're from out of town, don't think you can take advantage."

He held up his fat hands. "Wouldn't dream of it. In fact, I'll leave you gals to chat while we wait for the bad cop to arrive." He moved out the door, left it open a crack, but poked his head back in for a parting shot: "And by the way, please help yourselves to the water, *then* I'll deprive you of a bathroom break."

"Everyone's a comedian," Gina said once he was gone. "How the hell did this happen, Mandy? Is someone trying to frame you?"

"Why would they do that? Nobody even knows me here."

"It didn't happen by accident."

Nothing made sense as Amanda continued to shiver. She eyed Gina, who wasn't much help. "Why don't you hop down from that table and sit in a chair like a normal person? Flirting with Sergeant Rollins got us nowhere."

"Who says I was flirting with *Rollins*?" She slowly and sinuously slid off the table and wrapped her arm around Amanda's shoulders.

The warmth from another human felt way too good. Amanda leaned into her and closed her eyes. Maybe soon she'd wake up from this ridiculous nightmare. "Didn't you go to the hospital?"

Gina massaged the tension between her shoulder blades. "No, but I did steal Gladys's Mercedes and drove it straight here. I also phoned Ron while I was waiting to see you. Believe it or not, he's in the process of kidnapping Carl. He unhooked his IV, got him dressed, and was helping him into his car."

"They allowed Ron to take him?"

"Ron's a nurse, remember? He works at Mission Hospital, so everyone knows him. The patient was willing, Ron was able, so what could they do?"

"What about Gladys?"

"I gather she was down in the lounge getting coffee when Ron sneaked Carl out. She'll be hopping mad when she returns to the room and finds him gone."

"She'll also need a ride home," Amanda pointed out. "God, what a mess."

"Amen to that." Gina leaned her cheek into Amanda's hair. "Now all we have to worry about is what we'll do when the bad cop gets here."

CHAPTER TWENTY-THREE

Inconvenienced…

They did not have to wait long.

When cop number two walked through the door, Gina startled and stood upright, acting guilty—as if she and Amanda had been making out on the station house floor.

"What's happening, ladies?" He looked from one to the other. "I just need to take Ms. Rittenhouse's fingerprints. Is that okay?"

So far the bad cop wasn't so bad. This was the same officer who had searched her purse at the party and driven her to the station. He placed a small red plastic kit on the table that included an ink pad, roller, white cards, and hand cleaner. Amanda knew the drill. Been there, done that. She'd been eliminated as a suspect in the not-so-distant past and wondered if she'd be in the system. If so, she hoped the words "not guilty" were prominently displayed right beside her name.

The fellow seemed shy as he methodically cleaned her hands with alcohol. He was actually blushing when he helped her roll her thumbs, then other fingers onto the cards. By the time he imprinted her whole hand, he was sweating. She could smell his spicy aftershave, which made her rather sick to her stomach.

"You're wasting your time," she told him. "I never touched that jug." Or had she? Thinking back to breakfast with the boys, which now seemed a lifetime ago, she couldn't remember if she'd handled the jug or not.

The officer backed away, gave her a wipe, and regained his composure. "We'll see," he said. "If we find your prints on the object, we'll have our thief."

Amanda frowned. Not such a nice cop, after all. "How long will all this take?"

"Not long at all, as it turns out," said Sergeant Rollins, who stepped abruptly into the room. A shorter person followed close on his heels.

And then all hell broke loose. Cop number two jumped to attention so fast he nearly toppled the water cooler, then offered a comical salute. Even Rollins seemed flustered. When the short person—a woman—approached, it became abundantly clear she was in charge.

"This is Chief Toni Hall," Rollins barked.

Amanda wondered briefly if she and Gina were expected to snap to and salute as well. Instead they both stared at the chief—a middle-aged, short-haired blonde who filled out her black uniform very nicely. Amanda carefully focused on the big oval badge on her chest, rather than on her breasts.

Sergeant Rollins introduced them and Chief Hall shook their hands. Her grip was warm and friendly. So was her smile.

Her eyes lingered on Gina a moment, and then she turned to Amanda. "It appears we acted too quickly. You are free to go, Ms. Rittenhouse."

Chief Hall motioned to her officers that it was time for them to leave, stepping to one side as Sergeant Rollins backed out the door. Cop number two clumsily gathered up his red plastic kit, nodded to the women, and followed the sergeant.

Amanda was at a loss. "What happened?"

The chief sighed. "Usually I'm home watching *Masterpiece Theatre* on Sunday nights, but then a dear old friend came knocking on my door."

"So?" Gina interrupted impatiently.

"So, my friend confessed to stealing the face jug." Chief Hall shook her head in disgust. "I'm so sorry you were inconvenienced, Ms. Rittenhouse."

"That's it?" Gina slipped into her cape and gripped her pocketbook. "Your friend put us through hell. Who is she?"

"Never mind, Gina. Let's go." Amanda captured her friend's arm and pulled her into the lobby.

Chief Hall moved along with them, but when they neared the exit door she broke off to join a small group of cops surrounding a tall, distraught woman.

Amanda recognized the coat of many colors immediately. "Look, Gina, it's Millie Buncombe! She's the one who stole the jug."

Millie spotted Amanda at exactly the same moment and easily pulled free of her captors. Her long legs propelled her across the room, her gray ponytail swaying. She grabbed Amanda's wrists in her strong hands. "Oh, I am so sorry, dear. I never meant this to happen and I certainly could not allow you to take the blame."

Her dark eyes were red from weeping. Her extreme distress tugged at Amanda's heartstrings, and yet the woman had framed her. "Ms. Buncombe, how did the jug get in my pocket?"

"Lord, I am a stupid old lady!" Millie wailed. "I coveted Carl's little jug for my museum, but he made it clear tonight that I would never get it." She released Amanda and wiped her hands on her burlap dress. "So during the confusion after Carl fell, I slipped downstairs, snatched it off the pedestal, then went up to the coatrack on the mezzanine and shoved it into my pocket."

Amanda's mind raced. "But you put it in *my* pocket by mistake. I remember now, our coats were hung side by side."

"Shit, what a dumb fuck-up," Gina growled.

Amanda silently agreed. Millie's impulsive act was foolish and would cost her dearly. "I appreciate you coming forward. You didn't have to do that."

"I have to live with myself, don't I?" Millie said.

Chief Hall approached and gently took Millie's arm. "I wasn't able to talk to Professor Fischer, but I did speak to his friend. Ron Dunifon pressed charges on the professor's behalf, so I'm afraid I have to arrest you, Millie."

The big woman shrugged and allowed the chief to lead her off.

"What will happen to her?" Amanda wondered.

"She'll go to jail, of course, like she deserves."

"You're a hard woman, Gina."

CHAPTER TWENTY-FOUR

The morning-after blues…

Even before she opened her eyes, Amanda sensed sunlight flickering on her eyelids. The back of her throat tasted sour, and her tongue was swollen and fuzzy. Her head throbbed, and every inch of her body ached—especially her feet, since she had fallen asleep in her shoes, which felt two sizes too small. As she struggled to get oriented she reasoned she'd either been hit by a truck or had really tied one on last night.

The only pleasant sensation as she drifted toward consciousness was a cool breeze blowing across her face, scented of pine and far-away burning leaves. Eyes still closed, she pushed off her shoes with her toes, and from the absence of a thud, decided they'd fallen on carpet. Shifting onto her right side, toward the breeze, she felt warm, smooth skin against her arm, and instead of the breeze, the rhythmic puffing of someone's breath on her cheek.

Her eyes popped open to a sleeping Gina sharing her pillow. She was stark naked on her back, right arm flung up beside her head, left elbow bent with her arm across her chest, tucked under the cherry-topped peaks of her breasts.

Dear God in heaven, what had they done? The headache came on with a vengeance and her heart tripped double-time as she tried to remember. Praying her drumming heart would not wake her bedmate, she swallowed the sour taste and got her breathing under control.

Think...think...think! Somewhere along the line, she'd removed her black party dress. She still wore a slip and panty hose, and while Gina's lower body was tucked between the sheets, Amanda was splayed out on top of the spread, covered by a thin, untucked blanket. So theoretically, she was not *in bed* with the woman.

This technicality did nothing to ease her guilt. Surely they had not made love. She recalled no kissing, fondling, no intimacy at all. Near panic, she looked across Gina to the alarm clock on the night table and saw they had slept until noon. The window was open several inches. Beyond the gauzy, gently waving sheer curtain, a range of mountains slept in the noonday sun.

The light was unkind to Gina's slack face. It exposed each tiny age line, blue eye shadow separating into thin waves on her lids, residual lipstick clinging to the cracks—an achingly human portrait. Gina's vulnerability was endearing. It also convinced Amanda that she would remember making love to this woman, and she had not.

She stroked Gina's bare arm and whispered into her ear, "Wake up, sleepyhead."

Eyeballs shifted under Gina's lids, her feet twitched, she swallowed hard, and then she was awake. At first she seemed startled, but then she recognized Amanda.

"Well, hello there!" She tried for a seductive tone, but instead she was simply hoarse. "What happened?" She, too, suffered from the morning-after blues.

"You tell me." Yet details of the bizarre evening were rushing back—Carl's fall, the hours in the police station, the trip to the hospital to pick up Gladys. The woman had been furious, but she'd given them a lift home in her Mercedes. Ron had been occupied in Carl's bedroom with a seriously banged-up patient, but he had directed them to the liquor cabinet. "How much did we drink?" Amanda wondered.

Gina stretched and groaned. "Too damn much. We started with wine and finished with cognac—I think."

"God help us." It was all flooding back. She recalled stripping off her dress and collapsing on Gina's bed.

Gina saw her staring and pulled the sheet up to cover herself. "What day is it?"

"It's Monday afternoon. Don't you need to get home to Charlotte?"

Gina groaned and threw one arm across her forehead. "I am so screwed. I teach a painting class this evening."

"Maybe you can still make it." Amanda intended to sound encouraging, but at the same time, she didn't look forward to the trip. She needed a shower, food in her belly, and much more sleep. She pulled the cover over her head, closed her eyes, and heard gravel crunching in the driveway as a car arrived and parked. It wasn't Ron, because someone rang the doorbell. She hoped it wasn't Gladys returning for another shouting match, because last night when she'd briefly visited the house, her argument with Ron had been loud and brutal, and Amanda's splitting head could not tolerate another.

Feeling drowsy and slightly sick to her stomach, she listened to soft voices in the entry hall, followed by footsteps on the spiral staircase. They reached the upper level and moved down the hall to the bunk bed room. Wondering idly if Ron employed a maid who had come to tidy up and change her sheets, she was half asleep when a timid knocking started on their door.

"Gina, are you awake?" Ron called.

Gina reared up on her elbow. "Just barely. What do you want?"

"Are you decent? I'm coming in."

"No!" Amanda's eyes popped open. "I don't want him to see us together!"

"Too late now." Gina laughed.

"Have you seen Mandy?" Ron asked as he pushed into the room. "She has a visitor."

When Ron saw them in bed together his eyes bugged and Amanda's heart stopped. Sara was right behind him.

She stood frozen in the doorway staring, her mouth open in a silent scream of betrayal.

CHAPTER TWENTY-FIVE

A stare-down…

For what seemed an eternity, the four were frozen in suspended animation. Sara's eyes locked on Amanda in shock and disbelief.

Gina moved first, pulling the bedspread defensively up around her neck. "Who the hell is she?"

Ron fidgeted like he had fire ants up his trousers. "I'll leave you girls to it," he squawked in falsetto. "I need to go tend to Carl." And then he was gone.

Even paralyzed in this horrific tableau, Sara was beautiful. Her stricken green eyes were weary from travel and her forest green pantsuit was rumpled from what had surely been a God-awful drive, but she was still magnificent.

Amanda watched the amazing shift occur as Sara regained her composure and transformed into a no-nonsense shrink. She squared her shoulders and strode right up to the bed, hand extended.

"Hello, Gina. I'm Sara Orlando. Pleased to meet you."

"Jesus Christ!" Gina croaked. She could not shake Sara's hand without dropping the bedspread, exposing the swell of her right breast, but she did so anyway. "I thought you were in Washington."

"I'm sure you did." Sara coldly eyed them both. "I was there, but now I'm here."

Amanda longed to disappear from the face of the earth, but instead she found a tiny voice, "Listen, Sara, I know this looks bad, but nothing happened."

"Where have I heard that before?" Sara smirked.

Amanda waited for Gina to back her up, but the poor woman was in shock. Gina dropped Sara's hand, gathered the spread around her body, and quickly climbed out of bed. "If you two will excuse me, I need to take a shower."

"Make it a cold shower!" Sara called as Gina disappeared into the bathroom and loudly locked the door.

Her departure left them still engaged in a mortal stare-down. Amanda did not know what else to say or how to break the trance, so she let her heart speak for her. "God it's good to see you, Sara. I missed you and I need you."

Her impassioned words seemed to fall on deaf ears. Sara's perfect porcelain features remained as immobile as the famous marble statue of Venus de Milo. Her full red lips were tightly compressed, the twin emerald beams of her eyes cut into Amanda's soul.

"Please believe me," she begged. "You must know I didn't sleep with her."

Sara's gaze swiveled from the empty wine bottle on the floor to Amanda's black dress in a ruined heap. Gradually the corners of her mouth began to twitch and the edges of her eyes creased in a smile. Suddenly she was laughing and opening her arms. "Of course I believe you, babe! I missed you and want you more."

Needing no further invitation, Amanda flew from the bed and into her arms. She held Sara tight, rejoicing in the press of Sara's soft, full breasts against her ribcage as her own smaller breasts tucked above them. Sara kissed the hollow at the base of her throat, then tasted the salt of her neck as she nuzzled her.

When their lips met, Sara's tongue explored the soft lining of her mouth and tangled in a tipsy dance with hers.

As they continued to say hello, she urged Sara's hips closer and tighter until their hearts pounded in sync and, in spite of the hangover, she throbbed with urgent need.

When they came up for air, Sara laughed and said inelegantly, "You taste like a brewery."

Not to be outdone, Amanda said, "Well, you taste like a sausage n' cheese biscuit." It was Sara's favorite travel breakfast. She held her at arm's length. "I have a huge shower in my room down the hall. I'll wash you, if you'll wash me."

CHAPTER TWENTY-SIX

The invitation...

One thing led to another. The shower was vigorous, playful, and more than stimulating. They also managed to get clean, but not entirely satisfied. They eyed the narrow bunk beds and debated.

"It's not ideal, but I'm game if you are." Amanda shimmied suggestively under the towel draped over her shoulder.

Sara groaned. "God, I want to, but it doesn't feel right. I haven't been invited to stay here, and I can't use a stranger's house like a hotel." She moved to the window overlooking the driveway between the house and the barn.

Amanda joined her and saw Moby Dyke parked beside Ron's white Ford Fusion. For the first time since their amorous reunion, she wondered.

"How in the world did you get here so fast..." She hesitated before asking, "and where is Maya?" She half expected Maya to be lurking in the back of the van, waiting for the two of them to emerge.

Sara sighed and took her hand. "Long story short, Maya did not return with me. She's decided to relocate to DC to be with Shar."

"God, why didn't you tell me?" This was an astonishing turn of events. She could not imagine Maya, at the very pinnacle of her career as Charlotte's district attorney, giving up her job—even for love. Yet in retrospect, she knew how devoted the couple had always seemed, how long they had been together. In that moment, she fully forgave Sara. What had felt like betrayal in the moment now seemed like truly just a stupid mistake. "You must have worked some powerful magic to make that happen, Sara," she concluded.

Sara belly laughed. "You have no idea! It was touch and go for a few days, but after a little hand-holding, Shar and I convinced Maya that her relocation did not need to be permanent. Maya can even commute and work part-time as an assistant DA. The powers-that-be have already approved that arrangement, because they don't want to lose her. They will keep their house in Dilworth, and who knows, a congresswoman only serves two years. Maybe Shar won't be reelected?"

"God, I hope the voters keep her in office forever."

"So do I, so does Maya. We are all so proud of her. It'll all work out, I'm sure of it."

She squeezed Sara's hand. If anyone could have pulled off this miracle, it was Sara-the-shrink. She couldn't wait to hear more, but she was still stunned by Sara's presence. "Last night you said you were coming home, but I didn't take you literally."

"I was trying to tell you when Gina interrupted, remember?"

Amanda remembered well. She had promised to call Sara back, but with all the chaos at the police station and then the hospital, she had not gotten back to Carl's house until one in the morning and decided it was too late to call.

"So I drove all night, then called the Asheville police this morning. At first they gave me the runaround, but eventually they supplied this address. Crazy, right?"

"Crazy fantastic! I adore you, Sara. Now I can ride home with you instead of Gina."

A mischievous grin lit up Sara's face. "Actually, I was hoping we could stay in Asheville a few days—a mini vacation. I haven't been in the mountains for ages. We'll get a motel room with a king-sized bed."

Amanda was ecstatic. "Queen size works for me, but what about Trout's birthday on Thursday? I promised Mom."

Sara pulled her into her arms. "Today's only Monday. I promise to get us home on time."

They sealed the deal with a long kiss, then she looked out the window just as Gina drove up in her green Nissan truck. She threw open the tailgate, jogged into the house, and returned with her overnight bag.

"I must say goodbye to Gina," Amanda said quietly. "She's a good person, Sara. I think she'll be a friend to us."

"Okay, but no goodbye kissing, please. And while you're down there, will you bring my suitcase from my car? I could use some fresh clothes."

As it turned out, Amanda and Gina did kiss and even shed a few tears at their parting. They promised to get together—the three of them—when they got back to town. Secretly Amanda hoped that Gina would reunite with her beloved Red and they'd make it a foursome. Gina deserved much happiness.

"All set?" Sara asked twenty minutes later. They were dressed, packed, and ready to roll.

"First I want you to meet Carl, if he's up to it. He's such a nice man, Sara. He reminds me of my grandpa."

Ron greeted them as they descended the spiral staircase, like he'd been lurking in wait. He looked surprisingly fresh after the horrific night they'd endured, charming as ever in a brown cable-knit sweater, black jeans, and polished loafers. His raven hair was neatly combed back from his pale forehead, and he smiled as he appraised Sara—who looked pretty sharp herself, in Amanda's opinion. She wore a soft winter-white cashmere sweater and hip-hugging jeans. Seeing the two together—Sara petite and voluptuous, Ron six-foot-three and giraffe skinny—was a stunning contrast.

Ron took hold of Amanda's arm while smiling warmly at Sara. "Mandy, I hate to see you leave so soon, and I haven't even gotten a chance to know Sara. Carl and I have been talking. We'd love it if you two could stay on as our guests for a few days."

The invitation was so unexpected it took her breath away. Clearly Sara was shocked, too.

"Uh, I don't know, Ron. It's very generous, but Carl is recovering from his fall and we don't want to impose."

"Please, please, please!" he begged, including Sara in the entreaty. "Carl has taken a real liking to you, Mandy. It would mean the world to him."

The man seemed almost desperate, which was odd. She would have thought that after the crowd of admirers at Carl's party, and Gladys inserting herself into their lives, Ron would want to lock Carl away from the world and nurse him back to health in peace. On the other hand, maybe the men needed the buffer zone of company in the house to help them re-establish their equilibrium.

"What do you think, Sara?" Ron asked.

Amanda realized that Sara was waiting for a cue from her. Staying with the men was not her idea of a romantic vacation. Yet Ron was a great cook and a generous host, and he would respect their privacy.

"Can we have Gina's room?" she asked.

"That goes without saying." He looked knowingly from one to the other.

She gave Sara a tiny nod.

Sara responded immediately. "We'd be thrilled to stay here. Thanks so much."

CHAPTER TWENTY-SEVEN

Whiplash…

Ron whisked them down the hall to Carl's bedroom. Not knowing what to expect, Amanda was surprised to find the professor sitting up in a chair. As she came closer, she saw cuts and bruises on the left side of his face and a bandage wrap peeking out from the V of his flannel collar. When he smiled and opened his hands in welcome, she noticed his left fingers were bandaged.

"I hope this means Ron convinced you to stay," he said warmly as he appraised Sara. "I've already grown fond of Mandy, so I'm looking forward to knowing you, Sara."

Likely Gina had filled him in on their relationship, so Amanda was spared the embarrassment of elaboration.

"We can stay until Wednesday, if that's okay, and we thank you so much for asking."

"How are you feeling, Professor Fischer?" Sara began, but he insisted she call him Carl.

As he explained to Sara how he'd been saved from certain death by his red suspenders catching on a drainpipe, he patted his faithful bloodhound, Barney, snoozing at his feet. In the meantime, Amanda studied the room. By daylight, the master suite's window wall provided a stunning view of the distant mountains. It also included a door opening to the deck that wrapped around the back of the house.

While Sara chatted with Carl, Ron tidied up—making the bed and hanging clothes—and Amanda wandered along the ceiling-high shelves of pottery. The quality of the pieces Carl had held back for his own collection was even more exquisite than that of the work she'd seen at his gallery. The display included an impressive set of dinnerware, with a swirl of cobalt and crimson design on each plate that evoked a mountain sunset. It occurred to her that the unpleasant customer from last night's party, Al Cabella, would have paid a small fortune for this set.

"They don't wrap cracked ribs so much anymore," Carl was saying, "but in my case, I was gashed by the pipe so I earned a bandage."

"It must be very painful," Sara commented.

Carl chuckled. "Not to worry. They prescribed every painkiller known to man. Personally, I prefer scotch."

Amanda glanced at the bedside table. The many bottles included oxycodone and the heavy-duty opiate Dilaudid. Clearly Carl should not be taking those with his cocktails.

"Honestly, Sara, I'll be back at my potter's wheel in no time."

Amanda was pleased to see them getting along so well, but Sara had that effect on people. Years of counseling folks on her couch had made her a good listener.

Next Carl turned to Ron. "Would you mind bringing a fresh tin of rooibos for the girls and me, so I can brew a pot of tea?" He affectionately patted the fancy Breville tea maker set up near his chair.

An odd expression flickered briefly across Ron's face—a combination of irritation and panic—but it quickly passed. "Sure thing, Carl. I'll be back in a jiffy."

The moment Ron loped from the room, Carl switched gears so fast it gave her whiplash. His jovial features darkened as he frowned and said, "We need to talk."

Maybe Sara was used to such manic-depressive behavior, but she was not. "What's wrong, Carl?"

She stopped snooping and slid onto a plaid loveseat beside Sara so they were directly facing the man. Her heart beat louder as she waited for him to speak.

"I don't know how to say this, so I'll just say it outright," Carl began ominously.

But he did not continue. The grandfather clock ticked and Barney snored while they waited.

"Is this about your fall from the roof?" she gently prompted.

He pinned her with his intense blue eyes. "That's just it, Mandy. I did not fall. I was pushed."

Carl's shocking statement exploded the silence. It bounced against the grass cloth walls and window glass. Old Barney lifted his sad eyes and gazed at each in turn until finally Sara spoke.

"Are you sure about this, Carl?"

"Yes, I am quite sure." The pugnacious set of his jaw dared them to contradict him. "When it happened, I was too terrified to understand what had really occurred. Then later at the hospital, I was too drugged to focus. It wasn't until I woke up this morning that I remembered the swift pressure of a hand on my back."

"Whose hand?" Amanda gasped.

Carl groaned. "I have no idea. You were there, Mandy. You saw all those people near me at the edge. It could have been anyone, I wasn't paying attention. I was watching the sunset."

"Oh my God," Sara breathed. "Did you see anything, Mandy?"

"I'm afraid not." She'd been too busy hugging the wall. "I know both Gladys and Millie were near you."

Carl scoffed and shook his head.

"But you know Millie stole your face jug, right? Maybe giving you a little push was just the distraction she needed."

"That's ridiculous. Millie wouldn't hurt anyone. Besides, it wasn't a woman who pushed me."

She and Sara shared a look. Too many men underestimated the power and malice of a women, a mistake that could be fatal.

"Ron was nearby, of course, with his little bartender friend," Carl continued. "I saw some men I didn't know, including a big African American guy who wasn't one of the regular gallery crawl crowd. But these were all strangers, so why would they hurt me?"

Sara said, "You remember more than you think. Maybe I should hypnotize you?"

"You're kidding, right? I don't believe in all that mumbo-jumbo."

"Neither do I." Sara laughed.

All this was going nowhere. "Did you tell Ron?" Amanda asked.

Carl actually growled. Barney lifted his droopy head and whined. "Yes, I told Ron, but he refused to believe me. He had the nerve to suggest that I'd had too much to drink and my wobbly old legs just gave out on me. I tell you, I am furious with the man."

Obviously so, because Carl's pale face flushed red beneath his shock of snowy hair. Amanda was worried about the allegation, and yet a part of her agreed with Ron. Her first impulse when she'd heard about Carl's fall had been to blame arthritis, alcohol, or his lack of a cane.

"Maybe Ron is in denial?" Sara soothingly suggested. "No one wants to believe someone would deliberately hurt a loved one."

"Are you trying to psychoanalyze me, young lady? If so, stop right now."

Amanda suppressed a giggle. How many times had she said exactly the same words to Sara? "Did you tell the police, Carl?"

The professor considered. "Not yet. I was afraid they would think I was paranoid or senile. But Chief Hall is coming by soon about an entirely different matter. She is a sensible woman, so I have decided to tell her."

CHAPTER TWENTY-EIGHT

The fields beyond…

A cold, brisk wind lashed them as they stepped off the back deck onto the driveway. It tousled Sara's long black hair and lifted Barney's long ears as they walked toward the barn. They had ducked out of the house before Chief Hall arrived because Amanda had mixed feelings about seeing the woman again. The chief was pleasant enough, but Amanda was still stinging from her near-arrest the night before and did not look forward to another encounter with the local law.

They wanted to stretch their legs, so Carl had suggested they take Barney with them. But as they struck out to explore the fields beyond the house, the women wondered if the ancient bloodhound could keep up.

"I really like Carl Fischer," Sara confided as they strolled past the door to the barn. "What do you think?"

"Was he pushed? He seems to think so, but I can't imagine who would want to hurt him."

"Not that woman who stole the jug? Or Gladys?"

"No. Millie is okay. Stealing the face jug was stupid, but in the end she helped me last night. If Gladys is marrying the man, why would she?" She brought Sara up to date about the other strange characters she'd met, including Larry the surfer dude, Al Cabella, and the football guy. "They were all up on the roof, but again, why would they?"

Barney put his nose to the ground, tail swaying like a metronome, and picked up his pace through the knee-high brown grass. He seemed to know where he was going, so they followed. She enjoyed the sensation of wind on her face, working out the kinks in her tired muscles. Sara obviously did, too, as she raised up her chin and lifted her knees like a drum majorette.

"Something's definitely going on between Ron and Carl, though," Sara panted. "Don't know if he's jealous, or angry, but Ron is pissed at the man. Were they ever lovers?"

Amanda explained the theories she and Gina had concocted. "Bottom line—no. We decided that Ron wants a relationship, but Carl isn't having it."

They stopped moving when Barney paused to sniff a dead rabbit. A pair of turkey vultures hunkered down in a nearby tree waiting for them to move on so they could finish their lunch. The gray sky was punctuated by fast-moving silver clouds bordered by brilliant light where the sun shone behind them.

"Any indication that Ron would rather see Carl dead than married to Gladys?" Sara wondered.

"Maybe he'd rather have Gladys dead, but Ron is a gentle man. I don't think he's capable of violence," she answered as she surveyed the land. To either side of the broad field they were walking, the suburban development of Beaver Lake sprawled behind rough screens of tangled brush. The little lake itself shimmered like a smoky gray eye. Just ahead, a barbed wire fence carved out a property within the Fischer property, and she was surprised to see a decrepit two storied farmhouse swallowed by kudzu vine.

"Look, Sara, I bet that's the original homestead."

"Right. Likely that old house and the barn once stood all alone on this acreage."

"Let's take a closer look. Maybe we'll see a ghost or two."

Barney knew his way. With a small yip of excitement, he jogged to a secret opening where the fence had long ago been trampled to the ground and led them through. As the hound trotted forward, Sara threw out her arm, stopping Amanda in her tracks.

"Wait, someone's at the house! We'll be trespassing."

Amanda saw a basic white utility van parked on a rise just beyond the building. An olive green awning stuck out from one side of the vehicle, sheltering a gas cook stove, a folding table, and a single chair. Clearly the occupant was set up for camping.

"Wow, check out that awesome KTM Adventure R!" Sara thrilled.

Amanda had no idea what she was talking about until she saw the motorcycle parked in the shadow of a grape arbor. It looked like the Batmobile, black with an orange stripe. "Since when do you know so much about motorcycles?"

"Marc is obsessed. That model is an off- and-on road vehicle, a little Austrian number that costs seventeen thousand new," Sara reverently whispered.

Would wonders never cease? Every day she learned something new from Sara's endless encyclopedia of trivia. At the same time, Barney began a lazy, low-throated barking as a big man emerged from the van. She recognized him at once and quickly pulled Sara down behind a stand of bushes, where they wouldn't be seen.

"Shh, keep quiet! That's the football guy from the party. What the hell is he doing here?" Today he wore a tight, gray, long-sleeved T-shirt and ancient jeans with expensive Nike sneaks. She noticed that Barney's bark was a greeting, not a warning, and when the man handed him a dog cookie it appeared they were well acquainted.

"You think he owns this place?" Sara quietly asked.

"I doubt it, and I sure don't want him to spot us." She fervently hoped that Barney would not lead him to their hiding place.

Fortunately, the big man had a different agenda. After giving the hound a friendly pat, he dug into his pocket, pulled out keys, fired up his bike, and slowly drove down a narrow rutted path to a road not far from the property. Turning left, he disappeared in the direction of Asheville.

"I wonder what he's up to?" Sara said as Barney bounded back to join them.

"No good, I suspect."

CHAPTER TWENTY-NINE

Standoff...

When they neared the house, she saw a white Ford Crown Victoria in the drive and correctly deduced it belonged to Chief Toni Hall. She was pleased to see the chief was just leaving, yet it would be impolite not to say hello. She walked up and introduced Sara.

Chief Hall's eyes lingered a beat too long on Sara, and then she smiled at Amanda. "Look what Carl gave me." She reached into the pocket of her blue fleece jacket and brought out the face jug.

Amanda was astonished. "He *gave* that to you?"

Out of uniform, Toni Hall was less imposing than she'd been the night before. She wore black sweat pants bagged out at the knees and vintage white tennis shoes. Her laugh was raucous and friendly.

"He wants me to deliver it to Brother Wolf and donate it to the cause. He and Gladys discussed it. When Carl is feeling better, they'll organize a national online auction for this ugly little jug. They hope it will fetch its value of fifty thou, maybe more."

"That's a generous gift," Sara commented, wide-eyed.

The chief shrugged. "Oh, Carl can afford it. Likely he will benefit from a charitable donation tax deduction. Besides, he loves dogs—I love cats—it's all good." She picked what looked to be a yellow cat hair off her jacket, waved goodbye, and left.

Amanda explained about Brother Wolf on the way into the house and was surprised to find Carl waiting for them right inside the door.

"I see you spoke with Toni. Did she tell you the good news?" He appeared to feel better as he slowly walked toward his room with the aid of his gnarled cane. "I refused to press charges against Millie Buncombe. They're cutting her loose this afternoon."

"Why?" Amanda was flabbergasted.

"Oh, the old gal meant no harm. She just got overly zealous about that dusty old museum of hers. No doubt Millie would have preferred me to gift the face jug to her, but that was a step too far." He grinned and invited them to join him in the master suite, where the tantalizing aroma of red tea permeated the space.

"Pour for us, Mandy." He nudged her toward his fancy teapot and indicated that Sara should be seated. "Amazing machine. The tea basket moves up and down infusing the leaves to maximize the taste. I program it to brew at breakfast and bedtime, and I tell you, the health benefits of South African rooibos are endless."

"Yes, I know. We'd love a cup." Amanda's ex had been a tea enthusiast, while she, a coffee gal, was sick of the topic. "Did you tell Chief Hall that someone pushed you off the roof?"

He refused to answer until they were all properly seated. "Yes, but I'm afraid the idea upset her—not that she didn't believe me, just that she was frustrated. They did nothing to secure the scene, you see. They took notes at the time and interviewed a few witnesses, but everyone assumed it was an accident. Although Toni did say she'd look into it, I believe it's too late."

Amanda agreed. "Listen, Carl, Sara and I enjoyed our walk through your property, but we were curious about that abandoned farmhouse out near the road. What's the story? Does someone live there?"

He laughed and shook his head. "The old Anderson place. I don't own it. Farmer Anderson, stubborn bastard, refused to sell his plot. He actually believed his worthless progeny would keep the place up and pass it down, but instead the kids moved to town and the house went to ruin."

"So nobody visits anymore?"

"Sometimes the wild grandsons come round to drink and smoke pot. Last summer they had a weenie roast and almost burned the place down. Other than that, it's populated by native critters. Barney loves to hunt there."

At the mention of his name, the bloodhound curled at Carl's feet, opened his droopy eyes, and wagged his tail.

It was a delicate question, but she had to ask. "Is the Anderson family African American?"

Carl's laughter was a thunderclap. "Good lord, no! They're blond, blue-eyed Swedes, the perfect prototypes for the Aryan Nation."

Glancing at one another, she and Sara knew they had to tell. Amanda took the lead, describing in detail about the camper van, the motorcycle, and the stranger hanging out on the Anderson land.

"I saw this same man at your farewell party, Carl. Perhaps there's a reasonable explanation, but it seems suspicious to me."

The room got deathly silent. The professor's hand trembled as he put down his teacup. He was beyond disturbed—he was frightened. "I saw him at the party, too," he said at last. "He was near me when I fell. I'm afraid he's spying on me."

"But why?" Sara jumped in. "Why would anyone spy on you?"

"I have no idea," he snapped.

Carl Fischer's whole demeanor changed from the outgoing, cordial host he had been seconds ago to a hooded, defensive old man. Like a turtle pulling into its shell, he retreated from them. The transformation was astonishing, and it occurred to her that Carl was a man with something to hide. Just as quickly, she reminded herself that he had just experienced a horrible, life-threatening event that would naturally leave him shaken.

Fortunately, the tense moment was interrupted by the entrance of Ron Dunifon. He popped into the room wearing his nurse gear—a lime green, short-sleeved scrub shirt that made his long, pale arms look skinny and fragile, loose cut trousers, and sensible brown rubber clogs. His stylish man-about-town persona had evaporated.

"How are you feeling, Carl? Can I get you anything before I leave for the hospital?" Ron busied himself plumping pillows and picking up stray tissues from the floor.

"Stop fussing, I'm fine," Carl gruffly admonished.

The animus between them was palpable. They made no eye contact.

"Just asking," Ron continued cheerfully. "I won't be home till late."

"No, tonight I want you home by eight. I know your shift ends at seven," Carl said. "Gladys is coming over to cook for us—all of us." His gesture included Amanda and Sara. "I need you to join us, Ron. It's important."

Red blotches appeared on Ron's cheeks. "It's too soon to have company, Carl. You need to rest and recover."

"Gladys is not *company*, and you know it," Carl barked. "Come home for dinner. I mean it."

The uncomfortable standoff ended with a bang when Ron left, slamming the door behind him.

CHAPTER THIRTY

The bombshell…

"That was intense between Carl and Ron," Amanda said as she navigated Moby Dyke through the unfamiliar streets of Asheville.

"No kidding. They were baiting each other like cocks before a fight. If they don't resolve their issues soon, there'll be blood in the ring."

They were driving down Merrimon Avenue into the city, retracing the route Ron had taken to the River Arts District. She had promised Sara lunch and a tour. Recognizing several landmarks, she turned right on Clingman and then right on Haywood. Making a quick right on Riverside Drive, she soon found Cotton Mill Studios.

As she searched for a parking space, she told Sara more about her near-arrest the previous night. "I couldn't believe it when Chief Hall walked in and told me I was free to go."

Sara smiled. "She's a very attractive woman. Did you see the way she looked at me? Do you think she's gay?"

"Listen, the chief saw me with Gina last night and with you today. She thinks I'm playing musical girlfriends, that's why she looked at you."

"I say she's gay," Sara said with finality before scanning the busy complex. "Wow, this joint is jumping. I can see why an artist would want to rent space here, but don't you dare!"

Amanda parked and turned off the engine. "I never seriously considered it, Sara. I want to be with you, so Asheville was never a real option." Impulsively, she leaned across the console and kissed her full on the lips.

When the kiss ended, Sara gasped. "What's happening? You never act out in public."

"When in Asheville, do as the natives do—what can I say?" Suddenly she was very hungry. It was already four, and they had not eaten since before their walk, when they'd grabbed stale bagels before heading into the field. "Let's get some food before I drop dead."

They chose a patisserie located inside the mill and shared a plate of cheese and spinach savories, both opting for hot coffee instead of one of the exotic teas on the menu. Next they roamed the fascinating galleries in the building, saving Carl's space for last.

She was surprised to find two college kids carefully packing Carl's pottery. The volunteers were from the art department at Appalachian State University in Boone, where Carl had taught up until eight years ago.

"We never had a class with Professor Fischer," the female student explained, "but we get extra credit in our Art Business course for closing up his gallery."

"It's grunt work, if you ask me," the male student grumbled. "Once it's packed up, we deliver it to Fischer's barn. Any house mover could have done this."

"I hear Professor Fischer is giving this space to a painter, some local guy," the girl said.

This was news to Amanda. "What guy?"

"Who the hell cares?" The disgruntled boy shrugged.

Sara wanted to see the roof, but Amanda did not. So while Sara was upstairs, she gazed wistfully at the empty space. Once the shelves were removed and the walls covered with studio white paint, it would be a magnificent showroom.

"Any regrets?" Sara came up behind her and gently squeezed her shoulders.

"None," she lied. "Did you find any interesting clues on the roof?"

"Nothing. Are you ready to go?"

She was determined to show Sara Gina and Ron's work at the Woolworth Walk, but time was getting short, so they'd have to hurry. Taking a final look at the dramatic fall of afternoon light through the warehouse windows, the flickering patterns it made on the walls and floors, she imagined one last time how her metal sculpture would look displayed here, and then she said goodbye.

When they stepped outside, storm clouds were blowing in from the northwest, indicating rain was on the way. A familiar black limousine came gliding right up to the base of the steps where they were standing, Al Cabella's face clearly visible on the passenger side.

"Shit, what is he doing here?" Amanda moaned.

"Who is he?"

"He's that slimy customer from Carl's party, the one who wanted to buy a set of dinnerware."

Sara stared into the car. "He's kind of handsome, like a movie gangster."

Amanda pulled her back. "Let's go. I don't want to talk to him. If we both look the other way and hurry, maybe he won't recognize me."

Moving Sara was like yanking a kitten from catnip. Even as they rushed down the steps and past the limo, she peeked in at the driver.

"His chauffer is a gorilla, Mandy," Sara whispered. "I wouldn't want to meet these guys in a dark alley."

"Shut up and move!" Amanda hissed.

Once they were safely in Moby Dyke, Sara giggled. "Are you scared of those men?"

"For heaven's sake, Al Cabella is an art collector, not a mobster. But why is he here? He must know Carl is still recovering from his fall."

"Maybe he's here to buy someone else's work?"

Sara continued to poke fun until they entered the Woolworth's building. "Did you notice the limo had Illinois plates? The Mafia's big in Chicago, right?"

"Give it a rest, Sara." She led the way to Gina's booth.

Sara tried to resist being impressed by the big splashy abstracts, but she couldn't help herself. "She's good. I can see why my brother takes lessons from her, but he has a long way to go."

They moved on to Ron's realistic landscapes. Sara commented on his tight mountain scenes: "These are carefully rendered, but they lack passion."

"I agree, but wait until you see his portrait of Carl Fischer. You're the psychiatrist. Maybe you can tell if it's love—or hate— he's captured there." But when she looked around the base of the pegboard walls for the canvas turned inward, the portrait was gone. "That's funny. It was right here yesterday."

Both were startled when a young man came up from behind and tapped Amanda's arm. "Ron took it home with him. I guess he didn't want me to have it."

Larry Goldberg smiled from behind his black rimmed glasses. Instead of the surfer clothes from the previous afternoon or the waiter's tux from the party, today the tan blond wore dark trousers, an open-collared cream dress shirt, a sport coat in tweedy autumn tones, and brown loafers. Instead of looking like he'd just stepped off a beach, he looked like a fashion model from *GQ Magazine*.

"What are you doing here, Larry?" Amanda asked.

"It's better than hanging out at the YMCA, right? That's where I've been living."

She wondered if he'd spent all his bartending money on this outfit. She introduced him to Sara and they shook hands. By the way Larry ogled Sara, it was hard to believe he was really gay.

"I've gotten to know the exhibitors here. Sometimes they buy me lunch." He gave Amanda a plaintive look.

It caused her to remember how she'd shared her club sandwich with him. "Have you eaten today?" she reluctantly asked.

"Nope, I'm saving my appetite. I have a date tonight." Larry struck a pose, daring her to ask.

"Okay, who are you going out with?"

"Ron Dunifon." He puffed out his chest. "He's taking me to Isa's Bistro, then maybe dancing after." After dropping the bombshell, Larry winked and sauntered off.

Sara gasped in disbelief. "But Gladys is cooking dinner. I thought Ron was coming back to the house to eat with us?"

"Carl will not be a happy camper."

CHAPTER THIRTY-ONE

Company…

Amanda was right. Carl was furious about Ron ducking dinner. She had given him a heads-up in advance of Gladys's arrival and told him Ron was going out with a "friend." She'd neglected to add that the relationship between Ron and Larry was possibly more romantic than platonic. Luckily the early warning allowed Carl to cool down, so that by the time they were all seated in the kitchen watching Gladys fix spaghetti, he was relaxed and mellow.

Carl was drinking no alcohol, neither his preferred scotch nor the excellent cabernet sauvignon Sara had purchased on the way home. His abstinence caused her to wonder if his easygoing mood was attributable to the smorgasbord of pain meds at his disposal. She hoped not.

"I was never much of a cook," the professor said. "I love it when Gladys feeds me the food I crave—like red meat and pasta. All the good stuff that's bad for me. Ron fancies himself a chef, but insists I eat only fish and chicken. He won't even buy real butter." Carl made an ugly face.

Gladys smiled sweetly at him. "My dear departed husband liked rich food, and he was a physician. I figured if he said it was okay to eat heavy, then who was I to disagree?"

Amanda wondered if the late Dr. Uplander had died of clogged arteries. She also wondered if it was wise to compare Ron and Gladys in the same sentence. One could conclude that the chef who worried about Carl's health was the one who loved him best.

"I'm not much of a cook, either," Amanda admitted. Possibly she had inherited the inadequacy from her mother, who was pathetic in the kitchen. "But I can chop things without cutting off my fingers, so may I help?"

Sara was entertaining Carl with a lively account of their afternoon of gallery crawling, so while they talked, Amanda visited with Gladys, who gave her a sharp knife, a cutting board, and a bowl of peppers, onions, and tomatoes.

Her first impressions of Gladys had been of a privileged and pampered woman, but up close she saw that her gray herringbone wool skirt and white pussy bow blouse had seen better days. Although obviously expensive, they were old and worn. Black polish barely covered the raw scuffs on her pumps. Like the older Mercedes she drove, it seemed Gladys's wealth had passed its expiration date.

Not that Amanda gave a damn about any of that, but she did hope that Gladys didn't see Carl as a meal ticket. Admittedly, she had known Ron first. She liked him and empathized with the angst of unrequited love, yet she was determined to give Gladys a fair shake.

"Have you been a widow long?" she asked, trying to draw the older woman out.

Gladys licked the spoon she was using to stir her sauce and set it down with a thump in its metal tray. "Doc died twelve years ago and left me with nothing," she snorted. "He had a gambling problem, you see, and stupid me, I didn't know we were leveraged to the hilt till he was dead and gone."

Amanda hardly knew what to say. Clearly the woman was not in mourning. "Any children?"

"Sadly, no. We were never blessed. It's one of the things Carl and I have in common. We both love kids. He satisfied that need by teaching all those years, and I volunteer at Empowerment Child Care at the YWCA."

Amanda was impressed. She also noticed that Gladys's southern accent was quite different from that of other North Carolinians she'd met. "Were you born around here?"

"Lord, no. I hail from Birmingham, Alabama—not that snooty high society crowd, mind you. I grew up dirt-poor and dragged myself up with a lifeline of scholarships."

She proceeded to describe her rags-to-riches story, which culminated in a master's degree in social work. Amanda admired that. Being a scrapper did not make Gladys a gold digger.

Sara tossed a luscious salad while Gladys served the spaghetti. In deference to his injuries, Carl agreed to forego the outside sunset in favor of eating at a long bar facing the window wall, where they still enjoyed an impressive view of the sky beyond the barn. Amanda had not realized how hungry she was, and by the way Sara was gobbling, she was starving, too. Carl entertained them by sucking up spaghetti noodles like a kid, and for a moment, all the tensions of the past few days slipped away.

Until the doorbell rang, startling them all.

"It must be Ron," Gladys said without enthusiasm.

"No, he'd just let himself in the back," Carl said. "I'm afraid we have company. I'll check it out."

As it was clearly difficult for Carl to rise and walk, all three women offered to do the honors, but he waved them away with a shake of his cane. "This is still my house, ladies, so let me be the host."

Gladys frowned. "I wonder who it is? Carl never gets visitors this time of night. Anyone who has been here before knows to come round back to park. This is very strange."

"One way to find out!" Sara sprang into action and tiptoed in Carl's footsteps. She stopped just inside the arched doorway leading to the foyer, then peeked around the corner to observe the action at the front door. Amanda and Gladys stared after her, and when Sara returned, her eyes were wide with surprise.

"Who was it?" Gladys demanded.

Amanda heard two male voices she did not recognize moving down the hall toward Carl's master suite. They were laughing.

Sara's hands fluttered. "It's the gangster and his gorilla. Their limo is parked out front."

"What on earth?" Gladys was understandably alarmed.

Amanda placed a calming hand on the older woman's arm. "Sara's just kidding. I believe it's a man named Al Cabella and his chauffer. I met Mr. Cabella at Carl's party. He wanted to buy some of his pottery."

"He still does," Sara explained. "Carl took them back to his bedroom to show off his collection. I expect Mr. Cabella will purchase something tonight."

"Should Carl be left alone with them?" Amanda was suddenly panicky about the whole situation.

"What are you girls fussing about?" Gladys huffed. "Why wouldn't Carl be all right with those men? He's an adult. He's sold his work from this house many times."

Sara and Amanda glanced at one another. Obviously Carl had not shared his concerns with Gladys. If she didn't know he'd been pushed from the roof, it wasn't their place to enlighten her. By silent agreement, they decided to let it go.

"Of course, Carl is fine," Amanda said. "But maybe I should take them all some dessert?" She gestured at the plate of chocolate and ricotta cannoli on the sideboard.

But Gladys swept the idea away with a dismissive wave of her hand. "For pity's sake, give Carl a chance to make his sale. If those men buy, they get cannoli—otherwise, no."

The three decided to have coffee. Each poured herself a cup and moved from the bar to the comfortable wicker chairs facing out to the deck. By then the sunset had performed a dramatic curtain call and taken its leave. They all gazed out at the dark night.

"So Carl never married?" Amanda picked up where she'd left off.

Gladys shrugged. "No. He had his reasons, but he's old enough now that those reasons don't matter."

A cryptic remark if there ever was one. Again, she and Sara glanced at one another. Carl had never married because he didn't want to settle down? Because he was gay? When did one become so old it didn't matter? Amanda couldn't let it go. "What reasons?"

Gladys's carefully coiffed head jerked upright, and her pale blue eyes were dry ice. "None of your business, young lady, and I suggest you forget the whole thing."

"Sorry," she muttered and quickly changed the subject, asking Gladys if she had made the cannoli herself. As Gladys detailed the recipe, Amanda wondered about Carl's secrets. This was the second instance in which she'd suspected he had something to hide. Making a mental note to check the professor out on the Internet, she was lost in thought when they all heard a loud crash out on the deck.

"What the hell?" Gladys jumped to her feet and moved to the window. "Is Barney outside?"

"He was asleep in the corner." Sara pointed at the dog, who was now wide awake, growling deep in his throat and baring his teeth.

"Someone's out there!" Amanda heard heavy, running footsteps and saw the jiggling pinprick beam from a flashlight. "Jesus, who is it?"

"Maybe it's Ron coming home?" Sara squeaked. Clearly she did not believe it.

Neither did Gladys. "For Christ's sake, call the cops!"

While Sara pulled out her cell phone, Amanda ran into the hall. "I'm going to check on Carl."

The deck wrapped around the house, with an entrance into Carl's bedroom—was it possible the intruder had gotten inside? As she picked up speed, she looked through the door to the patio and saw a single headlight wobbling near the barn. At that moment, a motorcycle engine roared to life.

Dear God in heaven, let it not be too late!

CHAPTER THIRTY-TWO

Emotional vacuum…

Carl's bedroom door was ajar. When she burst in like a crazed maniac, three startled faces swiveled toward her in alarm. Instead of the chaos she'd feared, the men were busy packing up the set of sunset dinnerware she had so admired. Carl was perched on the edge of his bed, a smug smile on his lips as he instructed the chauffer in the art of bubble wrapping. Cabella was lovingly lifting platters off the display shelves.

"Is something wrong, Mandy?" Carl asked.

Feeling foolish, she caught her breath. "Didn't you hear that noise out on the deck? Someone was sneaking around the house."

By their blank stares, the men were unaware of any disturbance.

"No, really!" she insisted, looking pointedly at Carl. "I saw a motorcycle leaving. I'm sure it's the man I told you about."

That got the professor's attention. With some effort he stood, and with an almost imperceptible shake of his head, indicated she should not discuss the matter in front of his guests.

"I'm sure it was nothing of concern. We'll check out the deck later." He turned to Cabella. "I think we're almost done here. Please step into the hall with me, Mandy, while these men finish up."

She headed back into the foyer and waited until Carl joined her. Closing the door behind him, he moved her down the hall a few paces and urgently whispered, "Was it that black fellow who's camping out at the old house?"

"I didn't see him, but who else would it be?"

The professor nervously tapped the tip of his cane against the floor tiles. "What the hell does he want?"

Suddenly she remembered. "Whoops, Sara is calling the police!"

"Well stop her, for God's sake! The intruder is long gone, and I've had a belly full of cops. Toni Hall will think I'm nuts."

She rushed back to the kitchen, but Sara had already made the call.

"Well, call them back and cancel. Carl is fine."

Gladys exhaled in relief. "I don't know what the hell's going on here, but I want it to stop! I wish everyone would just go away and leave us alone."

By that time Gladys was pacing, arms crossed over her chest in a way that was both defensive and offensive, like she was holding back from striking out at anyone handy. Amanda didn't know what to make of her. It seemed the fighting instinct from her dirt-poor Alabama roots was at war with the sophisticated persona she wanted to project. Amanda wondered if she and Sara were included in the *everyone* Gladys wished would just go away and leave her alone.

Gladys caught her drift. "Oh no, I don't mean you girls— you are a delight. I wish those men would leave and let Carl get his rest."

Amanda gathered that Cabella and his chauffer would not be getting cannoli even though they'd made a purchase.

Then Carl walked in. He gave Gladys a reassuring peck on the cheek and got confirmation from Sara that she'd managed to stop the police.

"Mr. Cabella is leaving now," he announced.

Right on cue, Cabella strolled up with a Cheshire cat grin and gave Carl a wad of cash. The man wore a different Armani suit, oozed charm, and was as darkly handsome as he had been at the party. When he offered an obligatory nod of recognition, she was as put off as before by his smarmy attitude.

When the chauffer arrived, his arms loaded with dinnerware, Cabella excused himself and together they propped the front door open.

"Put it in the trunk, Mickey, and don't break anything," Cabella commanded.

At the same time, the door at the back end of the hall flew open and Ron Dunifon burst in, followed by Larry Goldberg. The two were laughing and stumbling. When they locked arms, it seemed a move designed to hold one another upright rather than an expression of affection. As they moved closer, she smelled liquor in the cold, cross-current wind tunneling between the two opened doors.

"Have you been drinking?" Carl barked at Ron.

"Just a little." Ron was defiant as he pulled Larry forward.

"Lord, what now?" Gladys moaned in disgust.

"Hi, guys!" Larry stupidly waggled his fingers at them.

Amanda saw a stain on the kid's fancy new cream dress shirt, and the fly of his dark trousers was partially open, leading her to wonder what kind of sex games they'd been playing in Ron's Ford Fusion. The top snaps of Ron's shirt were undone, showing off a sparse forest of black hairs on his pale chest. These guys weren't just tipsy, they were roaring drunk.

"Who are those goons?" Ron's words were slurred as he nodded at Cabella and Mickey.

"Never mind," Carl growled as he gazed at the spectacle before him.

Plainly Ron wanted to make a statement by flaunting the young man on his arm, hugging Larry closer, hoping to make Carl jealous. The entire exhibition was sad for everyone involved. Gladys had had enough. She threw up her hands and retreated to the kitchen. Tossing a look of sympathy in Amanda's direction, Sara went with her.

Larry extracted himself from Ron. "Hey, I need to take a piss. Where's the john?"

"You can use the bathroom in the master suite, down the hall on the left." Carl pointed the young man in the right direction and rolled his eyes as Larry retreated down the hall with his left hand tracing along the wall for balance. They kept watching until Larry found the room and groped his way inside.

"Why are you doing this, Ron? This isn't like you."

Amanda detected sorrow in Carl's voice.

"Two can play this game, Carl. Larry is my date."

Luckily, Al Cabella interceded. He looked from Ron to Carl, an expression of smug amusement on his face. "We're all packed up, Professor. We'll be leaving now. Thanks for everything, and it's been a pleasure doing business with you."

When the men departed, closing the door behind them, the wind tunnel was cut off, leaving the three of them in a suffocating emotional vacuum where she could hardly breathe. This was not her drama.

"When *your* friend is finished in *my* bathroom," Carl said coldly, "I want you to drive him home. If you're too drunk, perhaps Gladys would be kind enough to do it."

Ron took a wide belligerent stance. He gave Carl a play punch to the shoulder and glared down from his great height. "Sorry, Carl, Larry is spending the night. He'll be sleeping with me in the barn."

With that, Amanda fled to the safety of the kitchen and did not look back.

CHAPTER THIRTY-THREE

Night sounds…

"I expected fireworks," she confessed much later as she lay in Sara's arms.

Sara giggled. "Sorry, but I detected sparklers and Roman candles in that last kiss."

Amanda blushed. "Not *us*, silly, I meant fireworks between Ron and Carl. I half expected them to come to blows."

"So did I. That's why I left when I did." Sara rolled her leg over Amanda and gently brought her knee up between her thighs.

In the end, Ron and Larry had retreated peacefully to the barn. She and Sara had eaten cannoli with Carl and Gladys, and then Gladys had driven home. It was apparent that Carl was exhausted from the ordeal, and soon after, he had retired to his suite for his bedtime tea.

"It's painful to watch the three of them together, like a ménage a trois that will never work," Sara continued. She parted Amanda's thighs and cupped her warm, wet core. "I'm afraid Ron will have to move out if Carl and Gladys get married."

Amanda moaned in pleasure, completely uninterested in anyone's love life but her own. She wrapped her legs up around Sara, pulling them tighter together. "Let's light some more fireworks!" She reached down, urging Sara to enter her, but Sara had a different agenda.

She played with Amanda, lightly teasing her, finding the sweet spot just inside and circling its slippery essence while she spread the opening. Just when Amanda felt she could endure no more, Sara came in slowly, rhythmically, then harder and faster until Amanda arched with need and her orgasm shook the bed.

After that they switched, with Amanda on top. She took her time with Sara's lush lips, their tongues dancing together. Then she moved down to the soft mounds of her full breasts, with tips tasting of salt and honey. She lingered there until Sara gasped and guided her face down to its ultimate destination, where Amanda used her tongue and tortured her lover much as Sara had done moments before. Involved, concentrated, on the edge of orgasm herself, she ignored Sara's pleas of *now!* and kept it up. Like hovering over a stove waiting for a teapot to boil, she heard the ever-more violent roiling inside and came again just as Sara's whistle blew.

Much later, in the never-never time around three a.m., something caused her to wake. The sound could have been part of her dream, which included the irregular tap-tap-tap of two hearts beating off rhythm—or it could have been faraway footsteps coming, for instance, from the deck downstairs. Either way, the disturbance popped her eyes open. Their window was cracked about six inches, with a cold breeze pouring in, chilling her naked arms. She pulled the blanket up to Sara's chin and watched the gently swaying curtain, but the sound came no more.

Still she could not get back to sleep, so Amanda remembered she wanted to do research on Carl Fischer. Sara always traveled with her laptop to ensure she was always available to her patients, so Amanda decided to borrow it. She dressed in jeans and a warm sweatshirt, found a chair behind the bed so the light wouldn't bother Sara, and did a Google search.

The professor's professional information came up almost immediately. He had received his MFA from Indiana University in Bloomington and became a full professor there in 1975 at age thirty-two. He taught at IU for fifteen years, then quit to try his hand as a professional potter in an arts community in Brown County, Indiana. In 1995, at age fifty-two, Fischer made his way to Appalachian University in Boone, North Carolina, where he taught until retirement, and then moved to Asheville at age sixty-five. From 2008 to the present, Carl was described as "an exhibitor, property owner, mover and shaker in the town's River Arts District."

While all this was impressive and interesting, it offered no juicy personal data other than the fact that Carl had never been married. Conspicuously missing were his place of birth and what Carl had done up until age twenty-eight. Because he'd attended IU, she guessed that Carl was born and had grown up somewhere in the Midwest, but who knew?

Other than a LinkedIn account, the man had no social media presence—which was not surprising for a seventy-two-year-old. The only way to learn more about his personality, social life, or sexual preference was to ask him directly, which she was not inclined to do.

Disappointed, she shut down Sara's laptop and realized her stomach was growling. Sex always made her ravenous, and there was leftover spaghetti in the fridge. Her host had made it abundantly clear that she and Sara were to help themselves to food whenever the spirit moved them, so why not?

Taking a last loving look at Sara, who would sleep straight through till dawn, she put on her slippers, tiptoed down the upstairs hall, and carefully descended the spiral staircase to the hall below.

It was eerie, almost spooky, roaming around someone else's house in the middle of the night—or in this case early morning. She felt the hard ceramic tile under her feet, smelled the lingering traces of cooking—tomatoes and onions—in the chilled air, heard the creepy night sounds like ice cubes dropping in the refrigerator and the heater clanking on. And she saw light spilling from Carl's open bedroom door.

This was odd. Both nights since his fall Carl had turned his lights off by eleven, before the rest of them went to bed. So he must be awake now—restless, hurting, or maybe hungry? Figuring he might need some help or even a snack, she crept down the hall, knocked lightly, called Carl's name, and when she got no response, stepped inside.

At first everything seemed normal, except Carl wasn't seated in his chair reading or lounging on his sofa with a cherished cup of tea. Maybe he was in his bathroom, but she heard no flushing or running water, only Barney's heavy panting. She followed the sound to the king-sized bed, where the old bloodhound was draped sideways against a pile of pillows. His sad eyes followed her approach, and he began to whine. The plaintive sound brought her closer, and then she stopped cold.

The pillows were actually Professor Fischer sprawled under the spread. His head was flung back in an awkward position, mouth wide open, and his eyes stared up at nothing at all. She could not stifle her scream of terror. It reverberated around the room and ricocheted off the walls, yet Carl did not move.

For he was surely dead.

CHAPTER THIRTY-FOUR

Damned determined…

When she stopped screaming, she crept forward toward the corpse. Her feet moved against her will as her heart raced and tears flooded her eyes.

Dear God, this isn't happening!

Some hidden force propelled her toward the horror. She motioned to the dog, but he would not move, as if guarding the shell of this man he loved would somehow bring him back to life.

She could not drag her gaze from Carl's slack face, while perversely, his eyes seemed to follow her progress. His right arm was flung out, palm up, on top of his covers, like he had reached out to Barney in his final moments. She abhorred the idea of contact with his cold skin, yet she extended her trembling fingers and touched him, then recoiled in shock, because Carl's flesh was still warm. He could not have been dead long. She ran her hand down to his wrist to feel for a pulse…and found one!

He was still alive!

Though sobbing uncontrollably, she knew through her shock that she needed to get help. Panicking, she realized her cell phone was upstairs, but then she saw the landline phone on Carl's desk, illuminated by the watery glow from a green glass lamp—the same light that had spilled into the hall.

As she crossed the room on numb legs, Barney wagged his tail in approval. She picked up the receiver and dialed 911.

When she hung up, she sank into Carl's chair and lost track of time. She couldn't say if one minute or one hour had passed before Sara knelt and held her.

"I heard you scream! Are you okay, Mandy?"

Unable to speak, she nodded at the bed and Sara understood immediately. Abandoning her, she flew across the room and, like Amanda, checked Carl's pulse. "You called for help?"

Amanda nodded, half comatose with shock.

"Shit, this looks like an overdose. Don't move. I'll be right back." With that, Sara was gone in a blur of white terrycloth.

Amanda couldn't have moved if she'd wanted to. She heard Sara's clogs clattering on the metal spiral steps and sirens wailing in the distance. Only a short while ago, she had read Carl's résumé, the many accomplishments of his long life, and now she wondered if that story ended tonight.

Suddenly Sara was back. Ignoring Amanda, she ran to the bedside and arranged Carl's arm. Holding a small purple and yellow box near his inner elbow, she pressed down.

"What are you doing?"

"This is an Evzio injector. I'm giving him a shot of Naloxone to counter the opioid overdose." Sara worked quickly and efficiently. "His breathing is shallow, pinpoint pupils, and his lips are blue. Jesus, I hope it's not too late. I hardly feel a heartbeat."

Amanda was stunned. Where did Sara learn all this, and why did she carry that injector around with her? Before she could consider these questions further, commotion at the front door propelled her down the hall. The paramedics were pounding and ringing the bell.

"Where's the victim?" asked a fresh-faced redhead in a white tunic who looked about sixteen.

"Down the hall. You can come through this way or bring the ambulance around the side, where there's a door directly into Professor Fischer's bedroom."

The team opted to split up. The young redhead followed Amanda with a medical bag but signaled to the others to drive around. When they burst into the room, Sara was still seated on the edge of the bed ministering to Carl. After the medic pulled out his stethoscope, he gently eased Sara aside. She explained what she had done and showed him the injector.

The man listened to Carl's heart, lifted his lids, shined a light in his eyes, felt for a pulse, and finally exhaled. "Good job, ma'am. I believe you saved this man's life." He looked admiringly at Sara, then called out to Amanda, "Reckon you could get this dog off the bed?"

Relieved to have a job, Amanda debated. So far she'd been unable to reason with Barney, but she knew a few doggie tricks and had seen the hound's leash in a basket near the door to the deck. As she reached down to get it, the two other members of the EMS team arrived at the door. She went to unlock it, but it swung open of its own volition. She might have wondered at this, but was occupied with her mission. She picked up the leash, rattled its clasps, and sure enough, Barney slithered off the bed and loped eagerly in her direction. She snapped the leash on his collar and led him to Carl's chair.

"We'll take a walk later, buddy," she reassured him.

Together they watched in dazed silence as the medics did their work. The female on the team slipped an oxygen mask on Carl's face, while a burly bald guy wrestled a folded gurney open and wheeled it up close and parallel to the bed.

"Don't touch anything without your gloves," the redhead, who seemed to be in charge, warned his helpers. He nodded to the tray holding Carl's many meds. "We've got us a regular pharmacy here, but I think he took the Oxy. The prescription was filled only yesterday, but all the pills are gone."

"Suicide?" the female asked.

"Could be," he answered.

"No way!" both Amanda and Sara shouted in unison.

"Carl would never kill himself," Amanda stated with certainty.

"You never know, Miss Rittenhouse," a familiar female voice said from the deck door. Chief Toni Hall was followed in by two officers Amanda had not met. "When I saw Carl earlier today he seemed in good spirits, but he was obviously in pain. He just gave away that valuable artifact, and I know he was in emotional distress about Ron Dunifon."

"No disrespect, Chief, but that's just plain crazy," Sara interjected and walked up to join them.

"What do you know? Are you a psychiatrist?"

Sara tossed her long black hair. "Matter of fact, yes I am."

"She's also a damned good emergency responder." The redhead approached, having turned Carl's care over to the others. "The doc here administered an injection of Evzio, saved the professor's life. We'll give him some intravenous Naloxone in the bus, pump his stomach, and keep him on oxygen when we get to the hospital. If he was going into cardiac arrest, I believe he'd be dead already. I think we may be out of the woods."

"Well, that is very good news." The chief gave Sara a grudging look of approval, then addressed the redhead. "I hope nobody on your team touched anything here."

"No, ma'am, we wore gloves all the way."

Up close Amanda saw tiny crow's feet at the corners of the man's eyes and a few white hairs at his temple—not sixteen, after all.

"Okay, Rudy." The chief nodded her approval. "I want you to stick to the professor like glue until I can get an officer to the hospital to watch over him. And call me the minute you know more about his condition." She turned to Amanda and Sara. "What about you two, touch anything?"

Amanda sighed. "Yeah, sure, we've been staying here. We probably touched everything in this room."

On the count of three, the other two paramedics lifted Carl's limp body onto the gurney, strapped him in, and hurriedly wheeled him toward the deck. "I'll call this in so they'll be ready for us at Mission Hospital," the female said as she passed them. "I know Rudy's hopeful, but I have my doubts. This patient's color is not good and his pulse is thready. I'm worried."

On that dire note, the team departed, leaving Amanda worried, too. But she was very proud of Sara. It was everything she could do to keep from kissing her hero. Sometimes she forgot that Sara had been through medical school before going on to get her degree in psychiatry. She never talked about it and always shied away from praise. It still seemed unusual that she would carry an injector in her purse, so Amanda asked her about it.

"I don't want to talk about it," Sara said decisively, but after seeing what must have been a hurt look on Amanda's face she quickly amended, "We'll discuss it later, babe."

At that point, she realized that Barney was straining at the end of his leash, desperate to follow his master into the night. She stroked his silken head and comforted him the best she could, but not until the sirens faded did the animal settle at her feet with a last pitiful groan. More than anything, Barney's despair brought a fresh glaze of tears.

"Now what?" she asked the chief.

Toni Hall sank onto the couch and buried her head in her hands. When she recovered, she eyed them both. "You know Carl told me someone pushed him off the roof, right?"

They nodded.

"If that's true, then we could be sitting in the middle of a crime scene." She ran fingers through her short blond hair. "This will be a long night, girls, because if someone is trying to kill Carl, they seem damned determined."

CHAPTER THIRTY-FIVE

Everyone's a suspect...

Chief Toni Hall removed a spiral notebook and pen from her fanny pack. She recalled Amanda's full name, wrote down Sara's, and then smiled. "So don't touch anything else. The criminalists will be here momentarily to process the room, but tell me what we should look for."

Happy to be asked, they both reiterated that Carl had not attempted suicide. They cited his upcoming marriage to Gladys Uplander and the fact that he was looking forward to retirement as positive reasons for living.

Chief Hall countered by describing his failing health and turmoil with Ron as reasons to despair. "Those men have been close for many years, while Gladys is new on the scene."

Amanda sensed the chief knew more than she was saying. If, as Sara believed, Toni Hall was indeed a lesbian, perhaps she was attuned to the sexual tension between Ron and Carl. Did she think Carl was reluctantly choosing Gladys over Ron in order to free the younger man to move on to a more age-appropriate, healthier partner? God, what a depressing idea.

"What should I know about this room?" The chief prompted.

"Carl is passionate about his tea," Sara suggested. "He brews it morning and night on an automatic timer. Could someone have poisoned him that way?"

Toni Hall nodded respectfully and underlined something in her notebook.

"And the door to the deck was unlocked!" Amanda exclaimed as she recalled that detail.

"Jesus, Mary, and Joseph!" the chief swore. "I don't suppose either of you know if Carl habitually left his door unlocked?"

They both shook their heads.

"God, these damn country people think they're perfectly safe. They don't bother to lock up, then when the shit hits the fan it makes our job impossible."

Amanda watched in alarm as Toni's face turned beet red. "Well, Carl and Ron always locked the main doors front and back, so you'd think they'd follow through with Carl's side door," she meekly postulated.

"You'd think so," Toni bitterly agreed. "What else?"

Sara looked sheepishly at Amanda. It seemed she was telling her that she'd take the next round of abuse from the irate chief by dropping the next big stink bomb.

"Something else, Chief Hall," Sara bravely ventured. "We had a prowler tonight."

Sara calmly and accurately described the loud crash out on the deck, the flashlight in the dark, and the motorcycle speeding away.

As the attractive law officer's eyes stretched wide and the flush from her face spread to her neck, it occurred to Amanda that somehow in the past few minutes she had begun to think of her as "Toni" rather than "Chief Hall." Suddenly she was more human than robot.

Certainly Toni's reaction was predictable. She paused her wild scribbling of notes and blinked at Sara. "You think you actually know the identity of this intruder?"

Amanda picked up the narrative and told her about the mystery man she'd seen both at Carl's party and camped out at the abandoned farm. "Carl thought the man was stalking him," she finished.

Toni was incredulous. "But why would anyone stalk Carl? And what's worse, why the hell didn't Carl tell me about it?"

The questions had no answers. They hung in the air like poisonous gas while Toni processed and then pulled what appeared to be a black walkie-talkie off her belt and pushed a button. Although she rose and paced to the far side of the room, it was clear she was activating a BOLO for the guy and directing a squad car to the abandoned farm behind Carl's property.

She returned and stood above them. "So who else was here tonight?"

Although they knew the chief would not be pleased to learn about the parade of visitors to the Fischer residence throughout the previous evening, Amanda gave the full accounting of dinner with Gladys, then the arrival of Al Cabella and Mickey the chauffer. "All these people were on the roof when Carl fell," she added.

"The black limo had Illinois plates," Sara provided, then winked at Amanda—a cute little reference to her Mafia theory.

"Perfect." Toni sighed and again took out her radio. This time she walked all the way out onto the deck so they could not overhear.

Sara snatched her hand and kissed her fingers. "It seems our information will keep the entire Asheville police force busy this morning."

"You're right." Sara's touch released a bone-deep weariness. The whole sad affair made her want desperately to take Sara back to bed, fall asleep in her arms, and let the whole sorry world slip away—which reminded her, "Where is Ron, for heaven's sake? You'd think all this commotion would raise the dead."

Sara tightened her grip. "I hadn't thought about it in all the confusion, but yes, Larry, too. They were very drunk, but even so…"

Just then Toni returned, a grim expression contorting her features. She was followed by a man with a camera, two technicians carrying crime scene paraphernalia, and a fingerprint guy—Amanda recognized the red plastic kit. Everyone wore gloves. She figured the room, maybe the whole house, would soon be wrapped up in a yellow bow of crime tape.

"So where is Ron Dunifon?" Chief Hall barked.

In that instant, in Amanda's mind, the woman reverted from "Toni" back to "Chief." She dutifully explained about Ron and Larry and their boozy entrance last night.

"So they're sleeping it off in the barn?" The chief snapped her fingers and a fifth officer Amanda recognized came inside. "Sergeant Rollins, will you please go back to the barn and roust out the two sorry men inside? Knock hard!" she growled.

The sergeant saluted, and after a brief nod of recognition at Amanda, he waddled across the dark yard as fast as his fat legs could carry him.

"And Rollins!" Chief Hall shouted at his back. "Also contact a woman named Gladys Uplander. Instruct her to stay close. I want to interview her later today."

"Yes, Chief!" Rollins confirmed as he hurried away.

Amanda's first impulse when the chief had reentered the room had been to quickly jerk her hand free of Sara's grip, but now she defiantly hung on. "About Gladys, Chief, was that like you telling someone they're not a suspect, but please don't leave town?"

"That's exactly what it was like, Miss Rittenhouse," the chief answered coldly. "Everyone is a suspect—that includes you and Dr. Orlando. So until I say so, you are both grounded in Asheville."

CHAPTER THIRTY-SIX

Aiding and abetting…

They were told to wait in the kitchen, and of course Barney came tripping along at the end of his leash. Amanda recalled where Ron kept the hound's food, located his bowls, and gave him chow and fresh water. While Barney made happy eating sounds, Sara got busy scrambling eggs. She also heated some leftover spaghetti and garlic bread as a cloud-shrouded sun lifted above the mountain range.

"This meal is a little unorthodox, but I'm starving," Sara said as Amanda cleared last night's dirty dishes and stacked them in the sink.

"It smells wonderful, so bring it on!" Amanda sponged off the bar and set out paper napkins and silverware. Five minutes later, they were wolfing down breakfast and staring out across the back deck at the barn, where Sergeant Rollins was still knocking on Ron's door. "I wonder what's got Chief Hall's knickers in a twist? She seemed angry with us, but I don't know why."

Sara sopped up some sauce with her toast, added a forkful of eggs, shoveled it into her mouth, and swallowed before she answered. "She's not mad at us. She's just pissed because she got stuck here. Normally a chief's underlings would handle the scene. I gather because Carl's a close friend she got roped in. That's all I can figure."

Amanda knew nothing about police procedure, but she was still in awe of Sara's role. "I'm so proud of you. I'm sure you saved Carl's life. Good thing you had that injector. 'Be prepared' must be a Girl Scout motto, too."

Sara rose and poured them second cups of coffee. "You're fishing, babe, but I suppose I'm ready to tell you why I carry the Evzio injector." Before she sat, she pulled her barstool closer, so their knees touched. "A couple of years ago, I treated a fifteen-year-old heroin addict. She was a sweet, fragile kid from an abusive family—like most of my patients—and she was drug-free, or so we thought. We finished our weekly session, said goodbye, and that night when I locked up and went to check the restrooms, I found she had overdosed. Little Misha died in my arms before the EMS team got there."

Amanda pulled her close and kissed away the tears gathering at the corners of Sara's eyes. "I am so sorry. I can't begin to imagine how you endured that, but it wasn't your fault."

"It could have been prevented, but it will never be my fault again." She pulled away, sniffled a couple of times, and got herself together.

Amanda knew to let it go. Sara seldom shared the heartaches of her job, although Amanda wished she would. When Sara occasionally let down her guard, it was like she'd thrown a scrap of trust, but Amanda wanted it all. Sara was a unique combination of toughness and vulnerability. In spite of her no-nonsense reputation, Amanda had glimpsed the raw emotion bubbling like a pressure cooker just under her surface and did not want to force an explosion. Only more time together would relieve it.

They lost their appetites at the exact same moment, put down their forks, and moved to the sink. Sara rinsed and Amanda arranged the dirty dishes in the dishwasher.

"It looks like our vacation may be extended longer than we planned, so we might as well earn our keep." Amanda enjoyed the casual brushing of arms and hips as they completed the mundane task, and when she looked out at the barn, she saw that Sergeant Rollins had finally gained entry. "Look, Surfer Dude's come to the door. He's wobbly, but functioning."

"Ron will be devastated when he finds out what happened to Carl last night. I still can't believe they slept right through it."

They spied intently as Rollins entered the barn. Overcome by curiosity, they stepped out on the deck, hoping to overhear a snatch of conversation. They left Barney inside, whimpering and pawing at the glass door.

"Whoa, look at this!" Amanda cried, hugging herself against the sudden cold. "Someone toppled one of the picnic table benches. Must've been the prowler."

"Don't touch anything, Mandy." This back portion of the deck, like the side into Carl's room, was strung with yellow tape. Chief Hall and the techs had noted the toppled bench as well.

Just then, a stealthy footstep startled them from behind— the fingerprint guy with his little red kit. "Please step back into the kitchen, Dr. Orlando. I need your prints." He smiled smugly at Amanda. "We already have yours on file, ma'am."

Sara self-consciously clutched her terrycloth robe. "Mind if I change into clothes first?"

"Be my guest, but make it quick please."

As the officer backed into the kitchen, Barney decided he'd had enough of captivity. He wriggled past them and bolted off the deck, dragging his leash behind him.

"Aw shit!" Amanda took off after him.

"Where do you think you're going, Ms. Rittenhouse?" the officer called in alarm.

"Don't sweat it, I'll be right back!" she shouted angrily. Like Barney, she was fed up with detention.

"I'll catch up with you later, babe!" Sara called out as Amanda rounded the barn.

Barney had an agenda. After lifting his leg and peeing on an unlucky blueberry bush, the bloodhound let out a yelp and put his nose to the ground, hot on the prowler's scent. Although the hound was uncharacteristically fast, putting a lot of ground between them, she didn't need a crystal ball to know where he was headed.

Unlike yesterday afternoon when she and Sara had taken this stroll, the atmosphere today was heavy and windless. The cold gray sky pressed down with rain, long overdue. In the distance Beaver Lake smoked behind a scrim of mist, and she almost tripped on the dead rabbit, now reduced to a pile of fur and bone.

"Barney, wait!" she cried, and quite unexpectedly, the animal halted. He panted and watched her catch up to where his leash had snagged on a tree stump. Once she had him freed and in hand, they proceeded together through weeds stiff with hoarfrost toward the Anderson property and the abandoned farmhouse strangled in kudzu. As soon as she stepped over the trampled section of barbed wire fence, the ghost homestead appeared in the fog.

The white utility van with its olive green awning, the cook stove, table, chairs, and fancy motorcycle were there as before—this time illuminated by the twin beams from an idling police patrol car.

She froze in her tracks. *Oh my God, the chief's men caught the guy!* She made Barney sit as the drama unfolded. Soon the big man climbed from the van flanked by two officers, but far from being under arrest, he was laughing with the cops like they were long-lost friends. They all carried Styrofoam coffee cups and someone had provided a box of doughnuts.

What the hell? She watched in disbelief as the cops helped the guy close up his campsite. They took down the awning, loaded the furniture and stove, and finally rolled the bike up a ramp and closed the van door. This was too much. She had to intervene, and Barney was more than willing. Leaping forward, the dog again broke loose and bounded toward the men, woofing a joyous greeting. She ran after the hound as all three humans gaped in surprise. When she reached them, no one seemed happy to see her.

"Who are you?" the shorter of the two officers demanded.

She caught her breath. "I'm the one who told Chief Hall about this man. I'm staying with Professor Fischer, and he is trespassing!"

This morning the intruder wore a charcoal gray hoody over his muscled body. He disentangled himself from the exuberant Barney and pushed back his hood. His bald head glistened like an ebony bowling ball, and although he was smiling, the smile did not reach his cold black eyes.

"Hello again, ma'am. For the record, I am not trespassing. I have permission from the Anderson family to camp here. But as it happens, I was ready to move on even before Asheville's finest showed up."

The taller cop invaded her space and got in her face. "This man is Paul Stucky, and I can vouch for him. He always volunteers at National Night Out, our outreach program, and gives kids rides on his bike."

Furious, she backed up a few paces. So now she was the meddlesome female and they were telling her to piss off.

"Your *friend* Paul Stucky has been sneaking around the professor's house. Why is that?" She spat out the words.

No one was impressed. Stucky lifted his eyebrows and opened his hands, the picture of innocence. The short cop laughed out loud.

"Calm down and go home, lady," the tall one advised. "I reckon we've got this situation under control."

Angry and humiliated, she snatched Barney's leash and gave it a sharp tug. Turning her back, dragging the dog behind her, she felt three pairs of eyes watch her scramble over the fence and back into the field. Too angry to cry, she broke out running when she saw Sara come over the rise. Now fully clothed in jeans and a neon yellow windbreaker, Sara had caught up as promised. She was a patch of brilliant sunshine on the gray horizon and Amanda ran into her arms.

Sara hugged her. "What's wrong?"

She pointed to where the van and patrol car were preparing to leave. The officers shook hands with Paul Stucky, then they all climbed into their respective vehicles and drove off the Anderson lot.

"The police caught him, but now they're letting him go!" Amanda exclaimed.

"But why?"

"Near as I can tell, they're aiding and abetting a criminal."

CHAPTER THIRTY-SEVEN

Motive and opportunity…

They let Barney off leash and followed him home. A light rain began to fall, dampening their hair and shoulders and soaking their shoes, so they started jogging through the high weeds.

"I don't understand. No one takes this Paul Stucky character seriously but the two of us," Amanda complained as she ran. "Don't they find it suspicious that he was prowling around last night?"

"It doesn't make sense," Sara panted as they neared the barn. "But look over there, Sergeant Rollins is leading the guys away." She gestured at the three figures stepping into the drizzle. Larry was running out front, head down, hands jammed in his pockets as he hunched against the weather. Ron was clinging to Rollins, half-stumbling as they made slow forward progress.

"What's wrong with Ron? He seems sick, and he can hardly walk," Amanda noted as they got closer to the pair.

"Maybe he's grief stricken because Rollins just told him what's happened to Carl, or else he's suffering the bad mother of all hangovers," Sara suggested. "At least Barney's glad to see him. A dog is the only thing on earth that loves you more than he loves himself."

It never ceased to amaze her how Sara came up with quirky quotes at odd moments. "I need to talk to him." She pushed in between Ron and Barney and took hold of the tall man's arm. "Are you okay, Ron?"

Ignoring her, he turned his sad brown eyes to Sara. "I understand you saved Carl's life. Thank you." His voice trembled with emotion. His complexion was pasty white, his eyes rimmed with red. His tall, thin body was stooped beside the rotund sergeant as they inched along.

In her opinion, Ron's condition was more than just grief or a hangover. It was almost like he was on drugs. She cast a worried look at Sara.

Sara said, "Do you need a doctor, Ron?"

"He'll be fine," Rollins gruffly intervened. "Once we pump him full of coffee, he'll sober up real quick."

The officer was not happy about slogging through the rain at a snail's pace. The thin strands of his comb-over were plastered to his balding pate, and his jaunty silver barbershop quartet moustache had wilted to either side of his heavy jowls.

Ron placed a clammy hand on Amanda's. "He thinks *I* had something to do with Carl's overdose, Mandy. I have no idea what he's talking about."

She didn't know how to respond. Ron was a nurse, so he could likely get his hands on all kinds of narcotics. The cops were aware of the recent turmoil between Ron and Carl, so they might find motive. Certainly he had access and opportunity. She tightened her grip on his bicep.

"That's ridiculous, Ron. Everybody knows you'd never hurt Carl."

His agonized look said it all. He knew he was in trouble, with few friends or allies. Just because she believed in his innocence with all her heart did not mean anyone else did.

They all climbed onto the back deck, ducked under the railing of yellow crime tape, and entered the kitchen. Larry was already inside, wiping the raindrops from the lenses of his black-rimmed glasses with a paper towel.

"Shitty weather," he commented before tearing off another hank of paper towel to dry his short blond hair. "What's next, Sarge? How long do I have to hang around in here?"

"Long as it takes, son. Professor Fischer's at Mission Hospital fighting for his life, and we need some answers."

"He could be dead by now," Larry said offhandedly.

"Far as I know he's still alive."

Larry shrugged, offered a tight smile, and then watched in disgust as Ron started sobbing. Barney shook his long ears, splattering Amanda and Sara before moving to his water bowl and then to his bed in the corner for a good snooze.

Sara said, "The better I get to know men, the more I find myself loving dogs."

"Will you please cut that out?" Amanda growled.

Sergeant Rollins frowned. "We won't be needing you two just now, so why don't you go up to your room so we can conduct interviews here in the kitchen."

It was not a question. "He's sending us to our room for a time out, Mandy." Sara gave Ron a little punch of encouragement, then walked into the hall.

"It will be all right, Ron." Amanda pulled his head down and gave him a quick peck on the cheek. "Hang in there, and we'll all hook up for dinner," she said before following Sara upstairs.

They had little to say as the rain intensified and flung itself against the timbered roof of their bedroom. They could speculate ad nauseam, but nothing more could be known about the assaults on Carl until they had more information. So while Sara took the first hot shower and dried her hair, Amanda sneaked down to the laundry room, tiptoeing between the muffled sounds of police activity in the master suite and kitchen, to dry their sopping clothes.

When she returned, Sara was seated in the window staring out at the barn. Her long black hair, still warm from the blow dryer, scented the room with the fresh aroma of her favorite shampoo, which always reminded Amanda of clover in sunshine. Sara's hair flowed across the shoulders of her white terrycloth robe, framing her porcelain face and berry red lips—a dark angel in the weak natural light.

Amanda bent over and put her chin on Sara's head, then encircled her in her arms. "So what's happening out there?"

"The criminalists from Carl's room have moved on to the barn. They've been in and out a couple of times...whoops, *now* who's coming?" An orange and black rent-a-truck pulled up to the barn door and a young couple jumped out to confront one of the techs. Sara squinted. "Oh, it's the kids from Appalachian State, the ones who were packing up Carl's pottery at Cotton Mills Studios. They told us they'd be bringing his art to the barn, remember?"

"Good luck with that. They just got turned away, and the boy is pitching a fit." Amanda watched as the disgruntled male student shouted and waved his arms, while the girl hung back, calmly taking it all in. Eventually they climbed back in the truck and drove away.

"They'll be back when the girl decides it's appropriate." Sara gave her hair a sassy shake. "Because women and cats do as they please, and men and dogs should relax and get used to the idea."

CHAPTER THIRTY-EIGHT

Grouchy for reasons…

Amanda floated through an endless fog of vaguely threatening images that would not quite come together—misted lights, distant sirens, dogs, and dead rabbits—accompanied by steady sluicing water and thunderclaps. She was sweating and struggling to breathe. When a repetitive series of claps brought her to consciousness, she unburied her face from the pillow and rolled away from Sara, who had also been startled awake by the loud knocking at their bedroom door.

As Sara pulled on her robe and went to answer, Amanda recalled falling into bed with Sara, who was already asleep. After her shower, Amanda had been overcome by an exhaustion that ruled out any intimacy other than a tight snuggle and a drop into oblivion. Although the alarm clock claimed it was after four in the afternoon, the stormy sky beyond the window was dark as night. She yanked her oversize T-shirt down to cover her nakedness, then swung her legs out of bed to see who had invaded their privacy.

Chief Toni Hall shyly poked her head in the door, but did not enter the room. "So sorry to disturb you, but I wanted to let you know we're done here. The criminalists just left, and I'm leaving now."

The chief's hair, skin, posture, and uniform had all sagged over the long hours. Unlike Amanda and Sara, who had enjoyed the equivalent of nearly a full night's sleep, Chief Hall had not rested at all. As they waited for further enlightenment, it seemed the woman was debating how much to reveal about the case.

"So after you girls write and sign a statement about everything you know, starting with the party and Carl's fall from the roof, I guess you can leave town."

"You want us to write novels?" Sara stifled a yawn.

"Keep it simple and complete. Or I suppose you can wait and bring your statements round to the station in the morning. The secretary will type them, you'll sign them, and then you're done."

"You're telling us to get outta Dodge?" Amanda joined in the teasing. "Can you give us a little hint about what's happening, Chief?"

Toni Hall leaned into the doorjamb. "We've taken Ron Dunifon downtown. We're detaining him under suspicion of attempted murder."

"That's insane!" Amanda cried out. "No way on God's green earth would Ron hurt Carl. You know that, Toni. Ron loves the man."

Flustered by Amanda's use of her first name, the chief shifted foot to foot and avoided eye contact. She cleared her throat. "There's a thin line between love and hate."

Amanda and Sara laughed out loud. Amanda could hardly contain herself. "Pu-lease, Toni, you sound like a seventies R&B hit. Can't you come up with something more original? Tell her, Sara, that Ron would never do such a thing."

But Sara did not support her. "I really don't know, Mandy. In my profession I've seen love go terribly wrong, so I can't make a judgment on this."

Sara's words felt like a betrayal, but not wanting to argue, Amanda said goodbye to Chief Hall, then locked herself in the bathroom.

"Still mad at me?" Sara poured her a full glass of cabernet sauvignon, the last from the bottle they'd bought for the spaghetti dinner. She poured herself Jack Daniels on the rocks.

"Don't you feel funny drinking Carl's liquor?" Amanda could not shake her residual anger. The last thing she'd said to Ron had been, "We'll all hook up for dinner," and now her friend was likely cooling his heels in a detention cell.

"Sure it feels funny, but Gladys said we should help ourselves."

Amanda fidgeted on her barstool and stared out at the barn, which was barely visible behind the scrim of solid rain. As she watched, lights came on in the loft, dim as fireflies dying in a sealed smoke glass jar. She assumed Larry Goldberg was moving around, scrounging up something for his dinner. "That's weird, too. Do you really think Ron told Larry he could live in the barn for as long as he wants?"

Sara sat down beside her and placed a bowl of pretzels and chips between them. "For now I guess we'll have to take Larry's word for it. I'm just glad Gladys didn't invite him to join us for dinner."

"No kidding. There's no love lost between those two." Surfer Dude had popped into the house the moment they'd come downstairs, ostensibly to wash and dry his wet clothes, but mainly to inform them that the police were finished with him and that he'd been invited as a somewhat permanent houseguest. "Larry didn't seem at all torn up about Ron being in custody," Amanda finished bitterly.

"The kid's a freeloader."

"Cute, Sara. You decide right off the bat that Larry's a freeloader, but you won't vouch for Ron? It makes me sick."

Sara took a long swallow of whiskey and toyed with a pretzel. "It's different, babe. Larry's a jerk, an open book. Ron's a lot harder to read."

Amanda bit her tongue, understanding she was grouchy for reasons other than Sara's unwillingness to commit to Ron's innocence. She felt like a guest who'd overstayed her welcome. She had not wanted to say yes when Gladys called and invited them to stay for dinner, and worst of all, she was worried about Carl—the absent host. Everyone was taking advantage of hospitality he'd not explicitly extended.

Sara took her hand. "What can I do to make you smile? Would some more doggie quotes help?"

She was just beginning to soften when the doorbell rang. The only doggie present clambered to his paws to check it out, then trotted back with Gladys in tow. The woman left her dripping umbrella open in the ceramic tiled hall, which Amanda believed was bad luck, then stomped into the kitchen in the same battered pumps she'd worn the night before. Amanda wondered ungraciously if her shoe polish would run and decided Gladys smelled like wet wool.

"What a horrible night. I'm chilled to the bone," Gladys complained as she approached. "But it's good to see you girls!" she cheerfully amended.

Too cheerfully, in Amanda's opinion, considering her fiancé was clinging to life in a hospital bed. She and Sara mumbled their greetings, then Sara offered to pour Gladys a drink. Who was supposed to be the hostess here, anyway?

Gladys said, "Make it a double scotch. I wish Carl were here to have one, too." She draped her wet coat over a kitchen chair. "So what's for dinner?"

The remark sent them both into a panic and rendered them speechless.

Gladys laughed. "Only kidding. Carl keeps gourmet pizzas in the freezer, and we have salad left over from last night. Will that do, girls?"

Amanda did not know what to make of that. "So how is Carl? Have you been to see him?"

Gladys wore the same herringbone skirt and white pussy bow blouse, but the bow had drooped and bore what appeared to be a mustard stain. Clearly she did not intend to answer Amanda's question until she had her double scotch in hand.

Finally she settled in one of the wicker chairs with her drink, then did something Amanda had not witnessed in years—she took a cigarette from her purse and lit up. The gesture, coupled with a seductive crossing of her legs, reminded her of Tallulah Bankhead, an old-timey movie star and sexual libertine her grandmother had admired. Tallulah was from Alabama, like Gladys. The blue smoke curled toward the beams as Gladys narrowed her dark eyes, a conspiratorial grin on her bright red lips and said, "Fasten your seatbelts, girls—do I have an update for you!"

CHAPTER THIRTY-NINE

Diabolical plot...

They all settled into the chairs to sip their drinks while the pizza heated. Now that the wine was gone, Amanda lost her inhibitions about using Carl's liquor and joined Sara in drinking Jack Daniels.

"Please tell us about Carl," she pleaded.

Gladys lost the vamp attitude and stubbed out her cigarette. "The good news is that my dear Carl will survive this. They've stabilized him, pumped some of the poison from his stomach, and neutralized the overdose, but he's still unconscious. The bad news is that someone definitely tried to kill him." She stared into her scotch, seemingly mesmerized by the ice cubes.

Sara and Amanda exchanged glances of confirmation. The attempted murder was hardly a surprise, yet having it spoken as an established fact was still shocking.

Amanda exhaled. "I'm so relieved about Carl. Do the police have any solid evidence pointing to who did it?"

"Oh, you bet your sweet booties they do..." Gladys was interrupted by the ding of a timer. Leaving them in suspense, she got up to serve the pizza. Amanda dished up the salad while Sara poured more drinks all around. Instead of sitting at the bar, they all returned to the wicker chairs and set the food on the cocktail table.

Only after Gladys had tasted everything and indicated it met with her approval did she continue. "Well, they found massive traces of codeine in his blood and urine. The drug put him to sleep and then into a coma. It seems the pills had been dissolved into the water Carl uses in his tea maker. You know Carl brews and drinks at least one cup at bedtime, and last night was no exception."

So the lab had tested the Breville tea maker, as Amanda had hoped. Unfortunately, the findings indicated a premeditated crime, executed by someone who knew Carl's habits and had access to the tea maker yesterday sometime between his morning and evening brews. She clearly remembered Carl ordering Ron to fetch a fresh tin of rooibos before she and Sara took their walk yesterday. Obviously Carl's tea had not drugged him, or them, for that matter, since they'd joined him for a cup after their stroll through the field.

As she tried to imagine this diabolical plot and the extreme evil of its perpetrator, her pizza lay cold and uneaten. Her mind raced with the many possibilities. Certainly it looked bad for Ron, who had the medical skills to pull it off, yet so many others had traipsed through Carl's bedroom during the critical hours, including everyone present, Al Cabella and his chauffer Mickey—even Larry Goldberg had staggered into Carl's master suite to take a drunken piss. But Paul Stucky, the intruder on his motorcycle, still topped Amanda's list.

"How could that happen?" Sara asked. "Surely Carl would have tasted the drug in his tea?"

Gladys began to cry. "You'd think so, wouldn't you? They say codeine has a bitter taste, but have you ever drunk any of that awful tea he loves?" She wrinkled her nose in disgust. "And by the time he finishes loading it with sugar, it tastes like cough medicine."

Sara took Gladys's hand. "I wonder why the police are fixated on Ron?"

"Because the little shit did it!" Gladys dried her eyes with the tail of her pussy bow. "The cops found oxycodone pills in Ron's loft. Stupid man!"

Amanda was incensed. "*Too* stupid, don't you think? If Ron had done it, would he leave pills lying around to incriminate himself?"

"Ron was pretty drunk last night," Sara quietly pointed out. "Maybe he wasn't thinking straight."

"Or maybe he was set up." Amanda found the scenario entirely too convenient. She was sure the would-be killer had simply used Carl's pills to do the deed. She angrily scowled at Gladys. "Do you honestly think a gentle soul like Ron, who obviously loves Carl, would try to murder him?"

They gaped at one another for several long seconds. Amanda felt the tiny vein in her left temple pulsing, a sure sign of her fury. The grandfather clock ticked from the foyer and she sensed Sara holding her breath.

Finally, Gladys spoke. "You're right, Ron does love Carl," she admitted, as all the antagonism seemed to drain from her body. "It's plain as ticks on a white dog, and I tell you, honey, I know Carl loves him back. I'm the problem, you see—I'm the competition."

Surely Gladys heard their gasps of surprise as the conversation took on a whole new dimension. Since it was clear everyone had lost their appetites, Amanda carried the pizza scraps to the garbage and thoughtlessly gave Barney a full slice. The hound licked his lips and smiled on his way back to bed.

Sara refilled their glasses, throwing caution to the wind. "Are you telling us Carl is gay, Gladys?"

The older woman sighed and lit another cigarette, held the smoke deep in her lungs, and slowly released it before continuing. "We never discussed it, but believe me when I tell you he's the only man I ever slept with who doesn't want sex. He cuddles, he kisses, but then he sleeps. He claims he doesn't need Viagra. You figure it out."

"And you're okay with that?" She could not imagine such a thing.

Gladys snorted. "Well, I should be, shouldn't I? At my age, sex shouldn't matter. We're so good together otherwise—best friends and loving companions—so it works."

Gladys's words did not strike Amanda as a ringing endorsement. Perhaps she was naïve, but she thought passion was essential at any age, and she knew damn well Gladys did want that sex. "But you still think Ron is guilty?"

This time when Gladys stabbed out her cigarette she did so with finality, signaling the end of the evening. "That butch Toni Hall grilled me for hours just before I came here. I hope they can wrap this up soon so Carl and I can get on with our lives."

Gladys had not answered the question, and Amanda took offense at the woman's homophobic slur at the chief of police. It seemed a good time to say good night. "Look we're all tired," she said diplomatically. "Chief Hall gave us some homework to do, so we'd better get at it."

Agreeing to call it a day, Gladys roamed down the hall and retired to Carl's room. Responding to a plaintive look from Barney, Amanda let him out to do his business. When he came back inside, the bloodhound also padded down the hall to the master suite. She hoped Gladys would let him in.

"Are you ready, babe?" Sara asked.

"I was ready an hour ago."

She and Sara needed to mend a few fences, and Amanda knew a delightful way to accomplish that. But first, she thought as they climbed the spiral staircase, they'd need to drink some coffee and compose their statements.

CHAPTER FORTY

Unfinished business…

Wednesday dawned clear, fresh, and frigidly cold. The weather app on her phone said it was only twenty-eight degrees. And when she looked down from the window seat to where Sara was loading their bags into Moby Dyke, it struck her that neither of them had brought adequately warm clothing. It didn't matter anyway, since they were leaving Asheville today.

The phone rang in her hand, and Gina Molerno's name popped up on caller ID.

"So how come you guys are still there?" Gina had assumed they'd left on Monday, and when Amanda relayed the full story, Gina was incredulous. "You gotta be kidding me! Someone tried to kill Carl? Twice? And those numb-nut cops think Ron did it? My God, Mandy, you can't leave until Ron is cleared."

Gina's panic haunted her as she drove down Merrimon Avenue into town. They had said farewell to Gladys, waved goodbye to Larry, who had watched their departure from the loft of the barn, and now there was no turning back.

"I get it, Mandy," Sara commiserated. "It does feel like unfinished business, but it's not *our* business. I'm sure one of the reasons Gina is so worried about Ron has to do with her studio space. Without his sponsorship at the Woolworth Walk, she won't be allowed to show there."

"That's cold, Sara. You know Gina, Carl, and Ron have been friends forever. She's desperately worried about them both." The hot air from the car heater warmed her legs as the GPS directed them to 100 Court Plaza. "You should be ashamed. The reason Gina called was to invite us out to dinner with Lila Franken, that famous sculptor I told you about. She's trying to be our friend, and you're bad-mouthing her."

Sara winked disarmingly. "I'm just jealous. Don't forget, I did catch you in bed together."

Amanda laughed. Sara had no reason to be jealous, or maybe she did—a tiny bit. Gina's call had reminded her how much she'd come to like that outrageous woman, and she wanted to do something constructive to ease Gina's mind. "After we sign our statements, can we go to the hospital? I'd like to say goodbye to Carl."

"What makes you think he's conscious? Hell, what makes you think the cops will allow us to see him?"

"There's only one way to find out."

The statement signings went without incident. They did not see Chief Hall, Sergeant Rollins, or anyone who particularly cared about the case—a very anticlimactic ending to their involvement. So after some bad station house coffee and stale crackers from a vending machine, they left for Mission Hospital.

She recalled seeing the sprawling health center when she'd first driven into town with Gina. The many-storied buildings in the complex rose on either side of Biltmore Avenue, connected by a high-spanning pedestrian bridge. St. Joseph's Hospital was on the left and Baptist on the right.

"Where do we park?" The place was a maze of doctor's offices, imaging clinics, research buildings, and finally, an emergency entrance to the hospital.

"Well, Carl won't be in the emergency room since he's already been admitted," Sara ventured. "But there's a sign for Visitors, so let's follow the arrows."

They turned up a hill leading to the McDowell parking deck and saw a covered pull-through to a main entrance. While she took a bar-coded ticket to enter the gate, Amanda recognized a familiar black limousine with Illinois plates parked under the canopy directly at the front door. It was idling with blinker lights flashing.

"Jesus, Sara, it's Al Cabella! I'm sure he's here to see Carl, and in my opinion, they shouldn't let him anywhere near the man."

"I totally agree." Sara was grim as they hesitated at the gate. She turned to Amanda. "Look, you park while I go find Carl. You can catch up with us later."

But Amanda leaped from the van and slammed the door, leaving the keys in the ignition. "Thanks, Sara, but you go park while *I* confront these guys. Then I'll meet you in Carl's room."

Weaving between incoming traffic and an impatient ambulance, its siren burping to clear pedestrians, Amanda's progress was further delayed by a mini bus of senior citizens come to visit their ailing friends. As she jogged in place, a white utility van cut in front of the old folks' bus and pulled to the curb directly behind Cabella's limo. At the same time, she saw Sara take the driver's seat in Moby Dyke and peel away in search of a parking place.

Paul Stucky was in the van, scowling darkly as he tapped his stubby fingers on the steering wheel. He also idled with his blinkers on. *What the hell?* Her heart raced as she wondered at the coincidence of these two vehicles coming together. Without regard for her own safety, she dashed into the street amid honking horns and one obscene shout. Luckily, she made it to the other side, emerging right behind the limo. The pieces didn't fit, but clearly the puzzle involved Carl and the murder attempts, and for some masochistic reason, she felt compelled to put that puzzle together.

Adrenaline pumping, she made a fist and pounded on the chauffer's window. Sara was right; Mickey was a gorilla. As he powered down the tinted glass, his heavy jaw jutted forward and his dark eyes glowered below the bushy brow of his primordial ridge. He stared like he'd never seen her before.

"Where is Mr. Cabella?" she demanded.

The beast's huge shoulders shrugged under the fabric of his suit coat and he pointed to earbuds in his hairy ears, indicating he could not hear her.

She made a circling motion at her own ear, imploring him to remove the buds, but the man simply smirked and played dumb. She knew damned well he remembered her. He'd passed not three feet from her when he was loading the dinnerware Cabella had purchased at Carl's house, and although she had never spoken directly to Mickey, she knew he understood English. What was his problem?

Enraged, she reached through the window, snatched the wire loop to his earbuds and pulled them loose. The gorilla's long, knuckle-beaded fingers batted at her hands, then clamped them in a vise-like grip. Just as she cried out, an opposing force from behind encircled her waist and dragged her body backward, trapping her midway in a tug-of-war.

"Leave him alone, Amanda!" Paul Stucky's embrace compressed her ribs and squeezed the breath from her lungs.

Mickey released her not a moment too soon, preventing her wrist from being dislocated, and then she fought back. She elbowed Stucky with a one-two punch, eliciting a satisfying yelp of pain from her attacker.

"Leave me alone!" she screamed.

"What the hell do you think you're doing?" Stucky roared as he continued to drag her backward, away from the limo and toward his van. "You and your girlfriend Sara are like bad pennies—you just keep turning up."

Her struggle was attracting a crowd of onlookers. Several of the senior citizens seemed concerned, but were unwilling to intervene as Stucky strong-armed her to the rear of his vehicle, opened its back door, and shoved her inside.

"Back off, Stucky, or I'll call the police!"

"Why can't you leave well enough alone?" Stucky grunted as she kicked him with both feet. "You two are going to ruin everything."

At the edge of her vision, she saw a red-faced Al Cabella being escorted from the hospital by two uniformed security guards. She tried to call out for help as the pair led Cabella to his limo and opened the passenger door, but Stucky stifled her with his big hand, sealing her mouth.

"Shut up, Amanda!" Stucky leaned over her body and pushed her deeper into the van. "I won't hurt you, if you cooperate."

When his jacket fell open, she saw a shoulder holster and gun. Terrified, she understood that noncooperation was not an option. She stopped kicking and started crying as he lifted her feet clear and slammed the door, leaving her in near darkness. The cab was partitioned off by a wall, and the panel van had no windows.

She bumped her head against the kickstand of the fancy motorcycle as they began to move downhill. Then, as near as she could tell, Stucky turned left onto Biltmore Avenue. Kidnapped and alone, she sobbed in earnest as she imagined Sara searching the hospital and finding her gone.

CHAPTER FORTY-ONE

Abducted…

She needed to think, orient, breathe, and get her tears under control, but for several long blocks, panic completely displaced reason. The gritty floor under her hips and shoulders stank of oil and treated canvas. It jarred her body with each bump, sliding her back and forth with the van's stops and starts. Wedged between the motorcycle and the wall, her legs were cramping, so she inched toward the front of the vehicle and encountered a folded pad of fabric—the portable green awning. Rolling onto its relative comfort, she was grateful that now her bones would not rattle apart.

God help me! She wiped her eyes with the sleeve of her sweatshirt. Outside her prison, traffic moved, pedestrians chattered, and suddenly she understood that as long as Stucky was driving in the city she might draw attention to her plight if she could make enough noise. Balling her fists, she pounded on the steel walls and screamed for help. She kicked with her feet, but rubber soled sneakers did not make very effective hammers. Her captor responded by banging several times on the back wall of his cab and by turning rap music to a high volume on his radio. The music's heavy bass and frenzied vocals would easily disguise or drown her racket.

What could she do? In her hurry to get inside the hospital, she had left her shoulder bag, including her cell phone, in Moby Dyke. She had no way to summon the outside world, no cash, credit cards, or ID. Her clothing was inadequate to the freezing temperatures. This thought made her teeth chatter with dread. Certainly she had no weapon to defend herself against Stucky's superior strength—or his gun.

Who would help her? Dozens of witnesses had seen her abduction, so perhaps they would call the police. Al Cabella had actually watched Stucky pull her away from the limo, as had Cabella and the security guards escorting him to his car. Surely the security guards, at least, would take immediate action. Above all, she could count on her beloved Sara. But when she imagined Sara's confusion, the chaos of conflicting stories, her panic when she realized what had happened, Amanda cried all over again. Had circumstances been reversed, Sara's kidnapping would have paralyzed her with grief. But Sara knew all the players and vehicles involved. She would provide a detailed description and suggest some motive—whatever the hell that might be.

Suddenly Stucky took a fast, wide curve. The centrifugal force threw her into a hard roll, slamming her left temple into the sharp edge of what seemed to be a toolbox. Her hands flew up defensively, and a wet trickle of blood dribbled down toward her ear. Determining the cut was not life-threatening, her fingers explored the contours of the box, found the U-shaped clasp, and popped it open.

She was insanely elated that the box was unlocked, yet mindful of the sharp tools that might be stored inside. Carefully exploring in the pitch dark, she touched a hammer, screwdrivers, clamps and nails. Eventually her fingers closed on a flashlight and she cried out in sheer joy.

So now she had a stash of potentially lethal weapons, and light—blessed light! Without hesitation, she thumbed the switch, and the van's interior lit up like a Hollywood movie set. The ribbed steel roof made her feel like she was under an upturned rowboat, while the network of bungee cords securing the shiny motorcycle were like rigging on a sailboat. At some point, Stucky had offloaded his camp furniture. A network of metal shelving bolted to the far wall was neatly stacked with expensive electronic equipment, piquing her curiosity in spite of her debilitating fear and disorientation.

Mostly she realized she was not wedged like tuna in a can, but instead had wiggle room, space to crawl around, providing she could find her balance. Obviously Stucky was an organized asshole, and her best find was a carton of bottled water and a box of Kleenex. Yanking out a handful of tissue, she daubed at her temple and sponged up the blood. Gratified that the surface wound was already clotting, she took out more tissue to blow her nose. Finally she opened a bottle of water, greedily drank half down, and used the rest to clean the gore off her hands and fingers.

Feeling more human and a tiny bit hopeful, she wedged the flashlight so that the beam illuminated the shelving. Checking her wristwatch, she was shocked to discover it was only noon. She had been abducted less than half an hour ago. She unfolded part of the awning, wrapped it around her shoulders to ward off the cold, and began listening for police sirens. Surely they would catch up soon.

Yet all she heard was the steady thrum of tires on pavement, great speed whirring under her steel floor. She also noticed the absence of rap music. Stucky had turned off his radio, which meant he had no further need to drown out her cries for help, which meant they were no longer in Asheville, which meant yes, for some time now they had been on a highway, perhaps the interstate?

This did not bode well for her rescue. She scooted into the front corner to brace herself and wrapped her arms around her knees to shiver and consider. Paul Stucky had called her by name when he'd grabbed her. More surprising still, he had said, "you and your girlfriend, Sara," had called them "bad pennies." But he had never met Sara. He had no business on earth knowing anything about her.

Who the hell was he and what did he want? Crawling on hands and knees, she made her way to the far side of the van and pulled herself upright by hanging on to the metal shelving. The shadow of her head, silhouetted by the flashlight beam, jiggled as she studied a heavy-duty tripod folded up beside an instrument that looked like a periscope. The lens was protected by a hooded white steel tube about thirty inches long. It was a camera labeled COHU-HD with night vision. It guaranteed a visual range of thirty miles. *Miles!*

Amanda sucked in a deep breath and gripped the metal shelving, her own predicament momentarily forgotten as she finally understood why Paul Stucky had been camping out at the Anderson farm. He was spying on Carl Fischer—day and night—breaking camp only after the professor was taken to the hospital.

She exhaled with a sudden whoosh as the van made a sharp right turn and threw her down into the alleyway between the shelves and the bike. She skinned her elbow and tore the sleeve of her sweatshirt. Then when the van pointed its nose to heaven in a steep uphill climb, she slid backward headfirst into the vehicle's doors. The flashlight broke loose from its wedged position and rolled after her. She snagged it with her foot and dragged it to hand, restoring a measure of control in a game where she was the pinball in a dangerous maze.

The van stopped momentarily, leading her to believe they had left the highway and climbed an off ramp to a stop sign or light. Stucky accelerated into another right turn and jerkily weaved back and forth while other motorists honked in protest. She clung to the door handle and hung on tight, her heart tripping double-time as she dared to hope. Stucky's erratic driving seemed like a car chase. Soon the local cops would pull the bastard to the curb and she would be free.

The high-speed zigzagging continued for several miles until they squealed into another sudden turn, then slowed slightly as their tires bumped onto a rough surface, spinning gravel up like shrapnel at the floor beneath her.

She braced herself seconds before a horrendous impact. Steel upon steel, the van crashed into something dead ahead, nearly pulling her shoulder from its socket as she held on for dear life. The absolute silence after the rending of metal and tinkling of glass was surreal. She blinked and listened, but all she heard was the cawing of crows. In an absurd vision, she imagined the big black birds hobbling toward the wreckage of a black and white patrol car.

The silence was shattered by the opening and slamming of Stucky's door and heavy footsteps approaching. The monster was still alive! In pure panic, her flight instinct urged her to hide among the boxes that had flown off the shelves. Her fight instinct told her to stand her ground. Getting to the toolbox—a hammer or screwdriver—was not an option, so she gripped the heavy flashlight, turned off its beam, and held it high above her head. She squirmed to one side so that when her captor swung the door open, she would own the element of surprise.

A key turned in the lock, and the interior handle angled downward. When the door opened with a metallic squeal, Paul Stucky's dark face loomed large.

"Are you okay, Amanda?" His deep voice boomed.

In order to do this, she had to ignore his words and his big dark eyes. So she concentrated on the cut on his jaw. Blood dribbled down his thick neck, staining the collar of his charcoal gray hoodie. Her inhibitions evaporated completely when she saw the revolver in his hand, hung at the end of his dangling right arm.

She swung hard and connected with his left temple with a dull, sickening thud. Her wrist and lower arm jangled from the force of impact, but Stucky went down to his knees and then crumpled to the ground.

CHAPTER FORTY-TWO

Vai con Dio...

His right arm was flung out, hand open, palm up. The gun had dropped harmlessly into the nearby grass. The flock of crows squawked in protest and flew across the country field to take refuge in the branches of a dead tree.

Amanda climbed stiffly from the vehicle, surprised that her jellied knees still held her weight. Adrenaline overload was the only force keeping her upright. Panting and feeling faint, she stared down at her victim with bizarre objectivity. His eyes were closed, his full purple lips were slack and parted, and the blow she'd dealt him was in precisely the same place as her own injury—the one she'd sustained from the damn toolbox.

Was he dead? Had she killed him?

Unable to process, she debated whether to pick up his gun or feel for a heartbeat. The decision was made for her when she saw the slow rise and fall of Stucky's chest. Not dead. Every muscle in her body cried out in rebellion as she lowered to her knees and reached out for the gun.

"I'll take that gun, Miss Rittenhouse," a deep male voice said.

Startled, she looked up, expecting to see a police officer, but instead gazed into the dark eyes of Al Cabella. The crisp sleeve of his Armani suit reached in front of her as he picked up the gun with a snowy white handkerchief. Eyeing the object with a mixture of interest and distaste, he carefully wrapped and pocketed it. He then looked back and forth between her and Stucky with undisguised disgust.

"You are a mess. Were you trying to kill each other?"

She was stunned speechless, debilitated by a sinking in her stomach, but took his perfectly manicured hand as he helped her up.

"This maniac who abducted you has been riding our tail for the past hundred miles or so," Cabella grumbled. "Who is he? What's his problem?"

Although it was interesting that Cabella did not know Stucky's identity, she was uninclined to supply him with any information. "Did you call the police?"

Cabella shrugged. "Why would I do that? Mickey is an excellent driver, and we were able to outrun him until a few minutes ago." He poked at Stucky with one of his expensive Italian loafers. When Cabella swiveled his neck and whistled for Mickey, his sleek raven black hair, patrician nose and beady eyes reminded her of the carrion crows still cursing from the tree.

She backed away from Cabella in mounting fear. Why had he not called the police? If being pursued in a high speed chase were not reason enough, he had witnessed her abduction and didn't kidnapping warrant calling the cops? "Why didn't you call the police?" she asked again.

His condescending smile resembled a smirk. "We were in a hurry, Miss Rittenhouse. We are on our way home and did not want to become entangled in a useless investigation which has nothing to do with Mickey or myself."

So Cabella didn't want to be inconvenienced, to hell with her fate. "Can I use your cell phone, please?"

Ignoring her, he whistled more sharply and the chauffeur came loping around from the front of the van as fast as his bowed gorilla legs could carry him. He smiled bashfully with a set of large square ivory teeth and finished zipping up his fly.

"Sorry, boss, I had to take a leak."

"Never mind. Take care of that, will you?" Cabella pointed at Stucky, who was still out cold.

"Toss him in the woods?"

"No, you idiot. Hoist him into his vehicle."

Mickey shouldered Stucky's dead weight effortlessly and pushed him into the van, much as Stucky had done with Amanda. As she watched the pair in action, she had to agree with Sara— these two were mobsters.

"Mr. Cabella, that man needs medical attention. You need to call an ambulance." At least she was trying. If Stucky died, she would be guilty of murder, not just simple assault.

He smirked again. "We will call for help once we are back on the road. Do not worry, Miss Rittenhouse, we will give you a ride and you'll be just fine."

Sure she would. Taking her arm, Cabella guided her around to where the trunk of the limousine was punched in like the mug of a Neapolitan Mastiff, but the rest of the car was unscathed. "Can you even drive this thing?" she asked.

Cabella crossed his arms and glared at the wreckage while Mickey peeked under the rear wheel wells.

"Nothing's scraping, boss. We're good to go."

"Jesus Christ on a stick!" Cabella pounded the ruined trunk with his fist. "Professor Fischer's beautiful dinnerware is in that trunk. "I'm guessing it now looks like pottery shards from a Mayan ruin."

Both she and Mickey jumped at his outburst, and while Cabella continued to fume, Mickey opened the rear passenger door, pulled her free from his boss, and shoved her inside. She'd been transferred from one prison to another with absolutely no say in the matter.

When she tried to open the rear doors and found them locked, the enormity of her new predicament hit like a blow to the chest. She could not catch her breath and she shook uncontrollably. Lowering her head between her knees to keep from passing out, she could not control the panic. Gasping for air, she tried to calm herself by thinking of Sara and help on its way, yet they were in the middle of a nowhere field with no sounds of distant traffic and no signs of civilization on the horizon. The stink of cigar smoke in the confined space made her nauseous on top of everything else.

"Where are we?" she asked once the men were settled up front and Mickey started the engine.

"We were near the Tennessee line when we veered off to avoid your maniac friend," Cabella grumbled.

"We took a right on Cold Spring Creek Road, boss. The asshole was gaining when I swung into this shithole cow patch. Don't know where the fuck it goes." Mickey drove along the rutted road in the same direction they'd been moving when they crashed. "Can't turn round right here because it's all mush and we'd get stuck."

"So drive until you can turn around, you jackass."

They were on a nowhere road in a nowhere field, and God only knew where it ended. Head still down, she checked her watch and saw it had been two hours since her abduction. As they crawled along, leaving the man she'd attacked behind to die, the only positive development was that the interior of the limo was warm and the leather seats were soft. Gradually she stopped hyperventilating and shivering. Clearly she needed a plan, but so did the losers up front. They were as clueless as she was.

"You promised you'd call for help," she reminded Cabella in a wimpy little twelve-year-old's voice.

"You promised you'd call for help," he mimicked her.

So Cabella was acting like a twelve-year-old, too, but this big baby held all the cards and the gun. She settled back into the cushioned seat and closed her eyes. If she couldn't see it, maybe it would go away. She listened to the tires bumping on gravel, the bickering of more crows, and the heavy breathing of her captors. Just when she was getting into the rhythm, pushing the terror back, Mickey slammed on the brakes.

"Here's a turnaround, boss."

She dragged her eyes open and saw a rustic oval sign on a post marking a gravel parking lot. The cream-colored upper half read "Max Patch." The black lower half said "Pisgah National Forest" in cream script.

"Good job, Mick!" Cabella barked. "Pull in and point us back at Chicago." He turned to offer a smarmy smile. "This is where you get off, young lady. It will be an adventure. Even I have heard about this place. The Appalachian Trail should be out yonder, and it's a fine day for a hike."

Was he crazy? Beyond her window, wind whipped across the deserted lot, bending the leafless bushes and a scrawny sapling that marked the desolate spot. "You can't leave me out here! Please, it's freezing! I'll die!"

Cabella reached back and touched her cold cheek with his hot hand. "My chauffeur will give you his coat, won't you, Mickey? And I did promise I would make a call. Soon as we're clear of this God-forsaken place, I'll send you some help."

"He's a man of his word," Mickey solemnly intoned as he swung the limo around.

She heard a dull thump as the auto-locks released. Seconds later, Mickey, a proper doorman, helped her step from the limo. He shrugged out of his dark wool suitcoat, exposing a shoulder holster and gun tucked under his armpit, and tossed her the garment. Unfortunately she was shaking too hard to put it on.

Cabella cracked his door, placed a can of Coke and a pack of peanut butter crackers on the gravel, and then reclosed his door. When the car moved forward, she jumped back to keep her toes from being crushed.

"Ciao, Miss Rittenhouse," Cabella called as they sped away. "Vai con Dio!"

CHAPTER FORTY-THREE

Make a plan…

Frozen to the spot, she cursed the cowardly tears streaming down her cheeks and watched Al Cabella's limo drive away as fast as the rotten road would allow. The vehicle's smashed rear end grinned as the weak sunlight glinted off its torn chrome mouth. She did not move until it disappeared like a black speck on the panoramic horizon, bordered by what would have been, in better circumstances, a breathtaking view of the Blue Ridge Mountains.

Then she blinked and greedily picked up Mickey's coat. When she slipped her arms into its oversize sleeves, it still radiated the chauffeur's warmth, his sweaty gorilla essence. Though it stank of cigar smoke, she was grateful. The overly long sleeves functioned as gloves to her chapped hands, and when she explored its deep pockets she was rewarded with a large, clean handkerchief and a fistful of those little round peppermints wrapped in cellophane.

Her sneakers still glued to the spot, she closed her eyes and used the warm handkerchief to dry her tears. And although she did not exactly believe in God, she said a prayer to hedge her bets. Was there honor among thieves? Where did that phrase come from—Proverbs? As an agnostic, her knowledge of the Bible was severely limited, but her life experience told her there was no honor in men like Cabella and Mickey, and the odds of them making a phone call on her behalf were slim to none.

Slowly opening her eyes, she stared down at the handkerchief and was gratified to see no blood. Her wound had dried, or scabbed over, or whatever cuts did. At the same time, she wondered how long it would take to die of thirst, or starvation, or exposure out here on the bald. Wasn't that what they called these ranges on the border between North Carolina and Tennessee? She saw lots of dried grass and shrubs stretching as far as the eye could see, but no forest. Did that qualify as *bald*?

Cabella had said the Appalachian Trail was nearby. Did that mean that soon a group of hardy young hikers would appear and share their squirrel jerky with her? Or were those kids all cozy at home this winter day?

She groaned aloud. Tomorrow was Trout's birthday. That bizarre concept focused her spinning mind and she imagined Sara—how frantic she must be by now. What happened when she discovered that Amanda had been abducted at the hospital? She pictured everyone—Sara, Carl in his bed, Ron in his jail cell, Chief Hall, Sergeant Rollins, and even Gladys wringing their hands and mounting a search party. Maybe Barney the bloodhound had been conscripted into service. It would be a manhunt on scale with the one for Eric Rudolph, the notorious abortion clinic bomber who had also gone missing in the North Carolina mountains. They hadn't found him for years!

Suddenly she realized she was standing in the middle of an empty parking lot laughing hysterically. She was going bonkers. She staggered toward a large boulder on the periphery and sat her butt down.

Get a grip, damn it! She drew her knees up to her chest, finding that Mickey's coat was roomy enough to enclose her like a tent. Should she drink the Coke, eat the crackers, and suck the mints now, or later? Should she shelter here, or start walking? Tucking her face into the soft cigar-scented wool, she decided to make a plan.

CHAPTER FORTY-FOUR

BOLO...

Amanda heard them long before she saw them—at least two sets of sirens wailing beyond the horizon. Her plan had been simple by necessity: she had walked out on the bald to keep her blood moving but never strayed far from the parking lot, she had eaten all the crackers and mints and finished the Coke, she had huddled inside Mickey's jacket on top of the boulder, and then she had walked again. Now, climbing back up onto the big rock, sneakers gripping its bumpy surface, she watched the long road leading to Max Patch and soon saw a police patrol unit, lights flashing and siren screaming. It approached at the fastest speed safety would allow, and although she knew they were coming for her, she still waved her arms like a windmill. And although she wanted to be brave, her eyes again began leaking like sieves.

When the car reached the parking lot, sending up puffs of gravel dust when it braked to a screeching halt, she saw the white sedan had big red letters on the side that read "POLICE," and under that in blue, "WAYNESVILLE." She did not know where Waynesville was, assumed it was nearby, but when the two officers approached, she had never been happier to greet strangers in her entire life.

The skinny male officer held up his hand. "Can I help you down, Miss Rittenhouse?"

She latched on to him and almost fell off the stupid rock. The female officer, who looked like a teenaged girl with her braided blond pigtails and saucer blue eyes, helped catch her. They introduced themselves as Chip Roady and Cindy Lou Hanson.

"Are you hurt, ma'am?" the woman asked.

"I think I'm okay." She gratefully accepted their support and allowed them to guide her into the backseat of the car. The male cushioned the top of her head when he pushed her in, just like they always did with suspects in the cop shows. Was she a suspect? No handcuffs so far.

"Hey, did you guys pass a white utility van on your way to me?"

Cindy Lou slid into the front passenger seat. "We sure enough did, ma'am. The ambulance traveling with us took the injured occupant to Haywood Regional Medical Center."

Amanda was afraid to ask. "How was the man?"

Chip started the engine and laughed. "We used a slim jim to unlock the van door. He was pounding so hard we thought we'd found us a trapped bear. He was bleeding like a pig and cursing like a sailor when we pulled him out, and it's safe to say he's mighty pissed at you, Miss Rittenhouse."

She exhaled a huge sigh of relief and finally relaxed into the seat. She had not fully realized how worried she'd been about Paul Stucky. Even though he was a scumbag, she had never wanted to kill him. She told the officers Stucky's name.

"We know. He told us," Cindy Lou said. "He seems to think his shit don't stink, pardon the expression, and he cussed us out for confiscating his van. Stucky even refused medical help until we cuffed him to a gurney. Once they patch him up, we'll take him into custody at Waynesville until we can sort out this mess." She eyed Amanda, her smooth young brow knit with concern. "Did Stucky hit you, ma'am? Do you need a medic?"

"No and no," she answered abruptly. Amanda was already dreading the long debriefing that would surely tie her up for hours. "I'm sorry, it's just that I'm anxious to get back to Asheville. Folks will be worried about me."

"Tell us about it!" Chip rolled dark eyes under his brown buzz cut. "Asheville put out an APB—that's an *all-points bulletin*—on you and that white van around lunchtime. All the local departments are cooperating. We've had patrols on Interstate 40, a unit at each exit, and roadblocks at all the county intersections."

"You must be some hot shit, ma'am, pardon the expression, because Chief Hall in Asheville's been squawking all day." Cindy Lou blushed. "Now that we've found you, everyone can relax."

It was nice to know she was missed. On the other hand, for every action there was an equal and opposite reaction. Considering all the trouble she'd caused, they'd never cut her loose without putting her through bureaucratic hell. "How did you find me?" it finally occurred to her to ask.

"Don't you know?" Chip said as he turned off the dirt road onto a paved two-lane highway. "We got an anonymous phone call thirty minutes ago. The gentleman said he was a man of his word. He told us about Stucky, then directed us to Max Patch."

"That man was no gentleman!" Amanda objected. She told her rapt audience of two all about Al Cabella, Mickey, and how she'd been kidnapped twice in one day. By the time she finished, both officers believed she was stark raving mad.

"We have a BOLO—that's *be on the lookout*—for that black limousine." Roady confided. "Illinois plates, right?"

"Right, and a bashed-in rear end," Amanda added. "You need to catch those guys. They're in it up to their thick mobster necks."

Cindy Lou giggled. "Yeah, I hear what you're sayin', ma'am, but those guys saved your sweet ass, pardon the expression."

This was true, she thought sourly. Perhaps there was honor among thieves, after all. Thoroughly exhausted, she closed her eyes and rested her head. Had she been a tiny bit less self-conscious, she would have lain on the bench seat, curled up into a fetal position, and slept the world away. Instead, she breathed in the heater-warmed air, which smelled of Chip's aftershave and Cindy Lou's cloying perfume—much better than eau de cigar—and listened to the comforting swoosh of passing traffic as they returned to civilization.

She forced herself to clear her mind and think about beautiful things. Instead of counting sheep, she did as her grandfather had counseled, silently chanting "grass…grass…green green grass." The verdant imagery led her to imagine Max Patch in springtime. The brown weeds she'd walked through today became green green grass, the barren bushes transformed to the wild pink rhododendrons she'd seen in mountain photographs. And of course, she found Sara strolling through the meadow, hands outstretched.

Suddenly she jerked awake as those warm hands cupped her chilled face. Completely disoriented, she first saw brown cloud stains on the patrol car's headliner floating above, then the stony silhouettes of Chip and Cindy Lou up front. But she absolutely positively knew she was dreaming when Sara's face moved in inches above hers. Her amazing green eyes were rimmed red as she bent down and kissed Amanda full on the lips.

CHAPTER FORTY-FIVE

Mugshots...

"Thank God, Mandy, I was afraid you were dead!" Sara kissed her again, gave her a sideways nudge, and scooted in beside her on the bench seat.

Amanda blinked and tried to process. She ran her hands over the neon yellow of Sara's windbreaker and searched her eyes. "How can you be here?" At the same time, she realized the car had stopped moving and they were parked at a two-storied redbrick building with a soaring pillared entryway. "Where are we?"

"We're at the Waynesville Police Station." Sara nodded at a second police car parked directly beside them. "The Asheville cops brought me."

She leaned her cheek on Sara's soft breast and peered through the window at the two cops in the Asheville unit. She couldn't see the driver, but Chief Toni Hall was the passenger. Like the officers in this car, she was staring straight ahead, studiously avoiding Amanda and Sara's passionate reunion.

"But how did you manage this, Sara?" Even in her discombobulated state, she knew Sara's participation was likely against police regulations.

Sara grinned and gave her another swift kiss. "I told Toni we were married, that you were my wife!"

Officer Cindy Lou Hanson gasped with surprise, Officer Chip Roady's eyebrows shot up, but no one was more surprised than Amanda.

"I guess it worked," she gulped.

"It did. Toni was sympathetic, but I cinched the deal by pointing out that *I* had witnessed events at the hospital and *I* knew all the bad guys. I guess that gave the chief the cover she needed to include me in the rescue team."

She burrowed into Sara's arms and held on tight, face buried in the warm canyon between her breasts. Sara had outed them to the world—to cops, no less.

"Thank you, Sara," she murmured. "What happens next?"

"Good question," Chip spoke in a wobbly voice. "Are you in our custody, or Asheville's?"

"I can answer that," Chief Hall said as she rapped at Chip's window. He powered it down. "Miss Rittenhouse is coming back to Asheville with us. Now."

"Yes, ma'am!" Chip all but saluted, then he and Cindy Lou exited the vehicle.

"Sara, I have to use the restroom before we go," Amanda whispered.

"I agree." Sara sniffed loudly. "You might want to lose that awful coat; you smell like a cigar factory. You need to wash that blood off your face, too."

Everyone involved concurred with Sara's assessment, so moments later, supported by Sara's arm around her waist, she entered the station's ladies' room. She left Mickey's coat in a heap near the trash can, carefully washed around the cut on her left temple, patted her face dry, and said a silent prayer of thanks to whoever who had provided the bottle of lotion. She slathered it on her face and hands, accepted a touch of Sara's lipstick, and felt much better when she emerged from the john.

She thanked and said goodbye to her two police saviors, noting that Cindy Lou refused to meet her eyes, while Chip stared at her and Sara with open curiosity. Amanda didn't care. This whole gay marriage thing was new to everyone. Moments later, she and Sara were in the rear of the Asheville unit en route to Interstate 40 east.

Only then did Chief Hall turn to them. She ran exasperated fingers through her short blond hair and glanced at their hand-holding. "Good Lord Almighty, the two of you sure manage to bring a heap of trouble. I should have run you out of town a few days ago."

"I wish you had, Chief," Amanda answered with fervent sincerity. "But it's never too late. Sara and I were on our way home when Paul Stucky grabbed me. Our van is packed and ready to go, so if you drop us at the hospital, we'll be on our way."

The chief wagged a stubby finger at them. "Now you know it's not that easy, girls. You're already experts at giving statements, and we'll need two more. Besides, I need you to check out a few mugshots, Mandy."

The chief's pretty young driver giggled while Amanda and Sara groaned.

"It's almost six o'clock, Toni," Sara objected. "I'm taking Mandy home for a good dinner, a hot shower, and a full night's sleep."

"Sorry, duty before pleasure."

"No, *I'm* sorry, Toni. I'm putting my foot down. We'll cooperate, but not till tomorrow."

The chief's mouth turned down at the corners. "I'd prefer you do it now."

"Tough titties." Sara smiled and winked.

"I beg your pardon?" the chief said while her driver giggled again. "Do you talk that way to your patients, Dr. Orlando?"

"Only when they deserve it, ma'am. Thing is, Mandy's well-being is not negotiable. We'll meet you first thing in the morning, sign the damn statements, and you'll be home in time to feed your cats lunch."

"We can live with that, can't we, Toni?" The pretty young officer touched her chief's shoulder.

The telling gesture was not lost on Amanda and Sara, and when the chief turned away from them flustered, she knew Sara had won. The chief was indeed a lesbian. Soon afterwards, they entered the Asheville city limits and the chief's girlfriend parked at 100 Court Plaza.

"I told you our van's at the hospital," Sara said. "Take us there now, please."

"Can't you be patient for five minutes, Doctor? You can both wait here with Julie, and I'll bring out the photographs out to the car." The chief beseeched Amanda, "Please, it'll take only seconds…"

"No problem," she answered quickly, before Sara could further dominate the poor woman.

When the chief disappeared into the station house, Sara turned to the driver, a devilish look on her face. "Hey, Julie, I was wondering…are you and Toni a couple?"

Amanda gasped at the impropriety, while Julie blushed furiously. "Don't ask, don't tell," she said at last.

Again Amanda was floored. Sara was nervy, but Julie was crazy. In her position, Amanda would never, ever have offered such a reveal. Clearly the young woman must be a handful for Toni Hall. She quickly changed the subject.

"Julie, have you heard anything about Ron Dunifon?"

It took the officer a moment to change gears, but then she repeated, "Don't ask, don't tell. But I can say I don't think Mr. Dunifon will be our guest at the jail too much longer."

This seemed like good news, implying Ron might not have been formally arrested. She decided to try another subject. "The officers from Waynesville told me they had a BOLO out for Al Cabella's black limousine, with the Illinois plates. Any news on that?"

While Julie considered her answer, Sara lifted a quizzical eyebrow. After all, they'd not yet had time to discuss any of this.

"I guess it's okay to tell you, Miss Rittenhouse. Yeah, a Tennessee state trooper spotted the limo just outside Knoxville.

He found it alongside a county road. It had been abandoned and hidden behind a bramble hedge—no sign of the men."

"But where did they go?"

"Who knows? Hitched a ride into town? Bought or stole a new vehicle? We'll find out, ma'am. In fact, it's those men the chief wants you to identify."

Right on cue, Toni approached and slid into her previous seat. She passed a manila file folder back to Amanda. "Tennessee ran the limo's tags and just like you said, the car is registered to Al Cabella. His last known address was in West Garfield Park outside Chicago. That area enjoys the city's highest crime rate and your Mr. Cabella has committed many of them. Look at his mugshot, please."

With Sara peeking over her shoulder, she pulled out a full sheet detailing Al Cabella's offenses. The smirking thug in the photo had a skeletal head, a soul patch under thin lips, a broken nose, and a disfiguring scar just beneath his receding hairline.

"It's not him!" Amanda cried. "I've never seen this man before in my life!"

"It's not the Al Cabella we know," Sara concurred as she tightened her grasp on Amanda's hand.

"Then who the hell kidnapped you?"

It was a very good question.

CHAPTER FORTY-SIX

Musical breakfasts...

"Good morning, babe," Sara said before they untangled.

"Same to you, honey." In spite of some heavy weights dragging down the negative side of the scale, on balance Amanda was amazingly happy. She was alive, satisfied and complete in her lover's arms, and so far no one had been killed—neither heroes nor villains. "I need to call my mother, though. She'll be so disappointed that we won't be home for Trout's birthday."

Sara shifted position in bed, lessening the delicious pressure of her knee high up between Amanda's legs, and when she rolled slightly, breaking the seal between their naked bodies, Amanda moaned in protest.

"Diana and Trout will understand," Sara whispered, her breath warm against Amanda's ear. "Like I said before, I'm sure they'll save us some cake." She kissed the tender cut on Amanda's temple then worked her mouth down Amanda's neck, her breasts, said hello to her navel, and then finished with a kiss to the elbow she'd scraped sliding around Stucky's van.

"I won't tell Mom what's happened here. First she'll be worried sick, but next she'll want enough details to solve these mysteries herself. You know how she is."

"Right, like mother, like daughter—you're both natural-born sleuths. If we'd gone directly home yesterday like I wanted, instead of stopping at the hospital…"

"Then none of this would have happened," Amanda completed the thought. "You told me so!" She gave Sara a playful little nip on her chin, eliciting a surprised yelp.

"You wanna play some more?" Sara threatened. She came on top, capturing Amanda's wrists and holding them above her head on the pillow.

"Please no!" Amanda gasped with pleasure. "I've endured all the manhandling I can tolerate in twenty-four hours."

"You didn't say no to the *woman-handling* last night!" Sara laughed, rolled off, sat up and swung her feet down to the floor. "But now it's time to feed my wounded warrior some breakfast."

While Sara scrambled eggs and nuked bacon, Amanda sipped coffee and tried to make sense of it all. True to her word, Chief Hall had driven them to the hospital after she'd viewed the mugshots. Although Amanda hadn't found a picture of the suave man who had been posing as Al Cabella, she had identified Mickey—full name Michael Benito—and that was somewhat helpful. Benito, like the real Cabella, had a long criminal history related to the Chicago mob.

At the hospital they'd visited with Carl, who had seemed to be recovering nicely, paid to get Moby Dyke out of the parking garage, and then purchased Chinese food on the way back to Carl's.

They both would have preferred checking into a motel, but Gladys had called Amanda's cell phone and begged them to spend at least one more night with her in the professor's "big ole house."

"I guess Gladys felt cheated when we refused to share all the gory details of yesterday's adventure." Amanda giggled.

"Too bad. You were dead on your feet, Mandy, and it's not like we had any answers."

So true. In spite of all the drama, they knew less than before about why or who had attacked Carl. They sure as hell did not know why Al Cabella was not Al Cabella and would likely never find out.

"I'm glad Gladys was gone when we got up," Amanda added. "We escaped more questions."

"Amen to that." Sara slid two slices of buttered bread into the toaster oven. "Her note said she was on her way to the hospital to spend the day with Carl."

"At least we have the house to ourselves, so we can write our stupid statements in peace." They had already broken their promise to Chief Hall by oversleeping. At this rate, they couldn't meet her at the station until early afternoon.

"So Toni won't get home to Julie and the cats till dinner," Sara concluded. "Let them wait."

At that moment, Larry Goldberg burst through the glass sliders from the deck, bringing a blast of cold air scented with the sweet smell of marijuana. "Who are Toni and Julie?" he asked.

His entrance startled them both. Amanda had almost forgotten he was living in the barn, and by his clothing, Surfer Dude was taking full advantage. He wore the brown cable-knit sweater she'd seen Ron wearing several days ago, rolled up at the sleeves. She figured he'd borrow Ron's pants and shoes if he could get away with it.

"Good morning, ladies," Larry continued brightly when they didn't answer. "What's for breakfast? I'm hungry enough to eat Barney."

The old bloodhound half opened his droopy eyes at the mention of his name, while Sara and Amanda rolled their eyes at one another. No one was happy at Larry's intrusion.

"I suppose I can fix more eggs," Sara said as she set the plates she'd filled for herself and Amanda down on the bar. "But you'll have to wait till we've eaten. I hate my food cold."

"Thank you, Sara. I can wait." He leaned against the wall, wearing a silly smile and glassy stare.

Amanda was wondering just how much pot he'd smoked and how he could afford it when her cell phone rang. Assuming it was her mother, she was about to answer when she saw the name "Ron Dunifon" on her caller ID. Taken off guard, but certain she did not want to converse with Ron in front of Larry, she said, "I'll take this outside. You can eat *my* breakfast, Larry."

Ignoring the exasperated look from Sara, she stepped out on the deck and immediately regretted the decision. The chill November morning was way beyond bracing, it was downright frigid, so she squeezed into a sheltered corner to answer the call. The one-sided conversation, conducted at breakneck speed by Ron, who was trying to fit his words into a jailhouse time limit, took her mind completely off the cold. The astonishing information he imparted left her with more questions than answers, and because she was only able to utter a few monosyllabic responses, the best she could do was agree to his urgent request.

When they signed off, she could not wait to tell Sara the news, but again, did not want Larry listening. She stepped back into the warm house to check on how their breakfast was progressing, but instead of the harmony she expected, Sara and Larry were yelling at one another.

"Don't be a bitch, Sara! Why can't I borrow your van? It's for a good cause." Larry tossed his fork onto his empty plate and his handsome face flushed under his tan. "I'll be back in an hour. What's the big deal?"

"I told you, *we* need the van," Sara responded in her firm, reasonable therapist voice and turned her back on him as she began cooking for Amanda again. Instead of musical chairs, they were playing musical breakfasts.

Larry jumped to his feet, fuming and pacing. He appealed to Amanda for support. "Is she this stubborn with you? Does she talk to you that way? How can you stand it?"

Actually, Sara did sometimes turn her unflappable psychiatrist attitude on Amanda and it was infuriating. "Sorry, Larry, we do need the van. The chief of police would be most upset if we're not on time."

The word "police" calmed him some, yet he stomped to the sliders, letting in the chill as he delivered his parting line: "Okay,

I'll hitch into town. It'll be your fault if some pervert picks me up!" The glass panels vibrated as he slammed them closed.

"What was that all about?" Amanda rubbed the circulation back into her arms and sat back down at the bar.

"Oh, he wants to visit Carl in the hospital." Sara broke two eggs into the skillet.

"Why would Larry care about Carl? He only met him for two seconds."

"He claims he's concerned, but mainly he wants to buy that portrait Ron did of the professor."

"But the painting isn't Carl's to sell. It belongs to Ron," she objected.

Sara shrugged and brought Amanda her breakfast. "Who the hell knows about that kid? Maybe he wasn't going to the hospital at all. Maybe he ran out of pot and needed to meet his supplier." She fanned the air to disperse the eau de marijuana. "Did you break the news about missing Trout's birthday to your mom?"

She took a deep breath. "You better sit down, Sara, because that was Ron Dunifon on the phone, and do I have some news for you…"

CHAPTER FORTY-SEVEN

In the closet...

They had a mission and Ron had given them specific instructions. Sara got her yellow windbreaker, Amanda pulled on her sweatshirt, and then they put Barney on his leash and headed for the barn. Arctic wind whipped across the driveway between structures, hurling dried leaves at Moby Dyke and Ron's Ford Fusion. When they looked down the long entryway leading to Carl's house, Larry was a black speck in the distance trying to thumb a ride.

"I wonder why Larry didn't just use Ron's car?" Sara turned away from the wind to keep it from lashing her hair into her eyes.

Amanda grunted in disgust. "From what Ron told me, Surfer Dude would have taken it in a heartbeat if he could find the keys—no permission needed."

A large part of her conversation with Ron had been devoted to his anger about Larry camping out in the barn. Ron insisted he had never invited the kid to stay. He called him a moocher, a freeloader, even a hooker, and begged Amanda to toss him out.

"I'm glad you told Ron he'd have to do his own dirty work. It might be dangerous handing that kid his walking papers. No doubt Larry will argue that occupation is nine-tenths of the law."

"You're right, Sara. Besides, Ron will be home this evening. He got himself into this mess and he can jolly well get himself out." She handed Barney's leash to Sara and bent over the heavy flower pot near the door. "Hope the key's really under here…"

It was. She had not seen an old-fashioned skeleton key like it since the one her grandmother had used in her pantry door. As they unlocked, unleashed Barney, and followed him into the dark space, she realized how eager she had been to actually see Ron's barn firsthand.

Sara found a bank of light switches just inside and flipped them all on. "Wow, check it out! God, wouldn't we love having a place like this?"

The cavernous space was an appealing blend of old and new. The renovation had retained all the structural elements of the old "bank barn." The far end, a windowless wall of fieldstone, was built into a hillside. One-storied at the rear, two-storied at the driveway, the loft was hung over the front and had likely been the hay mow. They already knew from the light patterns they'd seen at night that Ron's bedroom was up there.

"I guess we'll find the clothes Ron asked for up in the loft. I'm glad we don't have to climb the old ladder to get there," Amanda said. The rickety original ladder was still attached to the wall behind a new spiral staircase much like the one in the main house.

Sturdy rustic beams supported the sloped roof, punctuated by skylights, and defined the first floor into a small kitchen with a dinette set and a living area—the rest was all studio. The dark external wall beams and small windows were in-filled with drywall painted pure white, and the stark contrasts were Tudor-like. A framework of livestock stalls had been left in place and were now shelved with storage for books and Ron's art supplies. The ingenious design was both open and richly intimate in its detail.

Once she'd taken it all in, Amanda was able to answer. "God yes! Having a home like this would be beyond amazing. We'd be so happy here."

The moment those words left her mouth, she wondered if Ron and Carl would ever co-exist happily here. Half the studio space had been cleared to accommodate the art and equipment from Carl's gallery in Cotton Mill Studios. Unpacked boxes, a crated kiln, and his potter's wheel had been delivered by the college kids sometime yesterday, while she was busy being kidnapped. In the other half, Ron's easels, canvases, and finished paintings had been stacked willy-nilly in his absence.

"It's so sad," she thought aloud. "At least the cops don't think Ron's a murderer anymore. They verified that the oxycodone pills found in his loft had been legally prescribed to Ron when he was recuperating from rotator cuff surgery last year."

"Well, they took their sweet time clearing him. I'm sure it wasn't easy being detained this long. Too bad the results of Ron's blood and urine tests weren't analyzed sooner."

Amanda heartily agreed. An odd convergence of facts had finally convinced the police that Ron was innocent. His blood test had revealed an insufficient percentage of alcohol to account for his extreme drunkenness. All along he'd maintained that he had no memory of the night Carl overdosed. He said he'd experienced a blackout. This testimony, coupled with the fact that he'd been so hard to rouse the morning after the incident, suggested the possibility that he'd been drugged. Sure enough, the advanced technique used to analyze Ron's urine detected Rohypnol in his system.

"Someone slipped him a roofie." Amanda shook her head. "In college we called it the date-rape drug. Ron told me the bar where he and Larry went after dinner has been cited seven times in the past few months because men have been drugged there, but why would someone do that to Ron?"

"Who knows? Maybe it was a mistake?" Sara led the way to the downstairs sitting area and the couch where Ron claimed to have spent the night before his arrest. The clothes he'd been wearing for his date with Larry—button-up shirt and sport coat—were crumpled on the floor. "So Ron slept down here and Larry took the bed upstairs—not the most romantic end to the evening."

"Guess not." Amanda was glad those two had not slept together. It didn't feel right. Neither did the roofie angle. A college friend who'd actually been date-raped had described sudden paralysis, a blackout, and waking up twelve hours later shaking and unable to speak. It seemed to her that if Ron had been drugged at the bar, he couldn't have driven back to Carl's, let alone conversed once he got here.

"Something doesn't feel right," she mumbled.

Sara laughed. "How does this feel?" She pulled Amanda into her arms, held her close, and nuzzled the soft spot under her neck. "Let's put it behind us, babe, and check out Ron's bedroom."

When they reached the top, Amanda was enchanted all over again. She ambushed Sara from behind and encircled her waist. "Oh my God, I could live with this!"

A heavily carved oaken four-poster bed dominated the large open space. It was set on a richly colored oriental carpet, which in turn lay on wide varnished planks of the original floor. A triangular window echoed the peaked roofline. It overlooked Carl's house and a sky filled with racing cumulous clouds.

"Can you imagine sleeping in that bed?" Sara breathed. "It feels like we're in a bird's nest."

She tightened her grip on Sara's waist and dragged her closer as they took it all in. A row of dressers was built in under the window and Ron's desk was angled in the corner. His laptop computer was open in sleep mode, its colorful Windows logo floating lazily across the bright blue screen.

Ron's portrait of Carl Fischer hung above the computer, with a pair of stubby candles in antique silver holders set to either side. "That's the portrait I was telling you about, Sara. What do you think?"

Sara gasped. "Wow, I see what you mean. It's not only a provocative work of art, it speaks volumes about the artist's passion for the subject. The message is conflicted, but one thing is certain—Ron's got himself a little shrine going here. Whether he's worshiping his god or his devil, it's hard to tell."

They stood in silent contemplation until Barney's whining from the bottom of the stairs broke the spell. "We better get a move on or we'll never get our statements to Chief Hall," Amanda said. "If we're too late, she'll arrest us for extreme tardiness."

She released Sara and they moved toward Ron's walk-in closet. The closet had heavy double doors joined by a wrought iron locking bar that swiveled up from a grooved latch. The room was original to the barn, causing her to wonder what special farm stuff had once been stored there. When they entered and turned on the light, they saw rods hung with Ron's substantial wardrobe and racks filled with his expensive shoes. A small porthole window let in natural light.

"He asked specifically for his green pullover sweater, brown corduroy pants, black jacket, and suede loafers," Amanda said. "God knows what he was wearing when they took him in for questioning, but he's in an orange jumpsuit now and complaining the color does not suit him."

Sara chuckled as she slid hangers back and forth. "I suppose His Majesty will want clean socks and underwear, too. What do you reckon—boxers or bikinis?"

Amanda had agreed to bring Ron's "get out of jail" clothes when they delivered their statements to Chief Hall, killing two birds with one stone, so they got busy and concentrated on finding the specific garments Ron had requested. As they worked, the little room got darker when a storm cloud blocked the sun. A splash of rain slapped the roof close above their heads and they heard a distant rumbling.

"Is that thunder?" she wondered.

Sara scowled. "Shit, I thought we were done with rain."

At the same time, Barney began to growl. The menacing sound from deep in his throat spooked them. She went to the porthole and peered in every direction.

"I don't see anything."

"Forget it. The dog's just bored and wants to get outside."

But as Amanda kept watching, the rumbling stopped and a dark figure appeared from around the corner of the barn. The hood of the man's charcoal jacket was pulled up over his head as he hesitated, looked both ways, then crept stealthily across the driveway heading for the house.

Transfixed by fear, she whispered, "Quick, turn off the light, Sara!"

"Why?"

"Just do it!"

The man tiptoed onto the deck, peeked into the kitchen, and tried the door but found it locked. Next he disappeared around the edge of the deck. She was certain he would try the door to Carl's master suite and then the front. Her heart pulsing in her throat, she could not speak, so she prayed he would just go away.

"What's wrong?" Sara turned off the closet light and joined her at the window.

"Shh…" She pressed her fingers to Sara's lips.

"You can shut me up, but what about Barney?"

The hound had escalated to ear-shattering barks guaranteed to alert the stranger. Sure enough, the prowler ran back around to the driveway and stared at the barn, which was lit up downstairs like a birthday cake. When the man lifted his face, his brown features and the edge of a large white bandage were clearly visible under the hood.

"I thought they threw his ass in jail!" Sara gasped.

"So did I! He must have driven his motorcycle up the back way from the abandoned farm. What the hell does he want now?"

Sara's fingers bit into Amanda's shoulder. "He's coming to the barn. God, did we lock the door?"

They had not—why would they? "You know Stucky will walk right in. Can we lock this closet from the inside?"

They groped around in panic but found no interior latch of any kind. Then in silent agreement, they pushed one of the heavy shoe racks against the doors. When the two sides of the door came perfectly flush, they heard a loud snick as the iron locking bar on the outside dropped into its grooved latch.

Now they were prisoners.

CHAPTER FORTY-EIGHT

Insult to injury…

It was a pregnant moment—like right after the other shoe drops, when no power on heaven or earth could reverse the event. They were trapped, and Stucky had entered the building.

"What can we do?" Amanda whispered once she could breathe.

Sara gripped her shoulders. "Look on the bright side, babe. When he comes up to get us and sees the closet locked on the outside, he'll assume no one's inside. Only a crazy person would lock herself in."

Well, Stucky already knew Amanda was crazy. After what she'd done to him yesterday, he'd be ready to kill her—kill them both. "We're screwed," she whimpered.

Sara did not disagree. Instead she said, "At least Barney's stopped barking. I'd forgotten that he and Stucky were such good pals."

Indeed the bloodhound was making doggie happy sounds, greeting the enemy by thumping his tail. She figured the best they could do was become still as stone, refrain from sneezing, coughing, or even breathing more than necessary. If they were really lucky, Barney might not expose them by pointing up the stairs.

No such luck. After Stucky shuffled around below looking for God knows what, they soon heard his heavy footsteps on the stairs and moved quietly to the back of the closet. Barney, who could not handle the spiral challenge, stayed behind howling his displeasure.

They froze and held hands as Stucky explored Ron's bedroom. They heard him move toward the desk. Seconds later his bulk settled into Ron's chair and his fingers clicked on the keyboard. But why was Stucky snooping into Ron's private life? Indeed, why had Stucky been so quickly released by the Waynesville police? As these questions collided inside her brain, she began to wonder if the whole mess had been about Ron all along. Was someone trying to frame Ron, or separate him from Carl by killing Carl? Nothing made sense.

Suddenly her train of thought was derailed by the shrill ringing of the cell phone in her pocket. It screamed and vibrated against her thigh as Sara's eyes expanded in shock and fear, no doubt mirroring Amanda's expression as she extracted the traitorous device. She barely had time to register her mother's name flashing on the caller ID before the locking bar lifted and Stucky viciously kicked the door inward, toppling the heavy shoe rack. She quickly declined the call.

"God fucking damn!" Stucky cursed, a gun at the ready in his hand. "It's the bad pennies again. You really do keep turning up."

"So do you, Stucky!" Sara growled with much more bravado than Amanda could muster.

She was terrified to again be staring into the barrel of this bastard's gun—he seemed to have an endless supply. He motioned with his weapon that they should leave the closet and they quickly complied, stumbling across the fallen shoes.

"What the hell are y'all doing in there?" he drawled. "Find anything interesting?"

She gained her voice. "Not unless you are interested in Mr. Dunifon's clothing. He asked us to bring his stuff to the jail. They're releasing him, which is more than they should have done for you. Why did they set you free, Stucky?"

"You mean after you tried to kill me?" He pushed his hood back, exposing his bandage, and then holstered his gun. His ebony face was beaded with sweat.

"You mean after you kidnapped me?" She did not know where her newfound courage was coming from, but she was done taking shit from this asshole. "They should have thrown away the key."

He grabbed her roughly by the arm, gave her a little shake, and then pointed at the stairs. "Let's go down, ladies. I'm tired of listening to that damn dog howling."

Sara led the way, with Amanda and Stucky close behind. Rounding the spiral, Amanda glanced up and looked out the window facing the house, hoping against hope that help was coming. Instead of divine intervention, however, she saw Larry Goldberg shuffling down the driveway in their direction. He'd been unsuccessful at thumbing a ride and was undoubtedly returning to the barn.

So far neither Sara nor Stucky had noticed their imminent guest, so she pretended to trip, hoping to distract them. Surfer Dude was unlikely to be their hero, but his presence might keep Stucky from shooting their heads off. She fell against Sara, and Stucky steadied her from behind.

"Clumsy woman!" he roared.

"Sorry, so sorry," she said, "but I feel sick. I'm gonna throw up. Can I go to the bathroom?"

The color drained from Sara's face. "I'll help her to the bathroom, Stucky."

"Jesus H. Christ!" His black eyes shifted from one to the other as Amanda coughed and gagged. He shoved her away. "You can go, but make it quick." He transferred his grip to Sara. "But your girlfriend stays with me."

Amanda lost no time rushing to the door she'd noticed in the kitchen area. She had guessed correctly, it was indeed a tiny bathroom. She went inside, locked the door, gagged some more and flushed the john. Unsure how this diversion helped them, she cast around looking for a weapon. Unfortunately, Ron shaved with an electric razor so she found no straight-edged blade with which to stab the bastard. She did see a small window high up and stood on the toilet seat to look out.

Larry had arrived at the back deck and was staring open-mouthed at a spot right below her window. When she peeked down, Amanda saw it, too—Stucky's fancy motorcycle parked there. Larry stiffened and cringed. Sensing danger, he crouched cat-like, scampered across the driveway, and hid to one side of the barn entrance. She had always sensed a toughness in this kid, a street-wise self-preservation that might serve him well, even against a thug like Stucky. On the other hand, even Larry was defenseless against a speeding bullet.

She watched as the kid began picking through a pile of junk near the steps. Suddenly he stood upright, an ax in his hand. Her legs almost buckled as he hefted its weight and touched a finger to its rusted blade.

Anticipating the confrontation at hand, her knees gave out completely. An antique ax was still no match for a bullet, and Sara could easily get caught in the crossfire. By now a man like Stucky was surely aware of the intruder, and he possessed a perfect human shield.

She had to distract him, so she screamed bloody murder and pounded her fists against the door. "Help!" she screamed for good measure.

Stucky bellowed. "Oh for Christ's sake, go see what's wrong with her now!"

Sara's feet ran toward her and she unlocked just as Sara hit the door, causing them to fall into each other's arms.

"What's wrong, Mandy?"

"Snake in the toilet!" she hollered.

That got Stucky's attention. He again drew his gun. It dangled at the end of his arm as he strode nervously toward them. At the same time, the barn door silently opened behind him.

Stucky spun around seconds too late because Larry, ax raised high above his head, delivered a stunning blow before his victim could raise his gun arm.

Sara and Amanda screamed as Stucky toppled. Although Larry had attacked with the blunt side of the ax head, it had come down hard on Stucky's bandage. She winced at the insult to his injury, but was thrilled to see the big guy groaning on the floor.

Sara dove for the gun and got it in hand just as Larry, panting and stunned by his own violence, realized Stucky was still moving. Larry shifted the oaken handle so the blade was forward. He raised it high again, prepared to kill, when Sara pointed the gun.

"Don't do it, Larry!" she cried.

CHAPTER FORTY-NINE

Windows...

"It's not worth it, Larry!" Sara screamed again. "Drop it now, or I swear I'll shoot you!"

Everything happened in slow motion. Amanda saw the fine blond hairs on the tanned backs of Larry's trembling hands, heard the gears cranking in his brain and his breathing slow as he gradually came to his senses, lowered the weapon, and dropped it to the floor.

"Thanks, Sara. I don't know what happened to me just then!" Larry was truly shaken. A shiver passed through his entire body as he struggled to compose himself. He removed his black-framed glasses and polished the heat fog from his lenses on Ron's brown cable-knit sweater. "God, I would have killed that guy. Who the hell is he?"

Before they could explain, Barney, who had kept clear of all the action, came slinking up to his fallen friend and sniffed the spot of red blood appearing on Stucky's bandage. She felt a tiny pang of guilt when Stucky attempted to lift his hand and pat the animal.

"He's still dangerous, Mandy," Sara cautioned as she witnessed Amanda's empathy. "I think we should tie him up."

"You can use this…" Larry proudly lifted Ron's sweater and slid a black leather belt from the loops of his trousers. "It's a Comfort Click, as seen on TV. When you put it around the dude's wrists you can tighten it real good and it'll stay put."

She was amazed by the kid's fixation on a pop product at a time like this, yet accepted the belt. "Okay, I'll do it."

"I'll hold the gun," Larry offered.

"No, *I'll* hold the gun," Sara firmly asserted.

"Cool. Then I'll call the cops." Larry took out his cell phone and jogged toward the front door, as though seeking a better signal.

Sara nodded at her, then followed the kid.

Amanda bent over Stucky and stared into his black, slightly glazed eyes. "Turn over," she commanded, but he did not move.

He moistened his lips. "Come closer, Mandy, I need to tell you something…"

Now what? She had no desire to let Stucky whisper sweet nothings in her ear, yet he was down and incapacitated and she was curious. She bent closer.

"Please, Mandy," he begged. "Go upstairs and look at the laptop."

"Ron's laptop? Why would I do that?"

Stucky's eyelids drooped and he had difficulty forming the words. "It's not Ron's, it's Larry's. You must see…"

Stucky was out. Unconscious. And clearly he was talking nonsense. Having no other options, she lifted his heavy arms up cross-wristed on his chest, like a dead man, and bound him with the Comfort Click belt.

"Okay, the cops are on the way!" Larry called, returning the phone to his pocket. "I'll go back down the lane and flag them in," he said on his way out the door.

"I suspect the local police could find their way here blindfolded," Sara wryly commented as they watched the kid jog down the driveway.

Amanda was conflicted. "You know, Sara, Stucky just told me to go upstairs and look at the laptop. He says it's Larry's, not Ron's."

"So what? Stucky's crazy." Sara frowned at the unconscious man lying with Barney's head on his legs. "Leave the laptop to the police, babe."

"No, I'm going to check it out." She sprinted toward the stairs. "You stay down here and guard our crazy prisoner."

When she arrived at Ron's desk, the Windows logo was still floating across the monitor. When she sat down and jiggled the mouse, the screen lit up with the Internet page Stucky had been reading when he was interrupted.

She immediately recognized the site by its green leaf motif as Ancestry.com. Her ex had been obsessed with genealogy. How weird was this? Next she saw that Stucky was right, she was looking at Larry Goldberg's family tree. Fascinated, she quickly traced backward starting with Larry, who had no siblings, to his parents' branch. She was surprised by the fact that both Larry's parents were dead. Then she was arrested by the fact that his mother's maiden name was Fischer. *Oh my God!* Larry's maternal grandfather had a brother named Carl Fischer, and if this was true, then her host could be Larry's great uncle! Surely this was impossible. From what Gina had told her, Carl had no living family, let alone a nephew.

She clicked on Carl's name to bring up his Ancestry bio, which was unusually short: Born Fort Wayne, Indiana in 1944—this would be the right age for her Carl—seventy-two. He graduated from high school and was eventually drafted to fight in Vietnam. Then came the stunner—killed in action May, 1969, at the Battle of Hamburger Hill, body never recovered.

She slowly lifted her hands off the keyboard as her mind raced with the implications. Dead was dead, wasn't it? But then, the body had never been recovered. She shook her head and stared at the computer. The cursor seemed to move of its own volition as she opened Larry's Documents. Scanning the alphabetical list, she hovered over a file labeled "C.F." and opened it.

Sure enough, Larry had assembled an impressive library of articles pertaining to Carl Fischer, including the one she had Googled citing his professional achievements, from his MFA from Indiana University, to his tenure at Appalachian, to the present. Had Larry noticed the same gap she had? The report offered nothing about the professor's life up until age twenty-eight. Had part of his previous life included a childhood in Fort Wayne, military service, and an untimely "death" in Vietnam?

Excitement building, she opened another article with the intriguing headline "Millionaire Professor Revitalizes River Arts District." As she skimmed the text, two aspects of Carl's involvement stood out—his philanthropy and his extreme wealth, which was estimated to be in the multimillions.

By then her hands were shaking and her mind reeled with questions. Why would a young Carl Fischer choose to disappear from the world? She glanced up at Carl's portrait in the shrine-like setting and recalled Larry's desperate desire to own it. What were his reasons?

She could think of several million of them.

CHAPTER FIFTY

Heaven or earth...

"Hurry up, Mandy. What's taking so long?" Sara hollered from the foot of the stairs.

"Just a second, I'll be right there." Determined not to leave empty-handed, she returned to Larry's family tree and hit the Print command. Taking a few minutes to connect the laptop to Ron's wireless printer, she made a copy detailing Larry's relationship to Carl, folded the sheet, stuffed it into her waistband, and flew down the stairs.

"Sara, we need to talk!"

Sara was seated at the small dinette with Stucky stirring restlessly at her feet. She had placed the gun on a nearby chair. "He needs a doctor. You'd think the police would be here by now."

She handed the printout to Sara. "You have to read this. I found it on Larry's laptop, and it shows how he's related to the professor. That would make Larry Carl's only living heir, so he stands to inherit millions if Carl dies!"

"Slow down, Mandy, have you lost your mind?" Yet Sara was reading the sheet.

"Think about it," Amanda insisted as the puzzle pieces fell into place. "Larry has a motive and he's had opportunities. He was on the roof at Carl's party, and he was alone in Carl's room the night he overdosed."

"But surely Carl would leave his money to Ron or Gladys. He's about to marry the woman, for God's sake."

Suddenly it all came together. "But Carl and Gladys aren't married yet, and Carl doesn't have a will."

"How could you possibly know that?"

"Because I heard him say so." Amanda had not remembered until that moment, but the night of the party Carl had told Millie Buncombe, who coveted his face jug, that he was not yet ready to make a will. "Don't you get it, Sara? Larry was standing nearby when Carl said it, and soon afterwards Carl fell off the roof. Larry had to kill Carl before he got married or made a will, or Larry was screwed."

"It's too far-fetched," Sara objected.

Then Paul Stucky's deep, shaky voice resonated from the floor. "No, it makes sense. I was wrong all along."

"He's awake!" Amanda was relieved.

"Yeah, but he's not thinking straight."

Stucky groaned. "Please untie me. We have to stop Goldberg before he gets away."

She and Sara stared at one another in utter indecision.

"Who the hell is this guy?" Sara said.

"Turn me over—right back pocket."

Figuring she had nothing to lose, Amanda got on her knees, but could not flip Stucky's dead weight alone. "Help me, Sara."

Together they rolled him onto his side so that Amanda was able to fish a flat, black leather wallet from his pocket. Inside a clear plastic sleeve, she found a handsome five-star gold badge. The distinctive shield said USMS.

"United States Marshal Service," Stucky explained. "My ID card's in there, too."

Indeed a stiff card bearing an image of the same badge identified Stucky as an officer of the Federal District Court, North Carolina Western District.

Amanda was shocked. "Why all the secrecy? Why did you kidnap me?"

Stucky flopped onto his back. "Will you please untie me now?"

The injured man would be of no help whatsoever catching Larry Goldberg, but one did not argue with a US Marshal. She began tugging at his restraint, but Larry's belt would not give. "Help me, Sara. I can't get it loose."

"I wish the stupid cops would get here," Sara grumbled as she pitched in.

Barney rolled out of the way as the women worked, but while they were heads down, lost in concentration, a cold breeze sighed into the room as Larry Goldberg silently entered the barn. By the time Barney growled, Larry had picked up a large carving knife and was standing directly above them.

"The cops aren't coming," he smugly informed them. "I never called." His calm, eerily high voice was terrifying.

Amanda's fingers froze on the belt, which they had only nominally loosened. Stucky fainted out again, and Sara was unreadable.

"But I heard you call them," Sara said in an even, reasonable tone.

"I was acting. It was a monologue." Larry grinned. "You didn't know I was an actor, did you? It's expensive living in Los Angeles."

No doubt, Amanda thought bitterly. A starving actor could do worse than inherit millions. Trying to keep her expression neutral, she stared at his face—anywhere except at the butcher's knife glinting in his hand.

"Stand up and move away from that man. Put your hands on the counter," he demanded.

As if they had a choice? Her legs quivered as Sara helped her up. They had been in dire situations before, and she had always been impressed by Sara's ability to keep her cool. She had the skill to talk a would-be suicide off the ledge, provided that person could listen to reason, but from the manic glaze in Larry's eyes, she feared he'd gone round the bend.

They reached the counter and flattened their hands on its cold marble surface. Barney padded along with the three of them, uncertain whether to growl or wag.

"Put the knife down, Larry," Sara suggested. "It's not too late to walk away from this. No one's seriously hurt, so let's talk about it."

Larry's shrill laugh echoed around the barn and bounced off the beams. "Doc, I've spent quality time with better shrinks than you, and none of them have ever changed my mind, so you might as well save your breath."

The psychopath intended to kill them! Amanda's panic became a living thing. It beat its wings in her chest, making it impossible to breathe. No force from heaven or earth could alter this madman's plan, because beyond stabbing them, he had no plan.

He moved closer, the sharp tip of his weapon inches from Sara's heart. Amanda smelled marijuana on his clothes and fear in his sweat. Desperate to intervene, her fingers trembled and clenched as she gauged the distance between them. She would grab the knife with her bare hands if that's what it took to save Sara.

She was prepared to lunge when her cell phone screamed from her pocket. The sound stopped time and Larry froze.

"Don't answer!" He spun to face her, the knife catching the fabric of her sweatshirt.

She fell back against the counter in sheer terror, and at the same time, Barney made a decision. He sprang forward and sank his teeth into Larry's leg.

The blade grazed her flesh as the kid bellowed in rage. He shook his leg in agony and turned his knife on the dog. From across the room, a chair crashed to the floor.

"Drop it, Goldberg!" Stucky shouted.

Sara was reaching for Larry's arm and Barney was tugging at Larry's trouser leg when the shot rang out. It exploded in their eardrums, then receded into a void filled with Amanda's scream, Barney's startled yelps, and the insane ringing of the cell phone still in her pocket.

In that expanded moment, Larry's eyes popped wide in shock. He dropped the knife, his body went limp, and he crumpled like a ragdoll onto the floor with Barney. While the dog sniffed the fallen knife, Amanda saw that Stucky had toppled the chair on which Sara had left the gun. He had managed to reach the weapon, roll onto his stomach, and even with his wrists still loosely bound, he had propped on his elbows and taken the shot.

When the phone finally stopped ringing, Stucky broke the silence. "Is he dead?"

Sara dropped to her knees and examined Larry, who batted weakly at her probing hands. "You shot him in the knee, Stucky. He'll survive, but he won't be surfing anytime soon."

The US Marshal lowered his head between his outstretched arms and closed his eyes.

Amanda also got down on her knees to be sure Barney was okay. The bloodhound, completely unscathed, whined and gave her a big sloppy kiss before padding over to guard his buddy.

Sara then crawled to her and gently lowered her to the floor. She lifted her sweatshirt and saw the small incision where the knife had cut her. The inch-long surface wound, just above her navel, was no big deal.

"A Band-Aid should do you," Sara joked, her green eyes brimming with tears. The tears became a flood as they both cried in earnest. Sara lay down beside her and pulled her close. She cradled Amanda's head on her arm and kissed her salty lips. "I'm so sorry, babe. I guess we should call the police for real now."

Amanda kissed her back, then swiveled her neck and saw two unconscious men on the floor. "Should we request one ambulance or two?" She reached between them and fished the phone from her pocket. When she swiped the home screen, she saw that the missed call, the one that had likely saved their lives, was from her mother. Impulsively, she activated voice mail.

Hi, Mandy Bear, it's your mama calling. Matthew is enjoying his birthday, but you girls aren't here yet. Please call me back and tell me how many plates to set out for dinner…"

Mom's warm voice embraced them and they began laughing hysterically.

"I'd rather be eating cake." Sara sighed.

"Amen," Amanda agreed, and then called 911.

CHAPTER FIFTY-ONE

Not over yet...

They dispatched two ambulances and two squad cars. The shrill sirens were audible long before they reached the barn, giving her and Sara time to properly settle at the dinette set, near Stucky's stirring body, before the first uniforms eased through the door in defensive crouches. Each officer held his gun in both hands, arms stiffly extended, darting eyes scanning for danger.

"All clear!" Amanda hollered.

The men halted and stared at her. Quickly processing the scene—two male bodies down and two unarmed women—the lead cop lowered his weapon and chuckled. "I reckon we can trust your word on that. At ease, boys."

The first two holstered their guns as two more followed. They all pulled out gloves and stood aside as a plainclothes cop, who seemed to be the boss, approached them. He introduced himself as Detective something-or-other, she didn't catch the name, and then he took a chair at their table.

"Rittenhouse and Orlando, right? The chief warned me about you two."

"She told you we were trouble?" Sara asked sarcastically.

"Trouble on steroids." The detective grinned. He was young, dark, and movie-star handsome. "Can you tell me what happened here?"

Amanda sighed. "That could take a very long time."

"Give it to me in a nutshell."

As she related the bare bones of what had just transpired, Sara greeted two teams of medics. She pointed at Stucky. "This is the good guy." And then at Larry. "This is the bad guy."

The first EMS team tended to Larry. As they strapped him to a gurney, he spat out obscenities and screamed for morphine. They quickly whisked him out the door. Once the siren from his ambulance receded, silence descended on the room.

The second team got busy with Stucky, who was by then fully conscious. Amanda recognized the boyish redhead in a white tunic and his female assistant. They were the same pair who had rescued Carl the night he'd overdosed. She recalled the redhead's name was Rudy, and when he bent over Stucky and scowled, it seemed all too familiar.

"Can you get this dog off his lap?" Rudy said.

Amanda called Barney and hooked her fingers into his collar while Rudy cut the belt off Stucky's wrist with a tiny surgical instrument.

He examined Stucky's blood-stained bandage. "How are you feeling, sir?"

Stucky coughed out a laugh. "My mama never let me play football because she worried that all those concussive blows would scramble my brain. I'd have been safer in the NFL."

The paramedic smiled at Sara. "Did you wrap his bandage, Doc? At least you didn't need your Evzio injector this time."

Stucky answered, "I got this bandage in Waynesville, thanks to Mandy here, who hit me with my own flashlight. But Sara saved my life." He reached up and took Sara's hand. "There's an old Chinese proverb: if someone saves your life, then you owe them for life. I owe you big time, Sara."

Sara squeezed his large brown hand. "Then consider the debt canceled, Paul. You shot Larry and saved *our* lives. Thank you."

Too much violence. As Rudy worked with Stucky, the uniformed officers examined, but did not touch, the ax that would have more than scrambled Stucky's brain had Sara not stopped Larry at gunpoint. They noticed the knife that would have eviscerated them, had Stucky not ended Larry's rampage by shooting him from the floor. As the adrenaline that had fueled her for the past hour drained from her bloodstream, Amanda was suddenly weak and trembling.

The detective, who had been listening to their banter said, "Clearly this chapter in the saga has many new twists and turns. Chief Hall has briefed me on the first part, and I'm sure Marshal Stucky will bring us up to date on the second."

Hearing the detective call her kidnapper "Marshal" tightened so many loose ends it gave her a headache. No wonder the local cops and the ones in Waynesville knew Stucky—he was one of the tribe. It explained why the Asheville officers who'd helped him break camp that rainy morning had brought him doughnuts, why they'd never jailed him in Waynesville. She and Sara were the dopes, the monkeys in the middle, and after all they'd been through they deserved some answers.

The detective said, "You women still owe Chief Hall your statements from yesterday. She's been pacing the station all morning waiting, so I will personally deliver you there as soon as the criminalists arrive at this scene."

"No, you will not," Sara firmly stated as she stood up and urged Amanda to her feet. "Mandy and I are leaving now and going back to the house to rest. Tell Toni we'll cooperate, but she'll have to come to us."

Much to her surprise, the detective laughed uproariously. "The chief told me you'd say that. Her exact words: 'If Sara Orlando puts on the brakes, don't argue. She's one stubborn woman.'"

"The chief was right," Amanda proudly agreed, taking her stubborn woman's arm. She called Barney to heel, clipped on his leash, and began their exit.

In the meantime, Stucky was wrestling with Rudy, who wanted him on a stretcher. Stucky shooed the much smaller medic away and followed the women to the door. "I'm stubborn, too, and they won't keep me in any hospital. Tell you what, girls, I'll hitch a ride with Toni, and we'll both come to visit. It's not over yet."

CHAPTER FIFTY-TWO

Homecoming…

Amanda called her mom and promised that they'd be home tomorrow but did not attempt to explain what had happened during the past five days in hell. That story would require a very long sit-down over a belated birthday party.

Amanda smiled while Sara, as promised, applied a Band-Aid to her wound.

"We're entitled to several pieces of cake, don't you think?" Sara kissed the spot, mothering Amanda as though she were a child. "I bet we've both shed a few pounds over the past few days, so bring it on!"

They had showered and dressed in clean clothes. Amanda had thrown her old sweatshirt in the trash. She was not the least bit sentimental about a garment with a knife hole where her belly button would be.

"Let's start by eating these." Amanda had scavenged a plate of Gladys's leftover cannoli from the fridge. They had been warming to room temperature on the desk in their bedroom, where they intended to write their statements for Toni Hall.

Sara pulled up a second chair and gave Amanda one of the two lined writing pads she'd found in the drawer when they'd written their first statements. "I don't know where to begin."

Amanda sighed, took a pencil, and swung her feet up on Sara's lap. "Not at the beginning, or we'll never get done."

As the hour progressed, accompanied by the ticking of Carl's grandfather clock from the downstairs hall, they nibbled pastry and a band of warm sunlight fell across the desk. Eventually even the sensational nature of the story she was writing could not keep her awake. Both she and Sara had reached the end of their emotional ropes, so she proclaimed that they were done and took Sara to bed.

Barney's excited barking jarred them to consciousness. They were lying hand in hand, fully clothed on top of the covers, chilled and disoriented.

Sara woke up first. "Someone's here."

They moved to the window and looked down to where a new ribbon of crime tape flapped across the barn door, but the criminalists had all departed. The cold and windy morning had transformed to a sunny afternoon, and the alarm clock said 3:15.

"Whose car is that?" Amanda wondered as an unremarkable gray sedan parked at the rear deck. Seconds later, Chief Hall stepped out disguised as a civilian. "It must be Toni's personal vehicle."

Paul Stucky, freshly bandaged, was barely recognizable in dress trousers, sport coat, and tie. True to his word, they had not managed to hospitalize him. Ron Dunifon and Carl Fischer exited the backseat. Their unexpected arrival inspired Amanda and Sara to cheer and high-five each other.

"Hail, hail, the gang's all here!" Amanda cried. "Ron's gonna kill me. I never did get those clothes to him." He was currently wearing something baggy and orange, yet his spirits were high as he jogged around the car to assist Carl.

"Carl looks great!" Sara noted as the professor good naturedly rejected Ron's support and practically bounded up the back steps. "Seems like all that bed rest gave him a new lease on life."

Wasting no time, they snatched their finished statements and flew down the spiral stairs just in time to join everybody congregating in the kitchen. Amanda hesitated momentarily, aware that she and Sara were not family, hardly even friends, so who were they to intrude in this joyous homecoming? But the shyness quickly passed when both Carl and Ron opened their arms to them. They took turns hugging, and when Carl held her at arm's length to search her eyes, she almost lost it. The love, concern, and gratitude in his clear blue eyes again reminded her of Grandpa Whitaker.

"Mandy and Sara," Carl intoned. "How can I ever thank you?"

"You know Sara saved your life, Carl," Toni piled on. "These two are nothing but trouble, but they've been useful—in their way."

"Was that a compliment?" Sara wryly asked.

"Don't let it go to your head." The chief held out her hand and accepted their statements. "At least you've done your homework. What took you so bloody long?" She winked.

The embarrassing love fest was interrupted by Barney, who could no longer tolerate human interference between himself and his beloved master. He pushed between them, jumped up, and covered Carl's face with big sloppy kisses.

Ron sidled up to Amanda. "You let me down, girl."

"Sorry about the clothes. You're right, orange is not your color."

He vamped and struck a deliberately effeminate pose. "I will correct that faux pas posthaste. Okay if I bust into the barn and change, Chief?"

Toni Hall frowned at the yellow tape seal on the barn door. "Oh, what the hell? Go get yourself dressed, Mr. Dunifon. I suspect I've squeezed you for all the information I'm ever gonna get."

"Police brutality," Ron informed them as he made a grand exit, his long legs carrying him across the driveway just shy of the speed of light.

"Drama queen," Stucky muttered, a wide white smile spreading across his face.

These were the first words Stucky had uttered since they'd arrived. He seemed dazed and withdrawn, not surprising considering the double blows to his head. If a black man could be considered pale, then Stucky qualified, and yet he was in a very good mood. As were the others. Even Carl and Ron seemed to have put aside the hurt that hung between them.

"So let's have our pow-wow," Toni said. "I have questions, so y'all just find a seat."

"First we drink." Carl extricated himself from Barney. He brought a bottle of scotch from a cabinet and chilled wine from the fridge. "Mandy, you fill the ice bucket, and Sara, get some glasses. We're all going to my room."

No one argued with the professor as he strode down the hall without one trace of his habitual limp. She and Sara did his bidding, Barney broke into a smiling trot, and they all followed Carl to the master suite. Toni Hall chose to remain standing and politely declined while the others poured drinks. Carl settled into his easy chair with Barney at his feet, while she and Sara took the sofa. Stucky leaned against the doorjamb leading to the deck, nursing his scotch and watching, as though he expected more trouble to come down the road. Everyone waited with bated breath for Toni to start the ball rolling.

The chief cleared her throat. "Well, Larry Goldberg has awakened from his knee surgery and he's singing like Madame Butterfly."

"Was he cognizant when you read him his rights?" Stucky frowned. "You don't want his defense lawyer complaining the kid was too high on pain meds to confess, making that confession inadmissible."

"Don't worry, his doctor assured us he was clear and coherent, even made him count backward to prove it. If his defense pleads insanity, however, it wouldn't be far off the mark, because in my opinion, Goldberg *is* crazy. He actually brags about how clever he was to conceive his plot."

Amanda was surprised that she and Sara were being included in this debriefing because they were hardly the principal actors. Yet they had played roles, so she wasn't complaining, and as she expectantly sipped her wine, she hoped the chief would include all the juicy details.

CHAPTER FIFTY-THREE

Larry's story…

"Once we found out Goldberg had been living in Los Angeles for several years, it didn't take long to find his criminal record—two priors for possession, and he did a year for dealing," Toni said.

"Kid's a real badass," Stucky commented. "Wish I could've spotted it sooner."

When Toni gave Stucky a sharp look, Amanda again wondered why the marshal was involved. He'd been creeping around the periphery all along, but not in any official capacity she could see. Would he get into trouble for kidnapping her or for shooting Larry? Her only knowledge of such things came from TV cop shows. She supposed there would be an internal investigation of his behavior, but so far he'd been Teflon Paul.

"Goldberg got interested in Ancestry.com while he was in prison and became obsessed with you, Carl," the chief continued. "His acting career never got off the ground, so he was penniless and hitched a ride all the way here to climb on his uncle's gravy train."

She noticed that Toni was staring at Carl accusingly, while the professor was gazing into his liquor as though all the answers were hidden there. He refused to meet anyone's eyes.

Sara shook her head. "So Larry planned to kill Carl all along for his money. He must be borderline psychopathic."

"Not necessarily, Dr. Orlando. Goldberg claims he originally intended to introduce himself and then ingratiate himself. Once he was in Carl's good graces, he hoped to move in and become part of the family."

"And bide his time until I kicked the bucket," Carl interrupted. "It's pathetic."

Toni wearily exhaled and sat on the foot of the bed. "He began by getting to know Ron Dunifon at the Woolworth Walk. Goldberg had heard rumors that you and he were a couple, Carl, so he considered Ron a threat. When he realized you two were on the outs, he figured he didn't need to worry about Dunifon and could get to know you directly, starting at your farewell party."

"So he gets to know Carl by throwing him off the roof?" Amanda was appalled.

"Again, he swears that was not premeditated, but two events propelled him to action. First he found out that Carl was marrying Gladys, and then he overheard Carl say he had not written a will. Goldberg figured he had to dispatch with Carl right away in order to inherit."

So it was much as Amanda had suspected. "But how did Larry manage to drug him?"

Toni smiled. "You were there. You saw Goldberg ask to use Carl's bathroom the night he and Dunifon came home drunk. Only Goldberg was not as drunk as he appeared—perhaps it was one of his better attempts at acting—and the drugging was more opportunistic than premeditated. He saw Carl's new bottle of Oxy just sitting there, he had heard from Dunifon about Carl's tea fixation, so he simply dumped all the pills into the tea maker guessing it might do the job."

"The kid's a regular pharmacist," Stucky said. "I heard what your guys found in his knapsack."

"That's right. Goldberg was carrying not only pot, but also Rohypnol. He slipped a roofie into Dunifon's nightcap when they went out to the barn. It was an insurance policy of sorts. If Dunifon woke up and went to check on Carl, it would have spoiled his murder for sure."

"But I'm not dead," Carl softly interjected, "so how will you charge the boy?"

"Attempted murder, two counts," Toni said. "Goldberg keeps whining about how nobody got hurt. He figured he'd have to face a drug charge, nothing more."

"So he really is crazy," Sara said, turning a worried eye to Carl, who was still gazing unhappily into his lap. "This must be especially hard for you. A long-lost nephew turns up out of the blue, someone with whom you might have had a relationship, but then the boy tries to kill you."

Toni chimed in, "That's true, Carl, and I'm so sorry. You once told me you regretted having no family, but now this."

They all watched the professor climb to his feet. As he walked to the window, his limp returning, it seemed the conversation had drained all his energy as he turned back to the chief.

"It's much sadder than you think, Toni, because Larry Goldberg is not my nephew. No way, no how. Whoever his uncle Carl Fischer was, it was never me." His voice picked up steam and anger. "I never served in Vietnam. May his uncle's MIA bones rest in peace, but I fear they are spinning in his unmarked grave with the trouble his nephew has caused. Larry almost killed me, and he's ruined his own life. My take on it? Lock the kid up and throw away the key!"

CHAPTER FIFTY-FOUR

Stucky's story…

Chief Toni Hall prepared to leave soon after Carl's outburst. Somewhat shaken, she gave Amanda and Sara little hugs and a parting shot: "Now I know you girls aren't really married. I have ways of checking, you know…" She paused to give Sara a stern look. "Still, you two are good together, but you might want to rethink your careers as amateur sleuths—if you hope to live long enough to actually tie the knot.

"I'll stay in touch regarding Larry's case, and you might have to return to Asheville for his trial, but otherwise you're free to go," the chief finished before walking out into the late afternoon sunshine.

"Stucky, I'll wait for you in the car," she called over her shoulder.

The chief's marriage remark brought heat rushing to Amanda's cheeks. Over the past few days, she and Sara had been caught up in a maelstrom of violence not of their making, so she'd had little time to think about their own stormy relationship. She recalled how adrift and unhappy she'd been just one week ago, standing beneath the soaring heart sign at Love's Truck Stop, and the memory caused a sharp pain just under her breastbone.

Since Sara's arrival in Asheville, they'd alternated between passionate physical closeness and fighting to stay alive, with no chance to regroup and plan the next phase of their life together. That would change soon, she thought, as she reached out and took Sara's hand.

Sara, beside her on the couch, smiled and squeezed her fingers while Stucky glanced at them with interest, but then turned his attention to Carl.

"Professor, you know this changes everything," he said.

Carl shrugged and poured himself another drink.

"Are you listening to me, sir? We need to make new arrangements." Stucky's intense message seemed to convey a hidden threat.

Sara spoke. "Stucky, you were the one prowling around the deck the night Carl was drugged. Why the hell were you camped out at the farm?"

Amanda jumped in. "Yeah, and what about all that expensive surveillance equipment in your van? You owe us an explanation."

But the big man smacked them down with a furious glance, and then turned back to Carl. "You knew who that man was, right, Professor? So you also know we have to take this seriously."

"I knew who he was. I recognized him immediately." Carl laughed bitterly. "He looks just like his father."

"So we make a new plan," Stucky said.

"No, we do not!" the professor roared, his mild features distorted with rage. "I need you to back off, Stucky. I want out… all the way out."

Carl's uncharacteristic outrage took them all by surprise. Even Barney got up, nervously wagging his tail, while Stucky's dark eyes were round with disbelief.

"I mean it." The professor picked up his gnarled cane and shook it at Stucky. "I want you off my back and out of my life."

Just then the sliders opened and Ron stepped into the room. He had showered and shaved, with comb tracks still visible in his dark hair, and he was festively dressed in crisp brown slacks and a bright green sweater. "Hey, guys, I thought I'd order in a celebration dinner."

His cheery intrusion into the tense atmosphere was as unexpected as a man from Mars. "What's happening?" he wondered as all three gaped at him.

Stucky sighed deeply. "I hear you, Carl, but there's paperwork. You'll have to sign off on this foolish decision."

"No problem, bring it on," Carl said. "But right now you better move your ugly ass. Toni Hall is waiting, and she's not a patient woman."

Clearly defeated, Paul Stucky offered a half-hearted salute, winked at Amanda, and left the room. They all held their breath as his footsteps rounded the building and he hailed Chief Hall. The silence continued until Toni's gray sedan left the property.

Ron was stunned. "What's Stucky's story?"

"It's a very long tale that needs to be told." Carl smiled fondly at Ron. "But first order that dinner and I'll make us fresh drinks."

CHAPTER FIFTY-FIVE

Carl's story...

It turned out Ron's idea of a celebration meal, designed to please Carl, was traditional Italian, including an antipasto platter, seafood bruschetta, mini crab cakes, fennel and orange salad, vanilla panna cotta, and tiramisu. He called a restaurant in town where they were obviously regulars and requested delivery.

Then the men glanced at one another, more preoccupied by the portentous event at hand than any thought of food.

"Are you ready to talk about it, Carl?" Ron asked.

"Let's move to the kitchen so we can watch the sunset."

They settled into the wicker chairs overlooking the deck while the sun dropped over the barn. As they sipped their drinks and Barney ate his dinner, Carl was reluctant to begin. His lips moved ever so slightly as he tried to find the right words.

"Who was the man you recognized, the one who looked exactly like his father?" Sara gently prompted.

Carl ran a hand through his bushy white hair. "Stucky was referring to the man you all know as Al Cabella, the guy who bought my dinnerware."

While Carl paused, Amanda's need to know was like a runaway train. "The man with the black limo, the one who kidnapped me, who is he?"

The professor cleared his throat. "He is Peter Roman, Junior, son of Pietro Roman, better known as 'Milwaukee Pete,' although both men are from Chicago. Pietro died in prison several years ago. He was doing life for a Mafia massacre where five were killed in a local restaurant. Peter Junior must have been five or six at the time, so I doubt he remembers much about his father."

Sara glanced at her as if to say 'I told you so.' She said to Carl, "Is Peter Junior a gangster, too?"

Carl laughed. "Back then they called it The Chicago Outfit, a cute way to describe the Italian-American organized crime syndicate. I wouldn't know about Junior's connections, but clearly Marshal Stucky believes he is dangerous. He's been dogging the poor bastard ever since he arrived in town."

"Well, something is fishy, considering the man is pretending to be Al Cabella," Amanda pointed out. "What is he hiding?"

Carl spread his hands. "Who knows? Maybe he prefers to travel incognito? Maybe he doesn't want his wife to know how much he spends on art?"

Everyone knew Carl was prevaricating. Ron watched him closely, waiting for the truth.   "Tell us what you know about Pietro Roman, his father," Amanda pressed.

"I grew up in Chicago, Mandy," Carl answered. "Mr. Roman was friends with my daddy, so I saw him often."

This was harder than pulling teeth. She suspected the elephant in the room was that Carl's daddy had also been in the mob. Ron moved to Carl's chair and sat cross-legged on the floor, as if his closeness could make Carl's testimony less painful.

"So tell us about your daddy," Ron coaxed in a voice hoarse with emotion.

"My father is dead."

Of course he would be, considering Carl was in his seventies. Amanda hadn't meant to convey her impatience, but apparently she had, because Carl frowned at her and spoke again.

"My father is dead, and Pietro Roman killed him."

The stunned silence was shattered by the doorbell. Ron handed Amanda his wallet and asked her to answer, not wanting to sever his tenuous connection with Carl. She hurried down the hall, half expecting a gang of mobsters with automatic weapons to be lurking beyond the front door, but of course, it was only the Italian restaurant guy. She swiped Ron's credit card, took the box of delicious smelling food, and by the time she returned to the kitchen, Sara and Carl were seated at the bar while Ron distributed plates and silverware.

The tense moment had passed. Fearing she had missed the punchline, she opened her mouth but Sara subtly shook her head, indicating that she should let the subject rest for the moment.

During dinner Ron nervously filled the conversational void by telling them how Carl had arranged for him to take over his space at Cotton Mills Studio. "I'm so grateful. I'll use part of the space for my own work, but rent out the rest. I intend to invite Gina to show there and you too, Mandy, if you'd like to exhibit your sculpture in Asheville."

Under different circumstances, she would have been over the moon, but tonight she was unable to think about anything but Carl's story. "It sounds like a wonderful opportunity. Thank you, Ron," she mumbled.

When they had finished dinner and were moving toward dessert, Carl pushed away from the bar and went back to his chair. Ron got coffee brewing and put the panna cotta and tiramisu onto plates. They all watched Carl stare unflinchingly at the gaudy pink and orange sunset putting on its show.

Ron waited until everyone was seated with coffee and a dessert of choice. "Carl, can you tell us how your father died?"

Still staring at the sunset, Carl said, "Daddy owned the restaurant. I worked in the kitchen earning money to put me through the American Academy of Art…"

When Carl faltered, they all knew where he was going.

"The restaurant massacre?" Ron whispered.

Carl nodded miserably. "Six came in with Mr. Roman. They were after a hated competitor who was eating his Saturday night dinner. Roman's foot soldiers shot the rival, but Pietro's bullet hit Daddy, who got caught in the crossfire. I was hiding like a coward in the kitchen, but I saw the whole thing."

"I am so sorry, Carl." Ron wrapped his arm around the professor's shoulder.

She and Sara also murmured condolences.

"Why didn't you share this with me before now?" Ron asked.

Carl aged before their eyes. "I should have, Ron. I know that now. But I was sworn to secrecy, and I am a complete fraud." When he pounded his fist on the cocktail table, coffee jumped from the cups.

"How can you even say such a thing?" Ron grabbed both of the older man's hands.

"I am a fake. I've lied for the past fifty-four years, but now it's over." Carl faced them defiantly. "My real name is Nick Rossi. I testified for the feds when I was twenty-eight years old, and I've been in the Witness Protection Program ever since."

To say Professor Carl Fischer had a captive audience was an understatement. They were all too shocked to respond.

"It's called WITSEC, a federal program operated by the US Marshal Service. That's how Stucky got involved. When Peter Junior borrowed Cabella's car and came to Asheville, it triggered an alert in Chicago. Even though my case is ancient history, Illinois WITSEC decided they couldn't take a chance, so they activated Paul Stucky from Western Carolina District to keep an eye on things.

"I didn't know anything about it, didn't know Stucky from a hole in the wall. But like I said, I recognized Peter Junior the moment he arrived at my farewell party—the spitting image of my father's killer."

"Weren't you scared?" Ron asked breathlessly.

Carl's hand trembled when he tried to pick up his cup. He set it down again. "I was not scared because Peter Junior did not recognize me. He was not coming for me. Far as he knew, I was a semi-famous old fart potter and he wanted to purchase my work."

"How could you be so sure?" Sara wondered. "Especially since you got pushed off the roof, then later you were drugged. Jesus, Carl, I would have headed for the hills!"

He laughed. "When you've been looking over your shoulder all your life, you know these things. Junior fooled Stucky, though. The two attempts convinced him that Junior was here to avenge his father's death in prison. That's why Stucky was sneaking around my house when he saw Roman arrive to buy pottery. He had been surveilling him in case of just such an eventuality. It's why he chased him away from the hospital. Stucky intended to arrest him at that point, before he escaped town."

"But why did Stucky kidnap me?" Amanda interrupted. "I was making a scene and Peter Roman was driving away—no time for polite conversation, so he shoves me in the back of his van? That seems totally ridiculous. "

"Paul's a brave lad, but he overreacted." Carl shook his head. "I think he could have handled that quite differently, and so does Stucky. He apologized to Chief Hall for abducting you. I understand he wanted to arrest Junior, but ramming the limo with his van was also overly confrontational."

Stucky could have apologized to me. On the other hand, she had conked him with a flashlight, and in the end, he had saved their lives. She turned to Carl. "How do you know all this?"

"Toni told me the whole kidnapping saga. Normally Paul's duties extend no further than guarding the local courthouse, so he was out of his element. I first noticed Stucky at my party. Then when you girls told me about the man camping at the Anderson farm, I put it together that WITSEC in Chicago had assigned me a local bodyguard. I confronted Stucky directly when I saw him hanging around my hospital room."

She had a million questions. "So you told Stucky that Peter Roman was not the one trying to hurt you. If he'd listened and believed, maybe he would have suspected Larry sooner?"

Carl stretched like he was lifting the weight of the world off his shoulders. "Stucky feels awful about that, like he really screwed up, but frankly I don't think anyone could have seen that crazy kid coming."

"Does Chief Hall know you're in Witness Protection?"

"No, but I suspect she will soon. I cannot emphasize enough that WITSEC keeps its business top secret. Field marshals are only given information in an absolute emergency, and even Stucky managed to keep his operation under wraps. But now that I'm quitting the program, my story will be declassified to pertinent law enforcement, but not the general public."

"I don't like it, Carl." Ron put both his arms around the professor and rested his cheek in Carl's hair. "I want you to be safe. Perhaps you should reconsider?"

Carl stood abruptly and shook his head. "It's over, Ron. This decision is not negotiable." He whistled to Barney and moved out to the deck. "Let's light the firepit and drink some cognac. We'll toast my freedom as the sun dies."

CHAPTER FIFTY-SIX

Our story...

The roaring fire could not completely chase the chill away, but Carl's story was so fascinating that Sara and she forgot to shiver. He explained that his murdered father had been quite wealthy, so Carl had inherited his first million and invested wisely, never spending one penny he had not earned. Witness Protection had relocated him to rural Indiana with a new name, new social security number, and new driver's license.

"By then I already knew I wanted to major in ceramics, so I simply picked up at Indiana University where I'd left off in Chicago."

Amanda knew Carl's biography from that point onward. She sipped cognac and noted with interest that Carl had settled beside Ron on the redwood sofa. He then put his arm around Ron's shoulder and left it there. Emboldened, she took Sara's hand. They were seated side by side on the picnic table bench, their hands in plain view. She did not care.

"Now that you've left the program, do I call you Carl, or Nick?" Ron asked shyly.

Carl laughed. "Oh God, that boy Nick Rossi died decades ago. All that's left of him is a genetic addiction to Italian food."

Ron was intrigued, looking at Carl in a whole new light. Amanda agreed it took a leap of faith. She'd automatically assumed Professor Fischer was likely Jewish, of northern European descent. Imagining him as a dark-haired, blue-eyed young Mediterranean was a challenge. Yet even the revelation of his romantic new persona did not explain Ron's laser-like focus on Carl, and vice versa. Something was going on between those two.

All evening the second elephant in the room had been Gladys's conspicuous absence, so Amanda just blurted it out. "Where's Gladys? I expected her to be here for your homecoming, Carl."

Sara's eyebrows shot up in surprise. "It's none of our business, Mandy."

Suddenly she realized the red flush creeping up both men's faces was not from the firelight.

"Gladys isn't coming," Carl said slowly as he deliberately took Ron's hand. "It's over between us. We're not getting married."

"I'm sorry," she and Sara muttered in unison, not knowing what else to say.

"Don't be," Carl heartily advised. "Gladys understands. In fact, I think she's relieved. I adore the woman. We'll remain close friends, and I'll help her out financially if the need arises, but we always knew the marriage would be a sham. She sensed I was gay, and when she visited me in the hospital this morning, I told her the truth. We came to our senses."

Ron was not surprised by this declaration. "Carl told me he's been holding back because of our age difference, but ever since I was arrested and he almost died, he's changed his mind."

Carl pinned them with moist blue eyes. "I've been running from everything for too long, I'm sure you understand. I'm too old to run any longer, and since Ron agrees, we still have time to write our story."

Suddenly she and Sara were crying, too. Sara's perfect porcelain skin, full red lips, and expressive green eyes glowed in the flickering light, and Amanda knew she was also thinking about their story, with a fresh new beginning.

"I figure I'll never need to write a will if Ron marries me," Carl chuckled. "As my husband, he's automatically protected. Would you ladies return to Asheville for a spring wedding?"

This time Ron was more than surprised. His eyes were huge brown saucers overflowing. "Are you proposing?" he managed to ask through his emotional overload.

"I'm proposing marriage and a few other things I won't mention in mixed company. Why don't you move in tonight?"

Ron was speechless, but Sara could talk. "I'm up for another visit to Asheville if you are, babe."

As a conflicted kaleidoscope of images from this town—both violent and loving—shifted through her brain, all Amanda could say was, "Sounds like a plan."

Bella Books, Inc.

Women. Books. Even Better Together.

P.O. Box 10543
Tallahassee, FL 32302

Phone: 800-729-4992
www.bellabooks.com